He'd almost lost her.

The previous night, for a few eternity-spanning moments, Jonah had thought Paige was dead.

He loved her.

The realization was almost as terrifying as the sight of her unconscious body had been. Now he could no longer ignore his true feelings. He'd lost his heart to a mysterious, self-contained woman with No Trespassing signs draped around her like Christmas tree lights. The feelings had been growing for weeks, along with a need to protect he'd only lately realized.

Jonah glanced at her again, the tenderness welling up, spilling over so that he almost blurted out his feelings then and there.

What do I do now, Lord? I'm in love with Paige Hawthorne.

Books by Sara Mitchell

Love Inspired

Night Music #13
Shelter of His Arms #31

SARA MITCHELL

A popular and highly acclaimed author in the Christian market, Sara's aim is "to depict the struggle between the challenges of everyday life and the values to which our faith would have us aspire." The author of seven contemporary and two historical suspense novels, her work has been published by many inspirational book publishers.

Having lived in diverse locations from Georgia to California to Great Britain, her extensive travel experience helps her create authentic settings for her books. A lifelong music lover, Sara has also written several musical dramas and has long been active in the music ministries of the churches wherever she and her husband, a retired career air force officer, have lived. The parents of two daughters, Sara and her husband now live in Virginia.

Shelter of His Arms
Sara Mitchell

Love Inspired™

Published by Steeple Hill Books™

STEEPLE HILL BOOKS

Steeple
Hill™

ISBN 0-373-87031-0

SHELTER OF HIS ARMS

Copyright © 1990 by Sara Mitchell
First published by Accent Books under the title *A Deadly Snare*

Copyright © 1998 by Sara Mitchell
Text revised for Love Inspired™ edition

If I speak in the tongues of men and of angels, but have not love, I am only a resounding gong or a clanging cymbal...[Love] always protects, always trusts, always hopes, always perseveres.
—*1 Corinthians* 13:1,7

Prologue

London, England
1944

The heavy door closed behind him, snuffing out all sounds of the party. Fog—wet and cold, almost impenetrable—enclosed him before he took two steps. He paused to tug the collar of his coat over his uniform, shivering in the silence of a dank November night.

Mindful of the nature of his errand, he quickened his steps down the rough, largely ruined walk. The last V-2, General Avery had told him while they pretended to chat, had struck only two blocks away the previous night.

He stopped suddenly, skin prickling. Off to his left ran the Thames, where the mournful wail of a passing trawler rang out with a muffled echo. He lifted his hand, patting the left side of his chest to make sure the information was still securely in place.

There it was again—the scrape of a shoe on stone. He melted into the shadow of a brick wall and waited. Droplets of fog condensed in his hair, on his face, dampening his neck even with the protection of his heavy coat. His mouth flattened. He knew they'd sent someone after him—he'd been followed from

France but thought he'd lost the shadow in London. They were worse than bloodhounds, more lethal than the deadly rockets. And they wouldn't quit, because what he had discovered was too important.

Clenching his teeth, he waited in ruthless silence. Just a couple more hours... That's all he needed. General Avery had promised him Christmas leave after he passed the diary on, which he had just done. After fourteen months of this unending nightmare, he could catch a hop to the States and give Molly and little Justeen a present they'd prayed for for three years now.

Slowly, eyes and ears tuned to even a small shift in the wind, he resumed a stealthy path to his car. It's almost over, he thought, though there was little satisfaction. The damage that nine supposedly loyal Americans had dealt their country was incalculable. They ought to line 'em up in the path of one of those V-2s...or send 'em to one of Hitler's death camps. He fought the rage at their treason, knowing anger could blind him as completely as the unrelenting London fog.

"Does God mind if we're angry at the Nazis, Daddy?"

How like his Justeen, he thought. So solemn, her serious four-year-old face lifted to him as she asked the question... He could barely remember what she looked like now. It had been so long—too long. But he'd be home for Christmas. Even if he'd never get any more medals, even if General Avery had warned him that the whole affair would be buried in the bowels of the War Department, he knew he'd done what he had to do, would do again if it meant exposing traitors.

The car loomed just ahead, a dark amorphous mass. His fingers burrowed inside his coat pocket, closing over the key. He slid in, breathing a sigh of relief as he closed the door with a barely audible snick. Almost home free. The hour or so drive wouldn't be much fun, but he'd done it. He'd done it!

I'm coming home, darlin'. It's been way too long, but I'm—

The back of his neck prickled in warning. He ducked, turning automatically, lifting his arm. But it was too late. A muffled thunk was the only sound the silencer allowed to escape from a pistol fired at point-blank range.

Chapter One

❧

Washington, D.C.,
August, present day

She was late. And—according to the latest traffic report on the radio station—if she didn't leave immediately for the professor's house she would be even later.

Paige Hawthorne glanced at her watch as she popped the last bite of granola bar into her mouth. On her way out the kitchen door she drank a glass of juice, exchanging the empty glass for the stack of unstamped letters waiting on the hall table to be mailed. By the time she reached her bathroom to brush her teeth, she'd stamped the letters and double-checked her desk calendar. On her way out the apartment door she rinsed the juice glass and put it in the dishwasher.

Efficiency and superb time management. That was how she'd earned her reputation, and Paige had no intention of tarnishing the image.

But it was a definite challenge, pulling double duty as research assistant for two demanding men with two equally demanding professions.

Outside, she smiled as she dropped the letters in the mailbox. What a *refreshing* August morning, for a change. A dying Gulf hurricane had emptied itself over the District of Columbia for the past two days, momentarily washing away the enervating humidity and leaving behind a crisp blue sky. "Good omen," Paige decided, her mind efficiently organizing an alternative route to Professor Kittridge's house in Arlington so she wouldn't be late after all.

Paige hated being late. It was a weakness, a sign of inefficiency, downright laziness. An affront to the Lord. Jesus had never been late—His timing was always perfect. Though she hadn't and never would attain that perfection, it wouldn't be from lack of effort on her part.

Besides, if she were late, Jonah would tease her.

As she dodged slow-moving cars and ducked down side streets to avoid traffic jams, Paige found her thoughts dwelling more than she liked on Jonah Sterling. To be honest, the best-selling author couldn't actually be described as "demanding." During the six months she'd been helping him with research for his next thriller, he hadn't even raised his voice. Not, of course, that she would ever give him a reason to, Paige reminded herself. Oh, no. No way would she risk having those dark indigo eyes look at *her* with anything less than respect.

She whipped onto the Beltway ramp in front of a too-timid driver and gunned her sturdy little car into the fastest moving lane. Over the radio, the announcer's mellifluous voice was cheerfully agreeing with Paige's assessment of how refreshing the low humidity was today.

Jonah Sterling has a very nice voice. The wayward thought startled her, and Paige tried to banish it instantly—but without success. "Get a grip, bookworm," she muttered, hoping the use of her father's pet name for her would enable her to impose his weathered, sunburned face and Midwestern twang over that of the intriguing British author. Paige lifted a hand to make sure her hair was in place, then caught herself and made a face at the rearview mirror.

"Should have brought coffee and doughnuts," she mused. There wouldn't be anything in the house worth eating besides the wretched jars of peanuts Professor K. stashed in every room. A swift glance at the car's clock warned her that stopping for something on the way wasn't wise.

Paige's hands tightened momentarily on the wheel, then relaxed. Jonah was a big boy. If he was hungry, he could get himself something to eat. He was not—repeat, not—her responsibility. And of course he'd be the first to agree with her. Not only was the writer amazingly undemanding, he was also agreeable to a fault.

"Put your feet up every now and then," he'd counseled more than once, the Oxford accent overlaid by that tantalizing smoky drawl he'd picked up from living in Virginia's Blue Ridge Mountains for the past decade. "I may be under a deadline, but I've no wish for a knackered research assistant. I also have a very accommodating publisher."

"Fine," Paige liked to retort. "Blow the deadline—but it won't be because of a lack of effort on my part."

She made it to the professor's house at seven minutes past eight. Still late, and she was grumbling imprecations when she pulled into the driveway. Fortunately, Jonah was late, too. Neither he nor his motorcycle were anywhere in sight, and the tension that had been gathering in her shoulders relaxed. Professor K. would already have left for his campus office, which gave Paige a little more time to organize the previous day's research for Jonah before she started in on the professor's latest project.

"Exasperating man," Paige muttered as she started down the walk, her gaze indulgent as she surveyed the jungle of the professor's yard.

Professor Kittridge's son and her father had been boyhood friends, and in fact the professor was Paige's godfather. Sadly, the son—what *was* his name?—had died in Vietnam, but Professor and Mrs. Kittridge maintained their friendship even after Professor K. accepted the teaching job in Washington, D.C., at Georgetown U. In the past years, especially after Paige's disastrous marriage, Professor K. had become the mainstay of her life, more grandfather than boss. Paige loved him almost as much as she did her own father.

She blinked hard, an unexpected swell of emotion catching

her off guard. Professor K. had suffered a lot of tragedy in his life, but he always tried to make sure Paige was all right. Thanks to the professor, most of her own emotional scars were healed, out of sight...mostly out of mind. Paige would have worked for him for free, though the one time she'd broached the subject he'd thrown a book at her. Fortunately it had been one neither of them liked—Paige still smiled at the memory.

"I might just sneak over here one afternoon and at least mow his lawn, though," she told a mockingbird singing away in the middle of a shaggy-looking sycamore. "Professor K., the neighbors are going to lynch you one night, I'm afraid."

Her eccentric boss refused to consider a town house or apartment, obstinately clinging to the home he and Mattie, his now-dead wife had lived in for the past quarter of a century. Paige paused to sniff a late-summer rose, speculating as she always did at what her mother could do in this wildly overgrown yard.

She had just turned the key in the lock when her ear caught a faint sound. It was coming from inside, and Paige paused, frowning. She stepped off the front porch and peered through the tangled branches of some crepe myrtle, trying to see into the picture window. Professor K. wasn't supposed to be here—he always left for his office on the campus at Georgetown by six o'clock to avoid the traffic and crush of commuters taking the Metro. Had he forgotten something, caught a ride home?

Puzzled and a little concerned, Paige climbed the steps again and pressed the buzzer a couple of times. In spite of their relationship, she had never treated his house as her own home. When the professor didn't answer the door, she went ahead and opened it with the key Professor K. had given her to use when she was researching in his personal library.

"Professor?" she called into the silence of the dark, musty-smelling entrance hall.

The fedora and cane were gone from the bentwood coatrack—Professor Kittridge was definitely not at home. Paige walked slowly down the hall to the bedroom he had turned into his World War II room. "Jonah? Is that you?" It would be just like him—instead of riding his beloved motorcycle—to take a notion to walk the five miles from the apartment he sublet, regardless of the difficulty or danger.

There it was again—a soft sort of shuffling, like shoes muffled by carpet, or clothing brushing against a wall. The strange noise had come from down the hall, toward the living room, and for the first time a prickle of uneasiness feathered the back of her neck. Paige gingerly pushed open the half-closed door to the World War II room. It was empty, but—

"No!" The volume of her own involuntary cry shocked her almost as much as the sight, which to a dedicated historian was shock enough.

The room had been torn apart with methodical savagery. Books lay in scattered piles all over the floor—the ceiling-high shelves that covered two walls were stripped bare. Papers littered every surface in the room. Even the files of the antique oak cabinet gaped open, its contents disgorged and flung about in mountainous disarray.

"What's going on here? What happened?"

Paige whipped about so abruptly her shoe slipped on the cover of a book. She staggered, and hard arms closed around her. Shocked, off balance, she automatically shoved against his chest. "Let go—I'm perfectly all right."

Jonah hugged her, then gently lifted her away a little. "Paige? You all right?" The dark blue eyes scanned her face, then lifted to survey the ransacked room. Just for a moment his hands tightened on her upper arms, strength and warmth flooding her with a bewildering sense of safety.

Thoroughly rattled, Paige blurted out, "I couldn't help it. It was like this when I got here. I'm sorry, Jonah. I'm—" She clamped her jaw shut, then carefully eased herself free from his arms. Rubbing her elbows with her hands, she swallowed hard and tried to compose herself. "I mean...I just arrived and found it this way. I haven't checked the rest of the house, though the living room wasn't touched. But I—"

His hand covered her mouth, his head bending until his lips brushed her ear. The gentle rasp of his mustache sent fresh goose bumps coursing down her arms. "Shh...I heard a noise."

Paige nodded vigorously, her eyes stretched wide. Jonah

smiled down at her, deepening the creases in his cheeks on either side of the bushy auburn mustache. The broad hand covering her mouth lifted, brushed her cheek. "Stay here—don't move," he whispered, then melted out into the hall with a soundlessness more frightening than his abrupt appearance.

Paige crept to the door, trying for the same soundlessness, and watched, heart still racing, her throat muscles taut. Jonah was moving stealthily down the hall, his body alert, exuding latent power. Like some sort of professional—a policeman, even a federal agent. Anything *but* a writer. If she hadn't worked for the past couple of months with a laid-back, self-effacing man who constantly misplaced his reading glasses, then grinned like a sheepish boy when Paige pointed them out, she would have ducked out the nearest window and run. At the moment she was almost more unnerved by Jonah Sterling than she was by the presence of a vandal.

Jonah looked dangerous, even from the back. His hair, the color of mahogany, was still tousled from his motorcycle helmet, and through the thin weave of his knit shirt, muscles Paige had never noticed rippled across his shoulders and back. Suddenly he stopped, crouched in a position to attack. Dry-mouthed, Paige tensed as well.

From the far end of the house came the grating sound of an unwilling window being forced open. In a flash Jonah sprinted down the hall and disappeared.

Noise exploded from the other side of the kitchen. What if he got hurt? she thought. Galvanized into action, Paige raced down the hall after him. Seconds later a darkly clad man with a stocking over his face charged into the living room just ahead of her. Jonah was right behind. The intruder turned and lashed out with a poker he'd grabbed from the fireplace. Jonah ducked, feinted to the right. Then—in a series of lightning moves incomprehensible to Paige's stunned eyes—he knocked the poker from the man's hand and flung him to the floor.

Tumbling wildly, the intruder's stocky body demolished a coffee table and rolled twice more before the man scrambled back to his feet, the fireplace shovel clenched in his hand this time. Jonah dodged, his eye never leaving the intruder, his hands poised in front of his body.

Paige searched around for a weapon of her own, her gaze falling on a small brass lamp on the gateleg table in the foyer. Cautiously she edged toward the table, but the movement brought attention to her; with a snarling grunt the intruder heaved the fireplace shovel at Jonah, then launched himself across the room toward Paige.

"Drop, Paige!" Jonah called. "To the floor!"

Paige's hand connected with the little lamp, and she hurled it at the intruder's face before dropping to the floor and curling up into a tight fetal ball.

A chilling yell exploded in the dark room, the battle cry of a Viking warrior—guaranteed to cause nightmares for weeks. But it wasn't the intruder who had issued such a bloodcurdling sound: it was Jonah. *Jonah?*

Cursing and holding one hand to his face, the intruder tripped over the lamp Paige had thrown. One of his feet actually hit her knees a glancing blow, but he didn't pause. Pounding footsteps hurtled down the hall, with Jonah in close pursuit. She still didn't lift her head.

She heard the sound of breaking glass, then...silence. Paige thought about uncurling and rising to her feet, but for some reason her body wouldn't obey her brain. She sensed a presence above her, followed by gentle fingers touching her hair, smoothing strands out of her face.

"You can get up now, love," came Jonah's soft voice, laced with frustration. "The blighter got away."

Chapter Two

It was almost dark. Evening shadows had lengthened, intruding on the uneasy peace that had hovered over Professor Kittridge's study since the police had left. In subconscious defense as well as necessity perhaps, every light in the room had been turned on to provide at least an illusion of brightness and security for the three people who were present.

Jonah Sterling slouched deeper in the professor's favorite overstuffed easy chair, letting the clipboard and pen slide with a soft plop to the rug. His thumb and index finger idly stroked the corners of his mustache while he watched Paige dart back through the room, her arms filled with stacks of papers. She carefully placed them on the floor beside the desk where she and Kittridge had been working for the past four hours. *Give it a rest,* he wanted to tell her, but so far he'd managed to keep the words locked behind his tongue. This was obviously her way of coping. Paige was already strung out, and he was afraid of tipping her over the edge.

"That's enough for now, girl," the professor muttered without looking up, almost as though he'd read Jonah's mind. "My eyes are too tired."

"Let me take over, then," Paige offered for the third time.

"Tomorrow you can cross-check the papers I'm uncertain about."

Jonah watched Kittridge throw down a stack of index cards and lift his head to glare at Paige. Perspiration gleamed on the bald head, and the half-dozen strands of graying hairs he normally plastered across the crown had slipped. Beneath the yellowish glow of the banker's lamp his aging face looked gaunt, the lines deeper. "If you don't take a break, I'll have Jonah chase you down and use some of his fancy kung fu moves on *you!*" he roared with the irascibility of an old grizzly.

Jonah's mouth quirked. "It wasn't kung fu," he said mildly, patting his shirt pocket, then his slacks.

"You put them on the table beside you," Paige told him automatically, pausing from her endless puttering.

Jonah turned, retrieved his reading glasses and stuffed them in his shirt pocket. Rising, he strolled toward the drooping woman fighting so hard to hide the fact that she was tired. "Why don't we all go out for a bite? It's almost seven-thirty," he suggested, stopping a few feet from Paige and thrusting his hands in his jeans pockets. With Paige, he'd learned to be very casual, very nonaggressive. One day he planned to find out what had happened to her before she'd become Kittridge's research assistant.

Neither Paige nor the professor were forthcoming on her personal life, and normally Jonah wouldn't have even noticed. When he was working on a book, he had a tendency toward tunnel vision, and in past years had doubtless offended a number of people—especially if they were female. He grimaced at the thought, wondering what it was about his unremarkable person that seemed to attract women. His ex-fiancée had once told him that if he was going to write books and act like a nerd, he could at least look like one, for crying out loud. Several women he'd since dated seriously had been just as hostile to his obsession with the written word.

Then he'd met Paige Hawthorne, with her short moon-spun blond hair and shadowed gray eyes full of pain and secrets. They only sparked with life when she was lost in some musty book she'd unearthed in a library, or—amazingly—some of

Jonah's copious notes on the World War II mystery he was working on.

"I'm not that hungry," Paige said now. "Maybe in a little while, after I finish straightening this last set of files." She waved her hand. "You and Professor K. go ahead. I'll stay—"

"With us," Jonah finished, giving her a peaceful smile. "You can finish the files later, if you must." He shook his head, studying her. She was composed, but still too pale. The freckles scattered across her long, narrow nose still stood out like tiny spatters of mud; her gray eyes were smudged with fatigue and remnants of shocked disbelief. But at least she had quit trembling. Jonah recalled the feeling of her slim, shaking shoulders as he'd tried to soothe her.

His gaze returned to her face. Paige was watching him, chin lifted and lips pressed tightly together. Daring him to comment, he knew. Earlier, he'd tried to tease away her fear, gently ribbing her that most people trembled after a shocking experience. Paige had only blushed, just like she was doing now.

Jonah sighed inwardly. For a few incredible moments this morning, his reserved, quintessentially professional research assistant had been delightfully addled. She'd also been confusing: why had she apologized for the mess in the house?

"I've got a few things I want to check in the 'Nam room," Kittridge abruptly announced. He stood stiffly, glancing from Jonah to Paige, then back to Jonah. "You two go on along. Just bring me a doggie bag. I'll be fine." A suspicious smile lurked at the corners of his mouth.

The professor's heavy-handed attempt to leave the two of them alone infuriated Paige and amused Jonah. It wasn't the first time the elderly man had pulled something like this over the past months. "If you're sure..." Jonah began, not disguising the humor. Suddenly his gaze narrowed, sharpened, caught by a fleeting expression of furtiveness on Kittridge's face.

"No!" Paige contradicted then with surprising force. "I think we should all go. We finished straightening the Vietnam War room—I even double-checked when you were working on the POW files. There's no need for you to worry about it anymore tonight. You need to eat. You haven't had anything but that sandwich I made you at noon."

Diverted, Jonah lifted an inquiring brow. "Relax, Paige—I promise we'll bring him more than a doggie bag."

She began twisting the cameo ring she always wore, round and round, almost as agitated as she had been that morning.

Jonah stepped closer. "Paige?"

She took a deep breath and her hands dropped back to her sides. "I don't think he should stay here alone," she finally admitted, the smoke-colored eyes steady, unwavering, armor firmly back in place. "Remember how the police said the intruder must have known our routine, or he never would have broken in at the hour he did? He wasn't expecting me to come, since I've been at the Smithsonian this past month and haven't been working here."

Kittridge started, his hand making an abrupt movement.

"What is it, Professor?" Jonah asked, keeping his voice easy, matter-of-fact. Throughout the painstaking interview with the police that morning, Kittridge had reflected nothing but outrage over the destruction, and wry amusement over Paige's incredulous account of Jonah's actions. "Did Paige say something to jog a memory, remind you of a detail that might help the police?"

"No. You're both getting carried away, reading too many of Sterling's novels. There's nothing going on here but a typical break-in, with robbery as the motive. Don't read more into it than there is." He ran his hand around the back of his neck, looking across at Paige. "I'm just grateful you weren't already here, girl." He cleared his throat, saying gruffly, "The police know what they're talking about. He trashed the rooms out of sheer cussedness over the lack of money or stereo equipment or other valuables he could have sold on the street. The damage to the rooms is bad, but it's better than damage to my goddaughter."

"I know." Paige moved to give him a hug. "I love you, too, even when you're a grouchy old bear. And I'm just as glad *you* weren't here."

"Bah!" Kittridge stomped over and snatched up Paige's

purse. "Here." He thrust it into her arms. "Go along, now.
The two of you get out of here and quit treating me like an
incompetent old man." He winked at Jonah. "Even if I am."

But all the way to the restaurant, Jonah wondered about that
look of shifting evasiveness that had stirred in the older man's
eyes.

"I'm sorry about disrupting your research," Paige said stiffly
forty minutes later, after the waitress deposited two steaming
plates of breakfast-for-supper, the house specialty.

His research assistant had been unaccountably remote, almost brusque, since they'd arrived, but with that telling comment Jonah finally realized why. The little hedgehog! Naturally
she thought the break-in and subsequent lost day were *her* fault,
her personal responsibility. After working with her for six
months, he should have known.

"Couldn't be helped," he returned, letting it lie for the moment and digging into his stack of pancakes. Americans certainly knew how to do some things up right. Good breakfasts
topped the list, to his way of thinking.

"I'll find and collate the rest of Professor K.'s personal notes
on the dissolution of the Gestapo tomorrow," Paige persisted,
ignoring her food. "I gave you the ones I happened on when
we were cleaning up, but in the confusion I'm sure I missed
some. We'll still probably have to go back to the Smithsonian,
possibly the Library of Congress, though—"

Her voice faltered into silence when Jonah put down his fork,
braced his hands and leaned over the table. "I've told you it's
all right," he enunciated, the crisp Oxford accent ringing
through his words—a sure sign he was losing patience. Right
now he didn't particularly care. It took a lot to stir him up, but
Paige knew right where to stick the spoon. "Will you relax
about it? I'm not half as concerned about the research for my
book as I am about you skewering yourself on the prongs of
your overdeveloped sense of personal responsibility!"

He grabbed the water glass and emptied it, then grimaced an
apology across the table. Though she'd never said anything,
he'd realized early on that Paige harbored a deep-seated ab-
horrence for any kind of confrontation. Jonah had queried Kit-

tridge after Paige had been working with him several weeks; all he'd learned was that she'd been married once and had some problems she was dealing with as a consequence. Her husband was dead. Jonah spent several moments eating in silence, chewing on his food and his thoughts.

To smooth over the awkward moment, he decided to bring up the intriguing discovery they'd made several days earlier when they were examining a World War II uniform on loan to Jonah by the dead soldier's daughter. "Perhaps this is as good a time as any to warn you that, after last week, I've been thinking of altering my plot. Remember what we discovered in the ribbon mount on Major Pettigrew's uniform? Endless possibilities there, wouldn't you agree. All far more intriguing than, say, speculating on the inner workings of the two-bit thug who trashed the professor's house."

Paige finally relaxed a little, her lips softening into an almost natural smile. "I remember. It is exciting," she agreed. "I suppose I may as well confess that I've imagined all sorts of theories myself, and I'm not even a writer." Entranced, Jonah watched her face go soft and dreamy. "Think about it…a mysterious list of names, hidden for over half a century behind the rows of ribbons. A key, too. What does it mean? Where's the lock for that key?" She colored a little. "I guess I've speculated more than I ought to."

"I doubt that. And I do know what you mean. I'd enjoy tracing those nine names, too." Satisfied, he stuffed a forkful of scrambled eggs in his mouth, then sat back, smiling across the table at her until he swallowed. "Unfortunately, there's this contract I signed, so I'm afraid we'll have to wait until this book's in the hopper before we can play detective." He tilted his head, stroking his mustache. "Would you like that, Paige? Playing detective? You're the best researcher I've ever been blessed to have working with me. If I compared you to a beagle or bloodhound would you pour the maple syrup over my head?"

"I might—but then it would have to be cleaned up."

"And I suppose you'd feel obliged to do that, hmm?" He

was teasing again, but it was almost as though he'd snuffed out a candle.

"Probably. It would have been my fault."

"Not if I provoked you."

"Christians turn the other cheek, remember?" She shook her head. "Never mind. It doesn't matter."

Jonah thought it mattered a lot, but now wasn't the time to pursue the matter. But one of these days—probably the same day he overnighted the manuscript to his editor—he and Paige Hawthorne were going to have a meeting of the minds. "So what do you think the key belongs to?" he asked, smiling at her. "We can at least have fun speculating over our meal."

Paige toyed with her napkin a few moments, then shrugged. "I'm convinced the key is to a diary—my younger sister Katy had one."

The waitress appeared to ask if they wanted dessert, and by the time they both laughingly concluded that dessert following breakfast ought to be too decadent for their taste buds but that neither of them could resist, Paige had lost the last of her aura of defensiveness and frozen aloofness. Jonah continued to unobtrusively study her. He was alternately captivated and irritated by her elusive personality. It was, he mused with an inward smile over his insatiable need to toy with words, like...like trying to capture moonlight on water.

Over dessert they continued to exchange ideas concerning the Major Pettigrew mystery, allowing the shock of the traumatic morning to recede even more. The more they talked, the more Jonah found himself toying with a plot change. Paige had a quick, inquiring mind, and frankly, some good ideas worth pursuing, at least in the fictional sense. Jonah hid a grin. His editor of course would kick up a fuss at the inevitable delay, but in the end Jonah could have pretty much what he wanted—one of the perks of attaining a worldwide reputation from eight bestsellers and a TV miniseries, he'd learned.

But power and fame could be dangerous. If used unwisely, it corrupted people.

He'd have to pray about it. God never allowed things to happen randomly, or without purpose. Ultimately it didn't matter that he'd been working on this story line for half a year, researching on both sides of the Atlantic. Living his faith was a process, not a destination, just as the thrill of writing a book— at least for him—was more important than the amount of sales. So. The uniform of a World War II major killed in action had been dropped into his lap. And Paige had discovered a tiny key, concealed behind the ribbons mount, along with a list of nine names.

Why were they there? Who were the people? Jonah felt the restlessness taking hold, the surge of adrenaline rising, pumping through his bloodstream. There was a story churning in his head, struggling to be born....

"Ready to go?" he asked suddenly, wanting to be alone, wanting to toy around with ideas, scribble down some plot threads. Hopefully he wouldn't have to chuck entirely the character of the reformed Gestapo agent who teamed with a renegade Resistance hero. On the other hand, his mother always told him that nimble minds never refused to seize possible advantages of alternative situations.

He'd pray—and see what happened.

"It wasn't there, I told you," the voice said. "And don't worry—I fixed it so there's no way they'd know what I was after. And they can't ID me. Whaddya take me for?"

The voice on the other end of the phone iced over with contempt. "I took you for a person who could get the job done without bringing the entire Metro Police Force breathing down your neck."

He rubbed sweating palms on his slacks. "I got away. They got nothin'. Nothin'!"

"Neither did you." The rebuke stung, but the coldly spoken threat that followed promised worse. "I want to know how much he's found out. Then I want him eliminated. Soon. I can't afford the slightest hint of dirt."

"He's got more papers and junk than the city dump. I can't just—"

"You have one week. The man threatened me. So you will

destroy the information with which he did so—and then you
will destroy the man.''

"What about the woman and that British writer?"

"If necessary they will be eliminated, as well. But only when
I say so.''

"I asked around—that Limey's hot property—not just a two-
bit hack writer. It'll take me a while to arrange things.''

"I'm not interested in excuses. If you can't do the job, I'll
find somebody else.'' The biting voice softened even more. "I
can arrange for anything I want. Don't let yourself become
something else I must...arrange.''

Chapter Three

Lips pursed in satisfaction, Paige snapped her notebook shut, then glanced at her watch. Nine-seventeen. She'd been working less than two hours, but already had finished cross-checking some sources in Professor K.'s fully restored World War II room. With a bit of luck, she would be able to—

The phone next to her elbow rang.

"Paige? Good. Glad I found you so easily." Jonah's voice flowed into her ear. "Plans have changed. Don't meet me at the Archives at two. Instead—" Paige heard the sound of rustling paper "—we're going to Georgia. Can you make it to National by twelve forty-five? I've booked us on a one-thirty flight. Don't worry—I'll clear it with the professor."

Twelve forty-five! That gave her less than three hours. What did he think she was, anyway? Paige stood straighter. "No problem. I'll be there. How many days?" Her voice was cool, professional, but she was thankful that Jonah wasn't looking at her right now.

"I think two ought to do it. A local museum in a small town about three hours south of Atlanta just received the donation of a phenomenal collection of World War II memorabilia. I was invited to check it out, if I cared to make the trip. You know me, right? If there's the slightest chance—I have to peer under the stone. Needless to say I'll need my favorite beagle with me."

At least *that* particular comparison had been in English. Paige felt the warmth in her cheeks, and was impatient with herself. Jonah Sterling was nothing but a big tease—he was all the time calling her some kind of nickname in some foreign language, his wide mouth smiling beneath his mustache, a twinkle in his eye. If she hadn't known better, she'd have thought he was flirting with her.

But she did know better. It had taken years, but she had finally learned—painfully—how to hide behind the wall of competency and intimidating capability, never letting herself respond to any of the masculine overtures that used to come her way. Men respected her, admired her. But in the past few years especially, she hadn't had to fend off any heavy-handed passes, or even lighthearted requests for a date.

God had taught her a lesson, and Paige had learned it well, all the way through her bones to her soul.

Jonah thought she was a "top-drawer" assistant, as he'd once told her. He was a kind man and a tease, but she was just his capable research assistant. The best he'd ever had, so he'd claimed. She didn't plan to let him down.

At least he asked, instead of ordered. Not like—

"Paige? You still there, or have you already left to finish a half-dozen tasks before you risk life and limb on the Beltway? Of others, I mean. You drive your little car as though it's a weapon."

"Around here, it's almost required to be assertive," Paige mumbled. "But I'm never aggressive—the police have really cracked down on those drivers." Abruptly she realized she was defending herself, almost apologizing. "I'll probably take the Metro so I don't have to worry about parking," she finished more firmly. Her mind returned with a thump to the present. *Professor K.* What about the professor? He'd be alone for at least two days.

Paige quashed that thought, too. "I'll see you at the airport." After a short pause she added, a dry note overriding the firmness, "I trust that you're aware of what the Deep South will be like in late August?"

"Can't be worse than the Sarawak Rain Forest in East Malaysia. See you soon, love." His voice softened. "And thanks."

He *would* throw that word out, in the low, melting tone that always unsettled her. *Love.* It was just a British term of affection, not even affection, really. More habit than anything, she supposed, because of course he wouldn't feel affection for her. She'd made sure of that. No, he'd just been distracted, trying to organize his thoughts for the trip. She'd learned how absentminded he could be, when he was lost in plotting.

Paige gathered all her notes, put papers away, straightened the desk, her mind a cauldron of seething emotions. Ever since she had met Jonah Sterling her life had been a roller coaster. The professor had introduced them, dropping the bombshell of Jonah's identity with Machiavellian glee. "Have someone who wants your much-lauded skills," he'd told her. "It would mean a leave of absence from your job at the Smithsonian. But you don't need to worry—I'll put in a word for you if this doesn't pan out. And...just to keep you busy, I've decided this would be a good opportunity to get started on the update of my prisoners of war book."

Professor K. had known Paige was restless, uneasy, that her job left her too much time to dwell on "unhealthy subjects," as he'd called it. But she had been totally unprepared for his bombshell. "You're saying J. Gregory—*the* world-famous J. Gregory—wants me to help research his next book?"

"That's the one. I've talked with him, and I think you'll enjoy this, Paige. He's not at all what I expected, frankly. At least make an appointment, talk with him yourself—I have a feeling you'll find the opportunity irresistible."

At the moment she wished she had resisted, Paige decided a frazzled forty minutes later. Here she went again, dropping everything to be at the beck and call of a man, bending over backward to please him regardless of the inconvenience. And she had no one to blame but herself. Jonah hadn't yelled at her, hadn't made his request a demand, much less threatened to sack her if she balked. No, this was a flaw in her character—some spiritual blindness or something she hadn't grasped. "Why, Lord?" she grumbled as she dashed into her apartment, flung a change of clothes in her hang-up bag and taped a hurriedly typed note to the neighbor's door across the hall. "Have I been too proud? Too...independent?" As a Christian was it her lot in life now to have to be meek, subservient, in order to teach her to be more Christlike?

David had told her that, many times. If she were a better Christian...if she were a better wife...if she were the Christian woman God intended her to be...then he wouldn't have to waste so much time teaching her himself.

"Stuff a sock in it, Hawthorne," she yelled out loud, even if she did clap a hand over her mouth and dart a quick glance around the empty room. "He's dead. David is dead. I won't let him dominate my life from the grave." She determinedly locked away the hurtful memories and headed for the door.

As she passed by her desk, she noticed the envelope with the key and list of names from Major Pettigrew's uniform. The previous week she had tucked it in one of her desk cubbyholes for safekeeping until Jonah decided what he wanted to do. He'd said he planned to share their discovery with Professor K. as well, though Paige had warned him the professor wouldn't appreciate the distraction from his Vietnam-era research.

"Trust me," she promised darkly. "I learned the hard way years ago. Even if you tell him you've discovered what really happened to Hitler, he'll just tell you that's 1940-something and he's working in the sixties right now, so you can just wait until he's through. And he won't say it politely."

Shrugging, she scooped up the items anyway. After all, she and Jonah *were* going to be pawing through other World War II memorabilia. When they returned from Georgia, hopefully Professor K. would be ready to listen, become as intrigued as she and Jonah. Paige was also hoping the professor might recognize one or more of the names. His prodigious memory rivaled Paige's, and many an evening they would engage in friendly competition, each trying to out-fact the other.

But when she arrived at the airport—three minutes early, she found not only Jonah but Professor Kittridge, as well. "What are you doing?'' She hugged his stooped frame. ''We're only going to be gone two days—there was no need for you to troop all the way down here to see us off.''

''He isn't.'' Jonah lifted Paige's hang-up bag and all but threw it on the security conveyer belt. ''He...ah...*insists* on coming with us.''

''I've got legitimate research there,'' Professor K. snapped after they had all passed through the security check, daring Paige with a fierce scowl to comment. ''I'll stay out of your way. And I won't even bother asking Paige for any assistance. You can ignore me, confound it!''

''It's not that,'' Jonah repeated with elaborate patience, but the words were clipped, his hands jammed deep in the back pockets of his slacks. ''I've already explained to you. It's not the fact that you're coming—it's that interview you're going to miss if you do. You've been trying for two months to arrange it, remember? All week long you've rubbed your hands in glee-ful anticipation. You've enjoyed keeping us dangling, refusing to tell Paige and me what it's all about. And now you're shrug-ging it off. Doesn't make sense, my friend.''

''The interview can wait.'' The professor wiped the back of his hand over his mouth. The gnarled fingers were trembling. ''It can wait,'' he repeated, ''but this other can't....'' His voice trailed away, and he abruptly turned his back.

Paige and Jonah exchanged looks, and in unspoken consent dropped the matter.

The flight to Atlanta was uneventful, and Jonah rented a car to drive the two hours south to the town of Warner Robins, Georgia. Professor K. slept the entire drive, but it was a restless, somehow uneasy sleep, and more than once Paige twisted to watch him in concern. He kept muttering unintelligible words.

''I think he's afraid and won't admit it,'' Paige finally ven-tured, unable to hide her worry. ''He's tried to disguise it, but that break-in really unnerved him. He's seventy-nine, after all. He wouldn't have stood a chance against the miserable punk who trashed the place. But I wish he had confided in me. I could have stayed behind with him until after that interview, then met you down here.'' She swallowed the lump that had risen unbidden in her throat. The professor had done so much for her...yet she hadn't been able to help him when he'd needed her.

"I don't think he came along because he was afraid to be by himself," Jonah returned. He sent her a quick, unreadable look. "He's too used to being alone. He didn't let you spend the night there last night, now did he?"

"Not for want of me trying."

"There you go."

He hesitated, and Paige studied the rugged profile, wondering at his frown. He sure needed a haircut. The shaggy, reddish brown hair was falling over his ears, brushing his collar.... "What?" she asked absently, then realized that her thoughts had scattered.

"I said that something's certainly weighing on his mind. Until this morning I would have said it was this interview he's had such a time arranging. To change his mind..." He shook his head, looking bemused. "Bit of a puzzle, that."

"Do you think he really has some people to see down here, or was that just an excuse? Seems a little too pat to be coincidence."

Jonah passed two cars and a slow-moving camper before replying. "Wish I had my Harley," he muttered. "I don't know," he finally answered Paige. He frowned, slid another quick glance across, then seemed to reach some inner decision. "When I stopped by his office this morning," he said slowly, thoughtfully, "and told him where we were headed, he jumped. Actually jumped, as if I'd burned him with a hot poker. Then he mumbled something about coincidence and God's timing and informed me that he was coming along. Nothing I said could change his mind."

Jonah hadn't been able to change Professor K.'s mind? Paige looked unseeingly out the window. That in itself made her uneasy—Jonah in a persuasive mood could charm knotholes out of a pine tree. "He wouldn't elaborate, provide you with any of the details? No names or places? I've been working with him pretty closely on the revised edition of that POW book he wrote almost thirty years ago, remember. Initially I thought he was tagging along because he couldn't resist double-checking his Vietnam entries.''

She lifted her hands, feeling helpless. Hating it. ''But that still doesn't make a lot of sense. He's spent *months* on the updated book, preparing comparisons of POW experience in Vietnam, Korea and World War II. There's no reason for him to be here, especially when he'll miss that interview.''

''Did he ever tell *you* who the interview was with?''

''No. But that's not as unusual as you may think. The department secretary should know, though. On the other hand...'' Her voice trailed away. A strange tightness was constricting her chest, along with an undefined anxiety she hadn't been able to put aside.

A half smile lifted the corners of Jonah's mouth under his mustache. ''Don't worry 'bout it, all right? We'll try pushing a little harder tonight. He's a stubborn, opinionated old rascal, and we might not get anywhere. But if it will make you feel better, we'll give it a try.''

Paige twisted around to gaze down again at the professor's sleeping form. ''He's never liked his right hand to know what the left is doing. I worked with him years ago, before I—'' she faltered, then mentally shrugged and plowed on ''—before I married. Professor K. might have told you.'' She glanced quickly across at Jonah's impassive face, then away. ''I quit after I married, but when my husband...died, I accepted a job at the Smithsonian. Professor K. still made a point of dropping by, keeping tabs. I didn't find out for two years that he would always call my folks to report in, promise to take care of me so they wouldn't worry. That's what I mean...''

Her fingers began drumming on the door handle, a rapid, restless tattoo. ''He seems to know everything about everyone else, but he won't share much of himself.'' And the knowledge hurt. ''I just hope he's not in trouble with his publisher, or the university or something. Some dispute he doesn't want me fretting about.''

Jonah's arm slid across the seat of their small rental car to give her a brief hug. Obviously he meant only to offer comfort. Paige knew better than to read more into it, yet for a shocking moment her entire being yearned toward that quiet, Gibraltar-size strength. It had been so long.

Then she stiffened, keeping her face averted, and forced herself to pull away. She felt Jonah's fingers gently tug the hair over one ear. Incredibly, he emitted a soft chuckle.

"Worry, little *koneko,* is nonproductive, though you do it very well. How about if we leave the professor in the Lord's capable hands and enjoy the trip?"

Paige shot him a fulminating glare, which he serenely ignored. Every time he called her one of those foreign names, she wanted to stuff the teasing words back in his too-amiable face. Obviously they were some teasing endearment, like calling her a beagle, but Jonah refused to translate any of them. Polite requests, stern demands, threatening to quit...she had tried them all, but they both knew she wasn't going to do anything. She couldn't—in spite of the political climate ruling the day—even claim harassment, because, well...because he wasn't.

But there was a deeper reason Paige never pushed. The tightness in her chest threatened to crack her rib cage, because she finally faced the bitter truth about herself. Her unblinking gaze focused on a man and woman in the car they were passing alongside of, and she watched their laughter, watched as the woman reached across and rubbed the man's neck. Jonah accelerated by, but Paige's last visual snapshot was the man's expression: the relaxed affection and...well, the intimacy.

Something she longed for but no longer prayed for, because she knew it wasn't going to happen. Especially with Jonah Sterling.

The next forty-eight hours passed in a blur of more old uniforms and medals, along with personal and official documents, maps, photographs and yellowing newspapers. Paige enjoyed the whole process, not only because she could lose herself in research, but because she and Jonah had been able to cultivate an excellent working relationship. In short, they were a good team.

The back-breaking hours also kept her from worrying about

Professor K., though she was never able to completely ignore the low-level anxiety. The first day, after dropping her and Jonah off at the Robins Museum of Aviation, the professor had disappeared in the rental car and they hadn't seen him until breakfast the next morning. Morose and abstracted, almost depressed, he hadn't even responded to Jonah's lighthearted teasing.

By the final morning, Paige decided to push a little. "...and since I brought the list of names and the key in case you and I had some extra time, maybe if both of us insist, he'll at least acknowledge the tantalizing possibilities."

"I don't know, Paige. I'm a little preoccupied myself right now."

"I had noticed." And it drove her crazy. What if the names and key really did mean something important—like where Hitler was buried? She knew her own imagination was creating too many fanciful scenarios, but still.... "At least showing him the list of names might divert him, persuade him to at least hang around the museum with us," she told Jonah.

"It's worth a try." His expression belied the words, however.

"You just don't want to be diverted yourself," Paige pointed out. "Honestly, Jonah, you're worse than Professor K. Come to think of it, when you're working you're worse than the most absentminded professor ever."

That earned her a chuckle and a teasing hair pull. Also—to her breathless consternation, an index finger stroking down her cheek. Paige turned away hurriedly to greet Professor K., who had just arrived in the motel coffee shop. "Morning. I have a surprise to share with you today." She hoped neither man would notice her heightened color.

Professor K. dropped down in the chair, propping one elbow on the table so he could rub his forehead. "You look like a little girl waiting to share a secret," he observed, the deep voice gruff with affection.

Paige dug the envelope out of her briefcase, handing it to him while she explained the story. Smiling a little, the professor rubbed his thumb over the key, then carefully opened the paper with the list of names. All the color left his face. "I don't believe it," he exclaimed, staring at the paper as though it were a serpent.

"Professor?"

"You all right, sir?" Jonah stood, moved unhurriedly to the older man's side and laid a hand on his shoulder. "What's wrong?"

"Nothing. It's nothing." He stood as well, shaking off Jonah's hand. "I...forgot something in my room. I'll eat later, after I drop the two of you off."

He'd closed up like the door to a bank vault and didn't speak again until they were at the museum. "I'll meet you back here by three," he growled, and left.

Stiff with hurt and bewilderment, Paige watched the car barrel back down the drive. Jonah stepped in front of her, blocking the view, and clasped both her clenched hands. "Let it go," he ordered gently. "He's chasing rabbits, probably. You know how eccentric he is, probably better than I, since you've known him all your life. But I do have a book to write—and I need your valuable—undistracted—assistance for the few hours we have left here."

She stared down at their clasped hands. Jonah's hands were large, warm, the fingers surprisingly rough for the hands of a writer. The comfort his clasp offered contradicted his words, once again throwing Paige into confusion. Gently but firmly she withdrew. "I wasn't going to give you less than my best," she promised, turning away.

He muttered something incomprehensible beneath his breath, probably in German or Swedish. Naturally, on top of everything else, J. Gregory could converse in at least four other languages. There was little J. Gregory couldn't do, apparently. "Paige, I didn't mean..." he began, then gave up and followed her down the walk.

They met the professor back at the motel late in the afternoon. Once again he refused to talk beyond a terse declaration that he didn't feel like talking. But back home in Washington late that evening, when Paige tried to insist that he allow her to spend the night, there at the house, he finally relented, at least a little.

"Let it lie, girl. You're worrying us both to death." He hung his fedora and cane on the hall tree, then pinched her cheek—his one gesture of affection. "I realize I've been a bear. I'll explain when I can, but not before. Now, run along home. You look tired. I'll be fine. Don't bother to come over in the morning—I won't need you for the next couple of days."

"All right." She hugged him, kissed the beard-stubbled chin. "You look just as tired, so promise me you'll go straight to bed, as well. Please?"

"Now, how can I refuse when you turn those big eyes on me like that? Go on, then, and scat. I'll talk with you in a couple of days."

Paige was halfway down the walk to the waiting taxi, when he called her name. She turned.

"You've been a real trouper, girl. Jonah's lucky to have you for his assistant."

"Professor, in some things, you're as transparent as a glass of springwater," Paige called back, keeping her voice light with an effort. "Don't forget to lock and bolt the door!"

"I'm not a child," he shot back grumpily, and slammed the door.

"I had to call, even though I know how you feel," the old man said into the phone. *"Heed the warning—or ignore it. I don't know how he found my address, but I do know what kind of man that professor is. He isn't going to just let the matter rest."*

"Your warning isn't needed. The professor is being taken care of." There was an ugly pause. *"I learned long ago how easy it is to get away with anything—if you have the position and the power."* The voice dropped even deeper. *"It's fitting, don't you think...Father. I'm just following your example...."*

An awkward pause hovered on the line. "You always were a vengeful, unforgiving child."

"I'm the son of a traitor who never got caught. Don't forget

that, old man. If you want to start denigrating character, look at yourself.''

"Your mother—"

"Is a social-climbing snob who has her head in the sand and turns her back on the unpleasant smells." The old man closed his eyes, hearing the pain beneath the bitterness and hatred. His hand, slippery on the receiver, trembled as his son spewed more hateful, hurtful words. "And if you want something done, you do it yourself. What's the matter? You trying to go all moral, atone for your past? Forget it. It's too late, about fifty years too late. Look at it this way—I'll be doing you a favor. I'll have the nosy professor taken care of—and anyone else who starts digging all the skeletons out of our family closet."

"I know. That's what I'm afraid of."

There was no response. After a second that stretched to eternity, the click and subsequent dial tone buzzed harshly in his ear. Defeated, the old man hung up the phone. He was afraid, and there was nothing he could do now but wait.

Chapter Four

The rhythmic ticking of the ceiling fan irritated Emil Kittridge. Annoyed, he glared upward, vaguely aware of a tense, even oppressive atmosphere hanging over his living room. He was too engrossed to pay much attention, however. At least the revolving paddles generated a welcome breeze, though the humidity still sapped his energy. Growing old had proved to be a confounded nuisance.

He reached for another handful of peanuts without taking his eyes off the notes he was reading. There was something here, something important he was missing. His frown deepened along with the sense of urgency, and with an exasperated grunt he took off his glasses, rubbed his burning eyes, then crammed the bifocals back on his nose.

Suddenly he sat up straight, feeling excitement rejuvenating his tired old bones. It fit! By jingo, it all fit. Thanks to that timely trip to Georgia, the last pieces had fallen into place, because he'd been able to corroborate the POW's story. He could finally document all the evidence—two witnesses, wasn't that what the Bible required? Well, he'd found them. And if his suspicions were correct, the whole *family* was cursed with a legacy of treason and unprincipled amorality.

Immediate action would have to be initiated, because election campaigns were already under way. Kittridge rubbed a tired hand over his face. If he didn't publicize his findings, the scurrilous man would be a shoo-in, according to the latest polls, if he chose to run. And human nature being what it was, Kittridge knew this man would run.

Outside under his picture window, something rustled the overgrown crepe myrtle, causing the branches to scrape the side of the house. The noise was almost as annoying as the blasted fan, Kittridge thought, his gaze returning to the list of names. Laying them aside, he picked up a spiral notebook and flipped to the last entries, near the back.

A muffled thud, like a body falling to the ground, caused him to jerk upright in the chair so violently he tore a corner off the page he was reading. Then the next-door neighbor's cat yowled a warning, and the air filled with the muffled screams of a cat fight.

Disgusted, Kittridge shoved back from the desk and stomped across the room to draw the curtains. He should have done that hours ago, anyway, when it got dark. For a long time he stood there, still holding the drapery cord, indecision warring with anxiety. Finally he returned to his desk, and tore a page out of the notebook. Now...where to hide it. His gaze moved over the room, assessing and rejecting likely places. Feeling a fool, he made his way from one end of the house to the other, eventually settling for what he felt was the best location, at least temporarily. If this information *was* what the intruder had been after, it would be safe enough here, Kittridge decided, especially if his suspicions were correct and the house had already been searched before it was trashed. *This time, Ben, I won't let you down.*

But he was going to have to break one of his long-standing personal precepts. First thing in the morning, he'd talk to Paige and Jonah, show them the notes. Paige had a good head on her shoulders, for all the nonsense that fool husband of hers had foisted on her. And Jonah...Kittridge chuckled. Now there was the kind of man his goddaughter really deserved. The pair of them might chuckle at his lack of subtle matchmaking, but Kittridge didn't care, if it got the job done. Might be time to have a serious discussion with Jonah. It was plain as white paint that Paige was not being honest about her own attractions, and Jonah's feelings about her.

His mind was wandering. Sighing, he massaged his temples, wondering for the first time if he should consider retiring. Mentally as well as physically, he was slowing down.

"Tomorrow," he muttered tiredly. He'd enlist Jonah's and Paige's aid tomorrow, to resolve the treason issue and see that justice—albeit decades and too many deaths later—was served at last. At least his son could finally rest in peace. Resigned to his decision, he plodded to the kitchen to make a cup of cocoa before he went to bed, abruptly feeling every one of his seventy-nine years.

He woke in the predawn hours, abruptly and completely. A wave of goose bumps peppered his skin, and he sat up, head tilted. Had that been a noise *inside* the house? Carefully he shoved aside the sheet and swung his feet to the ground, snagging the flashlight he kept on the floor by his bed. His knees cracked as he tried to sneak out into the hall, and he cursed both age and his apprehension.

There. Down the hall a shadow moved. Fighting fear as well as anger—how *dare* the little twerp break in a second time— he edged backward, never taking his eyes off the shadow. It didn't move—it was just a shadow after all. Relieved, he dropped the arm holding the flashlight, debating now whether or not to call the police. The corner of his eye caught a blur of movement. But...it was coming from the *other* direction. *What—*

The blow crashed into the side of his neck. Bright light exploded behind his eyes, hurtling him down a long, undulating tunnel. He knew he was falling, and then—nothing.

"And although no man can ever predict the hour, we rest in the knowledge that our heavenly Father has a place prepared for all of us who have put our hope in His Son Jesus. Let us cling to that hope, and the peace He offers even in the midst of our grief over departed loved ones...."

Paige sat, her eyes wide and unblinking. Dry. She still hadn't

been able to cry. She felt numb, cold as the gravestones surrounding them, empty as the skull of a long-dead dinosaur in
the Museum of Natural History. Jonah sat beside her, holding
her hand in his. She didn't even know when he'd taken it.

It's not true. Professor K.'s not dead. This is just a bad
dream....

The people around her blurred, the minister's words running
together in nonsensical patterns of sound. Images flashed
through her mind, scenes from out of the past roaring by as if
viewed through the window of a fast-moving train. The same
ugly emotions choked her, just like then. Guilt, pain...
fear...washing over her in a red tide. She would drown in them
and she didn't care.

"Paige?"

She looked numbly up at Jonah, then around. The service
was over. Friends and acquaintances had surrounded them, of-
fering condolences and snippets of the professor's long and
colorful life, murmuring that he'd died as he would have preferred it. It was a blessing, wasn't it. On the way to work.
Quick—mercifully quick. The minister patted her shoulder.

Finally they could go. "I want to go back to his house for
a few minutes." She stared up at Jonah. How strange. His face
was full of concern. For her? Surely not. She knew she looked
like a wax figurine. Black was not her best color. She wondered
why Jonah wasn't yelling at her, telling her she ought to change
clothes, that she needed to be more of a Christian about Professor K.'s death.

After a silence that could have lasted seconds or hours, Jonah
cupped her elbow in his warm, somehow supporting hand. "All
right," he said, helping her gently into the back of the limou-
sine.

The house felt empty, full of dank gloom, as if somehow it
knew that the professor had been stilled forever. He was gone.
He'd never pinch her cheek, call her "girl" in the gruff voice
again. At last, for the first time since the police had called her
three days ago, Paige felt tears sting her eyes. Behind her Jonah
quietly shut the door and turned on the hall light.

She stared at the coatrack, two hot tears sliding down her

cold cheeks. Almost hesitantly she lifted her hand to stroke the professor's cane, his crushed, ancient fedora. Surely if they took a couple of steps into the living room, he'd be there in his easy chair, munching peanuts. Beneath her fingers the smooth, worn handle of the cane felt strange, as though it knew her hand didn't belong there. And his fedora practically shrank away—

Something clicked in Paige's brain, a half-formed cranial synapse that dried her tears and froze her, midstep in the hall.

"Let's leave—this is too soon for you." Jonah's voice intruded, and Paige fought the arm wrapped about her shoulders.

"Wait." She looked frantically around the foyer, her fingers suddenly digging into his wrist. "Jonah...there's something...wrong here." Closing her eyes, she tried to concentrate, to focus on the half-formed message from her brain. Jonah's hand covered her clutching fingers, and Paige knew she should pull free, but right now all her energy needed to be directed on capturing that elusive sensation of wrongness.

When it hit her, she actually swayed on her feet as though struck.

"Jonah..." Calm. She must keep her voice calm, reasonable, even if she was screaming inside. "Jonah, the police said the professor was found at the Metro station, the one he takes to the campus."

"That's correct..." Jonah's tone was patient. "He apparently suffered a heart attack, possibly a stroke. He wasn't attacked, love—trust me. There were no signs of struggle—his briefcase was even still by him. The bruise on his neck came from hitting the concrete abutment when he fell. Paige—" He took her arms, gave her a gentle shake. "I know you're having a hard time with this and that's to be expected. But it would help if you'd cry, give in to the grief. It's okay to cry. You don't—"

She tore herself free. "Jonah—*listen* to me. I'm not hysterical, not trying to deny that he's dead. But it didn't happen at the Metro station." His gaze searched hers, and in rising fury she saw he was only humoring her. "Jonah, you have to listen to me. Professor K. did *not* go there the morning he died!"

Her teeth were practically chattering, but she forced the words out. "Jonah—I'm afraid Professor K. was murdered."

Chapter Five

Paige winced as she glanced at her watch. It was almost five o'clock. She'd been searching through Professor K.'s World War II papers for over seven hours now, but she still had nothing to show for it. She stood, performed a few bend and stretch movements to relax her muscles, then sat back down.

Seven hours today. Twenty or so over the previous two days, futilely presenting her case to Jonah and the police. Nobody— including Jonah—had listened. Everyone had been patient. Everyone had been gentle and polite. But in the end, everyone had been patronizing:

"Sure, something had been bothering him—his health. According to his doctor, he'd had to go on pills for high blood pressure recently. He was slowing down, getting old. Everyone noticed."

"Forgetting his cane and fedora—no matter how entrenched in habit he might have been—does not constitute enough evidence to initiate a homicide investigation, Ms. Hawthorne. There's nothing, remember, that indicates the break-in earlier this week had a motive beyond malicious destruction of property prompted by a dearth of items to steal."

"There's a good possibility it precipitated the heart attack, but that's the only connection."

"He was probably already slightly disoriented before he left the house, Paige. It's a miracle he didn't crash his car on the way to the station."

Paige finally quit arguing, but her determination had only hardened. Grimly rotating her shoulders and neck, she turned her attention back to the pile of notebooks stacked on the floor. It was late, and she knew she risked facing the quiet censure in a pair of midnight blue eyes...if he'd been here.

"Deal with it, Mr. Sterling," she grumbled, flipping open the notebook on top.

Jonah had received an urgent call from his editor that morning, and he'd shot off to the National on his motorcycle an hour later. Even if he finished his business in New York and got back to D.C., the odds were against him trundling over here. Why would he, after all? What Paige did on her own time was her own business, as long as it didn't interfere with the work she produced for Jonah.

On the other hand, he'd been a shadow shy of dictatorial since the funeral. Enough for Paige to...well, if not precisely *resent* it, but enough that she felt crowded. Crowded, and a little bit threatened. He might not be David—he wasn't David, but she still found herself sliding toward the dreaded mud hole of inadequacy again.

Paige surveyed the neatly organized mounds of paperwork surrounding her. She was proficient. Highly organized. Passably intelligent. Streetwise enough to come in out of the rain...well, all right. When it came to her personal life, she'd gotten pretty damp, and if she weren't careful, Jonah Sterling was going to leave her in the midst of another deluge, with no umbrella in sight. For some reason, she didn't appear to have much luck when it came to men.

Abruptly she stood up, deciding to take a break. When her thoughts wandered down that particular road she knew she was too tired to concentrate properly. And right now she couldn't afford to overlook any detail, however oblique. Something, somewhere in the house had to yield a nonrefutable clue that would force Jonah and the police to place more credence in her conviction that the professor had been murdered.

"But *why?*" she demanded aloud. The question—still un-answered—bounced off indifferent walls, and abruptly Paige snatched up a plastic paper-clip holder and hurled it across the room.

Then, sheepish and exhausted, she trudged over to pick it up, gather up every single one of the scattered paper clips, and return the holder to the desk. Her red-rimmed gaze fell almost haphazardly on the protruding corner of a notebook sandwiched between two textbooks. Out of sheer habit and compulsive ti-diness, Paige reached to align the notebook with the two vol-umes. The spiral caught, and Paige tugged the notebook out, intending to lay it aside and put the books away.

It was a smaller notebook than Professor K. usually used— about five by seven. Puzzled, Paige leafed through it, noting that most of the information dealt with the Vietnam era, which was strange, since this was his World War II room. Clever, Paige. You're a regular Sherlock Holmes. A page had been torn out of the back.

Curiosity battled with exhaustion as she sank into the chair again, pinching the bridge of her nose as her burning eyes struggled to decipher the professor's sprawling script. The years, "1965-'68," had been neatly scribed across the top; pages were subdivided by subject—battles, military references and the like. Below were names of men, the date the professor had visited them, and the coding system referring to the pro-fessor's files. He had been, she thought with painful wistful-ness, a fanatic for organization. A lot of her own research habits were directly attributable to Professor Kittridge's insistence that she "...document, document, document!"

A tear slid down her cheek unnoticed, and at first a name that had been added to the bottom of the page didn't register, because her mind was dulled by exhaustion and a sudden on-slaught of painful memories. "'James D—'" the writing looked hurried, almost scribbled "'—Med-der, Georgia.' Geor-gia? *Georgia?*"

Electrified, she swiped an impatient hand across her eyes. Was this one of the people Professor Kittridge had visited when he had insisted on flying down to Georgia with them? If so, and she talked to this person, maybe, just maybe she could glean a reason for the professor's odd behavior those two days. And if she discovered the motivation for his odd behavior, perhaps she would be one step closer to a motivation behind his murder. She glared at the wispy fragments of paper clinging to the spirals at the bottom of the notebook, signaling where the page had been ripped out. Why, she wondered, had he done that?

Paige tossed down the notebook and picked up the two textbooks, which turned out to be two bound theses...on the Vietnam War. What were they doing in here? She spent a fruitless ten minutes flipping through the two books, hoping he'd absentmindedly used the missing paper from the notebook to mark pertinent pages or something. But that would be so unlike him—he used paper clips, not scraps of paper, to mark pages.

Nothing. There was nothing. Sighing, she laid the books aside and turned back to the notebook. Could he have thrown the page away? Nope—never. Totally out of character. In all the years she'd known him, Professor K. *never* threw anything away, except perhaps months-old, moldy food even the neighbor's cat, Jasper, refused to eat. When Mattie had still been alive, she'd had to do battle constantly over newspapers and magazines. The professor even had a shed out back, filled with everything from rusting lawn tools to hundreds of empty peanut jars.

All right, then. He wouldn't have thrown that page away. That left only one alternative: he must have ripped the page out, for the express purpose of placing it somewhere else. Rapidly Paige searched through the piles of notebooks and index cards once more, just to be sure. Then, running now, she headed down the short hall for the Vietnam room. The files seemed to be in order, and yet...

Paige straightened slowly. "He must have suspected," she whispered out loud. She dropped into the chair by the library desk. "All along, he must have known..." But instead of talking with her, or even with both her and Jonah, he hadn't opened his mouth. And it had cost him his life.

Lifting her head to the ceiling, eyes wet, she clenched her

hands into fists. "God," she cried, her voice hoarse, "why didn't he share with me? Why didn't he ask for help?" *If only*—the most bitter phrase in any language.

Her head dropped and she buried her face in her hands.

After a while, she pushed back in the chair and stood. Then, her step brisk, she marched to the kitchen to buoy her body and spirit with some of the leftover food from the funeral. There was a lot to do.

Jonah maneuvered his motorcycle with almost reckless skill as he slipped in and out of the heavy traffic. Paige hadn't been at her apartment, which left him with one unpleasant alternative. He'd suggested before he left that morning that she hook up with some of her old Smithsonian mates and perhaps enjoy a leisurely meal in a restaurant. But it was obvious she hadn't. In fact, in the months they'd been working together, the only time she *ever* ate out instead of cooking a meal had been when Jonah or the professor had insisted.

The professor.

Mouth flattening, he gunned the bike past a slow-moving car and darted in front of another, then sped down the exit ramp. She was going to exhaust herself over her dogged notion that Professor Kittridge had been murdered.

At odd moments over the years, Jonah had privately acknowledged that his own single-mindedness could be difficult to adjust to, but he'd never worried about that unpleasant trait. Until now, when he could attribute it to someone else. Paige, he had learned, was more stubborn than a stone wall, and when her mind was made up, she was just as unmovable.

Too bad, he promised himself, but Ms. Stone Wall Hawthorne had met her match, as far as he was concerned. If he had to dismantle the wall of her erroneous conviction about the professor stone by stone, he planned to do so. Besides, there were more pressing matters she needed to address—namely Jonah's book.

Arrogant bloke, aren't we, J. Gregory, he chastised himself with a tired grin as he waited with a sea of cars for a light to change.

It was almost seven o'clock when he turned onto the tree-lined street where Kittridge had lived. Twilight cast lengthening purple shadows over the late-summer haze. In the quiet neighborhood the incessant roar of traffic had finally faded, and the only noise came from the muted sputtering of his modified Harley.

Jonah pulled into the driveway, killed the engine and stared in growing exasperation at the house. Every window blazed with light—Paige hadn't drawn the shades. Yanking his gloves off and tossing them on his helmet, he ran lightly up the steps. She hadn't locked the front door, either, and Jonah decided with the rashness of exhaustion to teach her a needed lesson. Apparently the intruder the other day hadn't been enough.

Paige was in the Vietnam room, crouched down on hands and knees with her back to the doorway. He cat footed across until he was standing just behind her.

"Now if I'd been a burglar or—"

The words died abruptly when Paige jerked sideways and grabbed a long knife that had been lying to her right. Then she leaped to her feet to face Jonah, who was astonished at the way she looked, the knife poised above her head for attack.

They stared at each other for an endless span of seconds before Jonah reached out and very gently, very carefully removed the knife from her upraised hand. "I can see," he murmured, "that I was misled by the carelessness of open windows and unlocked doors. Sneaking up on you now could be dangerous."

He tossed the knife in the air, catching it by the handle before absently tossing it again without taking his eyes off Paige. "Your reaction is certainly an improvement over the last time I startled you, but a trifle risky, don't you think, tempting circumstances like this? A weapon isn't much use when all your senses are focused only in front of your face."

Paige's complexion changed from pale to flushed. "How could you do that to me? You know I—" She stopped, hands automatically lifting to check her hair. Then she hauled them down with a jerk and glared. "You're just lucky I didn't have the courage to attack."

"Well, now, I could say you're lucky I didn't have to defend against your attack." Even as he watched, her embarrassment and frustration began to fade, her expression as well as her body stiffening into the poise he was coming to actively despise. Someone—probably her deceased husband—had done a number on the lady.

Jonah tested the blade with his thumb, hefted the knife in his hands one last time, then laid it on the floor. "You should have at least locked the door," he pointed out as mildly as he could, given his own irritation over her carelessness.

"Why? If the murderer wants to have a go at me, as well, he'd just break another window."

"I was hoping you'd spent the day in more fruitful pursuits." He propped his hip on the desk, studying her pale face thoughtfully. For some reason she was as taut as piano wire, and it wasn't because he'd startled her. "Paige...let it go. He wasn't murdered, and your obsession—no, don't shake your head at me, love—isn't healthy."

She picked up a small spiral notebook and smacked it against his chest. "Determination, Mr. Sterling, is *not* an obsession." She paused, and in a flash of insanity Jonah found himself wanting to smooth his thumb over the lines creasing her forehead. When she spoke again, the tone almost pleading, he wanted to take her in his arms.

"He didn't die of a stroke or a heart attack, Jonah," she said. "I found that notebook, found where a page has been torn out of the back. More significant, I found it in the World War II room, not the Vietnam room. And that's not the only thing."

Jonah flipped through the notebook, lifted his gaze back to Paige. "Tell me where you're headed with this, Paige."

"I've known—" her voice became flat "—knew—the professor since I was ten years old. He never threw anything away. Not even candy wrappers. It drove his wife crazy. And, Jonah—I can't even *find* his Vietnam notebooks, I mean the ones he normally uses. I mean, that he used." She pinched the bridge of her nose. "Sorry. I'm not making any sense, I know."

"Take it easy. I'm listening." It had been useless to argue with Paige lately, and when she was distressed, disagreeing with her caused her to retreat into a spate of apologies. Jonah scratched his forehead, twiddled with his mustache. "Um...this notebook. You think he deliberately tore out a sheet, then?" He tried for an encouraging look.

Paige nodded eagerly. "Yes! Don't you see? He *hid* it. I'm pretty sure they were some sort of clue as to why he was murdered. Maybe he's hidden the others, too. Jonah, you have to see—"

From outside the window came the plaintive "mrrouw?" of a cat. Paige jumped, but Jonah was on his feet and poised protectively in front of her before the sound faded. Claws scratched the screen, and the cat meowed again. Jonah and Paige looked at each other and burst into sheepish laughter.

"Jasper." Paige shook her head, walking over to the window. "He's so spoiled."

She opened the window and unhooked the screen, and the gigantic orange tom jumped with an inelegant thud onto the floor. After stropping himself on Paige's leg, he strolled out the door and headed for the pantry, his tail gently waving with pleasure.

"Professor K. got him hooked on boiled peanuts." Paige blinked furiously, her smile wobbling. "I don't know what will happen now that—"

A series of thumps, clattering and breaking glass erupted from the opposite end of the house.

"Oh, no..." Paige started for the door. "He's probably gotten into the pantry. I shouldn't have—"

Jonah caught her arm. "I'll go get the beastie. You start cleaning up, and I'll take you out for a spot of supper. I'm beat from my trek to the Big Apple."

"I can make something. There's still a good bit of leftovers from the funeral. I don't want to throw anything out. Thought I could donate some to the neighbors, or maybe a local shelter—there's too much for it to go to waste—"

Her voice trailed into silence when his fingers brushed her cheekbone. "We'll work it out. Later. Right now, let me take you out. Please..."

"I—all right." She glanced around, still flustered, Jonah

saw, though he wasn't sure whether it was from the missing page, Jasper the cat—or the impromptu spot of intimacy he'd been unable to resist. "I'll clean up," she mumbled finally. "Don't be angry at Jasper, Jonah. He can't help it if he's clumsy and spoiled."

"But no one would ever say the same for you, would they?" Jonah murmured tenderly, prompting a stunned look flashing his way from suddenly tear-darkened eyes. "Don't worry!" he called back over his shoulder as he strode out of the room. "I won't hurt the cat."

Chapter Six

He returned some moments later, holding Jasper in his arms and scratching the tom's ears and neck. Purring noisily, the cat kneaded his paws in Jonah's forearm, undisturbed by the fact that Jonah had just spent the past ten minutes cleaning up the mess his feline foraging had made of the pantry. "I've—um—brought Jasper back here. Maybe we should let him exit the way he came in."

"Probably." Paige was studying him with the frown back between her eyes. She opened her mouth as if to speak, shut it with a shrug. Then she said, "Jonah, when Jasper surprised us, why did you jump in front of me like that?"

He should have known Paige was too observant—and too curious—to let the matter rest. "Mmm...instinct, I suppose." He reopened the screen and gently shoved a reluctant Jasper out the window. "Um...I spent an interesting summer in Bangladesh once. Still tend to react...off-the-cuff, shall we say, when I'm startled."

"Oh, really?" Paige drawled, her expression dubious.

Jonah faced the fact that he was stalling. He watched Jasper settle on the grass to fastidiously clean his left hind leg, and tried with little success to think of a way to drop a lighted match into a pool of petrol without having everything explode.

"Jonah, what are you not telling me?"

Sometimes he wished the woman weren't so infernally astute. Sighing, he turned around, and with reluctant fingers reached into his hip pocket and tugged out a sheet of notebook paper. It had been folded many times into a tight little square. "I found this on the floor in the remains of one of the jars our friend Jasper broke." He paused, then added roughly, "I'm afraid you might be right about the professor's death, Paige. It's very likely it wasn't an accident. I'm sorry."

Silence spread. Fingers shaking, Paige reached for the paper, carefully opened it. Her stricken gaze lifted to Jonah's. "He really was murdered," she said numbly, "wasn't he..."

Jonah lifted the notes out of her hand. "Well...he was certainly eccentric, but not even the professor would have done something like this—" he fanned the paper in the air "—unless he felt this information was too dangerous to leave lying about. But dangerous to whom? And how?" He studied the neatly scrawled page, his mind racing. "What I don't understand is why he didn't talk to us, share whatever it was that was making him so nervous, so suspicious."

"Somebody killed him."

Jonah glanced sharply at her. She was trembling, her eyes staring sightlessly, lips quivering in a face drained of color. "Paige—" He laid a comforting hand on her shoulder.

She jerked away. "Leave me alone." She turned blindly, slumping, arms crossed over her stomach as if she were in deep pain.

Jonah stuffed the note back in his pocket, raging at himself for his insensitivity, and reached for her. At first she only suffered the embrace, her body stiff. He forced her head to his shoulder, whispering soft nonsensical phrases in her ear, until she finally gave in and held him, just held him, her hands clinging to his shirt. He couldn't bear to see that frightened look shadow her lovely features. He wanted to comfort her, protect her. Strands of silvery blond hair hid her face, and Jonah swallowed hard, feeling the fragility of her slender form, inhaling the poignant aroma of old books and an elusive scent he could only identify as...Paige.

* * *

They were sitting in the breakfast nook of Paige's apartment, empty plates and used silverware shoved to one side of the table. The odor of crisply fried ham hung heavy in the air—as thick as the atmosphere. Avoiding Jonah's gaze, Paige stacked the plates and arranged the cutlery on top; she would have moved the dirty dishes at least to the sink, but Jonah's hand whipped out to her wrist, stilling the action.

"You've cooked the meal, over my objections," he said, a crisp British edge to the phrase. "Cleanup can wait."

"We can talk while I clean."

"We can talk, then we can *both* clean."

"It won't take five minutes. I can clean and think at the same time."

"Mmm. I can't."

A rueful smile flickered, and she finally looked him straight in the eye. "Well...that's a surprise. I hadn't realized there was something you couldn't do."

Needing the security of a familiar routine, Paige had cooked the simple meal while Jonah read through a stack of Professor K.'s notebooks. She had also needed, on a deep subconscious level she winced at admitting, to show her competence at something. Rationally she knew she was not responsible for Professor's K.'s death, any more than she was responsible for his closemouthed independence. But pain—and corrosive guilt—still twined about her spirit, so she fought with the only weapons she had, one of which happened to be superlative kitchen skills.

"There's a lot I can't do," Jonah said, his gaze roving over her in an uncomfortable sweep. "But that doesn't include tying you to that blasted chair if you make one more attempt to play Superwoman in the kitchen." He was smiling, but the deep blue eyes were serious. "I'm knackered from the New York trip and the infamous Washington traffic. At the moment I need your brainpower more than your efficiency." He spread the creased piece of paper on the table. "Help me think—this bit of writing isn't enough on its own to take to the police."

For several moments they studied the page in silence.

"A family," Paige muttered. "'Has to be same family,' he says. But what family? And see here—up in the left corner? He's written a name. Is it part of the family he's referring to? I think it's Ben, but I don't know if it's a first name, or an abbreviation for a last name...three initials..."

Jonah leaned back, lacing his hands behind his head. He looked at the ceiling and quoted the scrawled, cryptic phrase that was driving them both crazy. "'Too much to be coincidence. Has to be the same family. Bad blood—sins of the fathers...' Why couldn't he have been more specific?"

"I told you," Paige repeated tiredly. "He was like that. If he discovered something really bad about an individual, he had to be careful—even with researched documentation—about what he put on paper. A lot of it was just the way he was, but my father did tell me that the professor was once involved in a pretty nasty legal snarl. When I asked Professor K., he only told me that one lawsuit for slander was one too many. Period. He and Mattie never mentioned it again, so neither did I. But I know that's why he hid this paper, instead of talking about it to anyone. He'd want to verify all his facts first."

"Mmph," Jonah grunted. "Can't say as I blame him, especially concerning the police. I have a nasty suspicion their response won't be any more encouraging than it was for your initial assertions." He propped his elbows on the table, dropping his head so that his hands could rub the back of his neck.

He looked defenseless and weary, but Paige's gaze caught on the way the kitchen light brightened his hair to the richness of a fox's coat, and she watched the strong bones of his wrists as he rumpled the thick mass with his fingers. "I can't just let it die," she said, forcing her gaze back to the table instead of Jonah.

"Neither can I." He shoved away from the table suddenly and began pacing the small kitchen. The glitter in his darkening eyes reminded Paige uneasily of lightning in storm clouds. "I don't like the feel of this. The professor must have hit a highly sensitive nerve, because someone was willing to commit murder to prevent him from investigating further." He paused, staring unseeingly at the shopping list Paige kept fastened to the refrigerator with a magnet. "My books are works of fiction, but the characters have the same drives and motivations as real people. If someone resorts to murder, there are only a couple of classic motives compelling enough to—in the murderer's mind, of course—justify that course of action."

"Greed, revenge," Paige supplied, nodding.

"And passion," Jonah finished. "Jealousy, rage...even love." He stopped. "Paige? What is it? Think of something?" He dropped back down across from her.

"Nothing." She couldn't look at him. Would she ever be free of David's ghost, and the searing embers of his raging emotions? Even after all these years, the memories still burned. Unlike Professor K.'s, David's death *had* been an accident. But Paige knew—far better than Jonah realized—the far-reaching consequences of out-of-control human passions.

"Paige," Jonah repeated, leaning forward. "You've that look on your face again. Talk to me, tell me what you're thinking."

She took a deep breath, waited until she was sure her voice wouldn't wobble. "I was just thinking that you're right—there have to be powerful forces at work here. Of course society being what it is, there are less social restraints to help curb those dark human passions you're talking about. The wrong color of a hat, the wrong accent..." Saying the wrong thing at the wrong time. Forgetting a meeting. Burning a casserole because...because—

"Let's not get carried away." His hand briefly covered hers, stilling the restless movement of her fingers before withdrawing. "Stick to what we know about the professor's death, and those implications." He waited until Paige nodded, waited until she finally lifted her head and met the midnight gaze. "I'm not trying to overdramatize this, or frighten you, but we're going to need all our wits about us." He took a deep breath, then finished grimly, "Something the professor learned triggered a murderous response. And that means, unless we discover the motivation, there's a strong possibility that the killer may strike again."

"I...sort of came to that realization halfway through scrambling the eggs.'' The feeble attempt at levity helped, but not much. She still felt as though her nerve endings had been fried along with the ham. "I also realized that the whole mess somehow has to tie in to that list of names I showed him. The ones from Major Pettigrew's ribbons?"

"Mmm. Possibly." His voice and expression stayed neutral.

"I know you think I'm stretching it, but it's all we have to go on until I get back over to his house, look up the codes and hunt down the rest of his Vietnam notes. See if there's any significance."

He sat up straighter. "You're not to go there alone."

The brusque, almost curt tone shriveled her insides, and Paige fought the instinct to meekly submit. "I don't want to," she admitted, staring at her laced fingers. The knuckles were mottling, and she forced her grip to relax. "But I'm the only one who knows the code to his files. He never even told his personal secretary. If you want to join me, fine. But I'm going over there."

"Not alone." Jonah folded his arms across his chest, mouth beneath the bristly mustache a thin, unsmiling line.

The uncompromising dominance was as unexpected as his skill at martial arts. It was also far more devastating to her resolve. Heart beating like a captive bird's, Paige jumped up and began clearing the table. *It's happening again, Lord. I'm letting it happen again. Lord? Please don't let it happen again.* "I'll just straighten the kitchen first. Do you want the leftovers? Maybe I should take them to Jasper."

"Paige."

She stopped, breathing light and fast, her back to Jonah. He didn't make a sound, but she felt his approach with every strumming nerve in her body. If he raised his voice, she didn't know whether she would crumble—or explode. She felt betrayed, trapped, and even though she knew the feelings were irrational, she couldn't seem to lessen their intensity. Out-of-control emotion. Another mistake. Real Christian women were *never* out of control.

"Don't go over there tonight. Please." Jonah's quiet voice

held a note of pleading now. He was right behind her, but made no move to touch her.

Pleading? "I have to." Paige turned around, then almost shrank against the sink. He was close—so close she could see each individual eyelash, the straight bristly mustache hairs. Swallowing, she fixed her gaze on the rumpled collar of his shirt. "I have to," she repeated, standing very still. "I won't be able to sleep, anyway."

After a long tense moment, Jonah's expression abruptly softened, and he took a step backward. "All right. All right, love." He hesitated, then asked, "Why did you cringe from me, Paige? That's not the first time, either." The look in the dark blue eyes was indescribable. "What have I ever done to make you afraid of me?"

"I'm not afraid of you," Paige retorted, even though it wasn't entirely true. She was *terrified* of the feelings Jonah Sterling had resurrected, deep inside the bolted cold-storage locker where she had buried them. For half a year she had managed to see him only as her employer, but somehow in the past weeks he had slipped past her guard. She busied herself with clearing the table and loading the dishwasher. "I'm not afraid," she repeated. "You were ordering me around as though I were a child, making demands you have no right to make."

"You're right," Jonah returned, his voice carefully neutral again. "So how about if I just tag along, as...a friend."

He helped her clean up, his movements swift and economical. Helplessly Paige allowed it. David would have spent a good thirty minutes lecturing her, battering her with an arsenal of derogatory words, all designed to shame her into showing proper penitence over the error of her ways. It had only required one quiet, noncombative sentence from Jonah. *I'm no better now than I was five years ago. Forgive me, Lord. Please don't punish me, though I know I deserve it.*

Jonah's hand closed around her arm, halting the mental self-condemnation. "Someday," he promised softly as they headed out of the kitchen, "you're going to tell me what happened to you. Who it was that makes you flinch from me now."

She grabbed her purse off the couch. "Don't, Jonah."

"It was your husband, wasn't it?"

Paige froze, then opened the front door, set the lock and turned on the porch light. She turned back, flicked a glance upward at the impassive face. "It's none of your business," she said, then fled down the steps.

Chapter Seven

Even though she objected, Paige waited in her car with the doors locked until Jonah conducted a thorough search of the professor's house. She would never have admitted to him that, in truth, she was cravenly relieved by the show of protectiveness. Growing up on a farm in the Midwest had trained her to cope with snakes, wild animals and tornadoes. It had not provided skills or experience to fend off robbers and murderers.

"Thanks," she told Jonah after he waved an all-clear and she joined him inside. "I still wonder if you're overreacting, but..."

"We're scrounging for clues to solve a murder," Jonah pointed out, his hand fisting to lightly tap her chin. "A *real* murder. Cut me some slack, all right."

"You're sounding almost like a homegrown American."

"Ouch. You can play dirty, Ms. Hawthorne." He winked at her, then abruptly sobered. "First thing in the morning we take whatever information we unearth to the police, regardless of the scantiness or implausibility. I'm not risking your safety, or mine. I realize nobody listened to you earlier, but things have changed." He studied her a moment, his thumb and forefinger stroking the corners of his mustache. "In a way, I suppose I can look on this as fodder for my own story."

She stiffened, turning to examine the dust-covered antique candle box sitting on the foyer table. The professor had used it as a repository for keys, wallet and anything else in his pockets. Paige jerked her gaze away. "I can still search on my own. I realize this is taking valuable time away from your research, and your book—"

"Is in first draft stage, coming along nicely, so forget the apologies." He pushed her toward the hall. "Let's get to work, try to come up with something concrete enough so we won't look too melodramatic when we dump the whole affair in the laps of the local bobbies."

A reluctant smile inched across Paige's face. "I won't make any more cracks about your Americanisms if you'll curb your Britishisms."

"Deal." He smacked his hands together. "Where shall we begin?"

"Why don't you run down to the deli and grab some snacks while I get started? I threw out the last of the leftovers from the funeral, and I know you'll be wanting some munchies while you wait." She kept her voice casual, almost indifferent, though her palms were damp and her mouth dry. "Go on. I'll be fine. You've made sure the place is empty, and I promise I'll lock the door after you."

"I don't think," he began, then stopped, peering down into Paige's face. She thought she'd done a fair job of hiding her tension, but Jonah was more observant than anyone she'd ever known. "That's a good idea," he said, changing tack. "It will be a long evening if my only snack food is stale peanuts. You...you're sure you'll all right? Staying alone, I mean?"

Throat muscles tight, Paige nodded. He couldn't know that he'd just blessed her with something far more precious than a roomful of priceless gemstones, or a wall hung with prestigious awards. He isn't David. Jonah let her tease, argue, disagree...he even let her have her way when he wasn't comfortable with her decision. She didn't realize she was staring at him, until his hand lifted to tuck a strand of her hair behind her ear.

"Take care. Lock the door. I'll be back in ten minutes." Jonah stepped out on the porch, then poked his head back inside, a look of roguish glee dancing in his eyes. "Would've been five if I had my bike instead of your car."

For several emotional moments after he left, Paige could only stand in the foyer, her gaze glued to the front door. No, Jonah Sterling was definitely not David. She locked the door, took a deep, steadying breath, and headed down the hall.

The professor's filing system reflected the man: idiosyncratic, complex and painstakingly thorough. Determined to have something to show Jonah, Paige plunged into the first filing cabinet and instantly lost track of time.

Jonah grabbed half a dozen snack items without really noticing. He hadn't liked leaving Paige—in fact, every instinct was protesting, but making an issue of the matter would have backed Paige into yet another corner. Refusing to leave her alone would have hurt her—and damaged their tenuous relationship—in some elusive but important way. Jonah simply couldn't do it. When she'd stood there, those rain-washed eyes watching, as if waiting for a blow, it had taken every scrap of self-discipline not to sweep her into his arms and kiss the pain away.

Muttering in a mixture of Japanese and French, he paid for the snacks and dashed back out to the car. He'd only been gone seven minutes, but it felt like seven hours.

Two blocks back down the street the steering wheel jerked in his hands and the car lurched sideways. Jonah managed to pull over to the curb and switch off the engine. Then he pounded the wheel in a burst of irritation. Of all the times to have a puncture!

After grabbing a flashlight, he opened the door; the hot night closed in around him, thick and opaque with the cloud cover obscuring the moonlight. The nearest street lamp was a good fifty feet away. He was yanking open the trunk when a car pulled up behind him and stopped.

A man, almost invisible except for the pale blur of his face, approached. "Need some help?"

Jonah straightened, turned in relief. "Thanks. I'd appreciate it. I'm in a bit of a hurry—" The words died in his throat, warning tightening his stomach muscles into steel cables. There was something about the man's stance...the shape of his body. The hand hovering at his waist as if—

Jonah dived, catching the man on his shins and knocking him to the pavement, just as he pulled a gun from beneath his jacket. A swift sideways chop with the side of Jonah's hand stunned the assailant enough to give Jonah time to roll backward, placing Paige's car between himself and the gun. A car was approaching from the other direction. The gunman, who had just scrambled back to his feet, was caught directly in the glare of the headbeams.

Crouched behind Paige's car, Jonah heard a foul curse, then the sound of scrambling footsteps. A car door slammed, and as the other car drew even with Paige's, the gunman's car roared to life, burning rubber as it shot off down the street.

Jonah stood, shaking and sweating, thankful for long-buried reflexes honed to perfection during the course of his youth. Stupidly, he just stood there, not moving until the gunman's car careened around a corner. That car—it had followed him into the convenience store parking lot. There was no way this had been a random attempt at carjacking, or robbery. The paralysis suddenly broke. Wild with fear over Paige, Jonah raced back to the convenience store at a dead run. He called the professor's house as soon as he finished talking to the police.

Excitement rose when Paige unearthed three names and addresses that should be helpful, and she carefully stacked the file folders in a neat pile on the library table. That hadn't taken nearly as long as she had expected. She turned back to the cabinet, glancing at her watch, and started in disbelief. Over an hour had passed. An hour. Where on earth was Jonah?

Concerned, she stood in the middle of the room, hesitating, feeling foolish. More than once Jonah had chastized her about assuming responsibility for someone else's actions, and she didn't want to hover over him as though she had a right to expect him to leave behind a detailed itinerary. Then, as though she'd conjured him up, through the closed door came the faint sound of a ringing phone. The surge of anxiety waned. That would be Jonah, of course, since nobody else knew she was here. Knowing Jonah, he'd decided he couldn't live without one of those uniquely Southern moon pie snacks he loved. The convenience store three blocks away must not have had any, so he'd gone on a hunt. Relieved, Paige started toward the door.

A ball of fire exploded through the window behind her, shattering the panes in a shower of glass. It landed with a roar on the library table, skittered across and fell to the floor in a conflagration of ignited papers. Tongues of flame licked up the legs of the table, snaked across the threadbare carpet and attacked another mound of papers. Smoke and gaseous fumes billowed, filling the room with choking black smoke as the library table and more papers ignited.

Just as suddenly the lights went out, plunging the house into darkness—except for the writhing red and yellow flames.

The files—the papers! Father in heaven—the papers! Horrified, Paige could not tear her eyes from the burning documents. If she didn't save those papers, she'd never prove that Professor K. had been murdered. She took three steps, then convulsed in a paroxysm of coughing when the billowing smoke engulfed her. Her eyes stung, filling with tears.

With a crackling roar, the fire shot up the drapes.

Coughing violently, Paige dropped to the floor. Had to get the papers. A fiery tendril trailed a meandering path across the carpet toward her. Hypnotized by the sensuous slow motion, Paige stared at the popping ribbon until with a sound almost like a sigh it attacked the dried-up philodendron next to one of the bookcases.

Behind her a blast of heat hit her back; she scrambled around—and watched flames block her path to the door.

The professor's papers were gone. And unless she acted quickly, Paige herself would be engulfed by the inferno. She spared a last agonizing second to renounce a lifetime of work, then began crawling toward the room's other window, and her only hope of escape.

Couldn't see.

Couldn't breathe.

Racked with coughs, praying desperate little incoherent

prayers, Paige crawled along the floor, her blurring vision straining to see past the choking smoke and flames.

Have to make it to that window or I'm going to die. Dear Lord. Is it time for me to die, too?

The floor was hot, her face was hot, her lungs were burning. She shuffled at a sloth's pace in the flickering red and orange light, cringing when the burning drapes collapsed with a crackling roar. Gathering strength, the flames engulfed the first set of filing cabinets.

Panic lashed her. The fire was closing in around her. She banged into the wall. Her hands flailed wildly, searching. *Where was the window?* It had to be on this wall.

She jerked her hands back. The walls were searing hot.

Another paroxysm of coughing doubled her over. She wiped a sooty hand across her burning eyes. She had to find the window. Her hand brushed against a smoother, cooler, surface, and she almost sobbed aloud in relief.

Now to get it open. Her fingers wouldn't cooperate—where was the catch? It wouldn't budge. She'd have to break it. *Sorry, Professor. I'll pay for it....*

Paige thrust herself to her feet, swaying. She grabbed the first object her groping hand brushed against, her fingers closing convulsively around it. With the last of her strength she lifted her arm, then heaved with all her might.

Chapter Eight

Paige fought a heavy suffocating shroud. *I'm not dead,* she tried to say, but fire and smoke still poured into her throat. She gagged.

"Take it easy. You're okay, miss."

She had to break the window. *Had* to break the window. She tried to move her arms, but they were bound tightly to her sides.

Something covered her mouth, her nose. She struggled. It hurt to breathe.

"Paige? *Paige!*"

She was floating, being shaken like a rag doll, squeezed like—like—she coughed again, and pain brought her, finally, back to full consciousness.

"Paige..." Jonah's voice, hoarse and strained, spoke next to her ear. Something soft brushed against her temple. Paige opened her eyes, blinking. In the darkness Jonah's face was bathed by a bloodred glow from a wall of fire, straining skyward. She tried to say his name, to explain, her breathing labored as she again tried to rise. She had to do something—save something.

"Easy—" A paramedic was kneeling on her other side, a portable oxygen tank next to him, and Paige finally realized there was a mask over her mouth and nose. "Easy, ma'am. Just breathe normally."

How could she breathe normally when her lungs were on fire? Her eyes and nose burned, her skin burned...and her head throbbed as if someone had taken a bat to it. But the quiet voice repeated instructions over and over, while Jonah's hands held her still. Paige quit struggling and concentrated on trying to breathe without the searing pain.

In the black and scarlet night the deep rumble of throbbing engines competed with the roar of the fire. Shapeless figures darted in and out of the darkness, their shouts and instructions sporadically rising above the rest of the noise. Eventually she realized she was lying in Jonah's arms, but she was far too weak to protest. Someone had draped a blanket around her shoulders. One of her hands clutched the edges with fingers that felt like jumbled toy blocks.

"Paige...love, you can relax. It's all right. Everything will be all right. You're safe."

She felt his hand stroking her other arm, gently tugging it out from beneath the blanket. "Jonah?" She winced. Muffled through the oxygen mask, her voice emerged in a harsh, smoke-roughened whisper. "I can't move my fingers."

"I know. It's okay." He continued the calming strokes.

Paige managed to turn her head, shift her gaze down to her lap. Locked in her rigid fingers was a solid brass bookend shaped like a pair of books. The back of her hand was covered with cuts and scratches, still oozing blood.

"It's the professor's...*his papers!*" She coughed and started to struggle again. "I have to—"

It took both Jonah and the paramedic to calm her. Jonah finally put his hands on either side of her head, forcing her gaze to remain on his face. "There's nothing you can do, love."

"Just relax, ma'am. You've hit your head—we'll be getting you to the hospital in a few minutes, as soon as the ambulance arrives."

Trapped in the warm cage of his fingers, reading the unwelcome truth in his eyes, Paige finally quit resisting. With a last lingering caress she barely felt, Jonah's hands drifted away from her face to gently prise the bookend free of her convulsive hold. A shudder rippled down her body. She lifted her hand to touch her throbbing forehead.

"I'm a mess. I need to change—I'm sorry." The dribble of words emerged without conscious thought, but even though Paige knew she should hush, the words spilled out anyway. "It was my fault...."

"Hush," Jonah murmured. "Hush, now. It's okay."

"Still in shock a little, I'd think," the paramedic commented on the other side. His fingers pressed against her wrist, checking her pulse. "Let's get her loaded into the ambulance."

"I'm fine." Paige stirred, blinking to clear her vision. "Hospital can wait—I need to stay here. Talk to the police. The fire—it was arson. Someone threw—" She choked, gasping with the pain. "There might be something...the professor's—"

"Someone will talk to you at the hospital—did you say her name was Paige? Someone will take your statement there, Paige." The brusque, professional voice was kind, but firm. "Right now you just need to be still and relax."

"How bad do you think it is?" Jonah asked. His voice sounded strained, with a deep gravity somehow as chilling as the fire was hot.

The paramedic hesitated, but Jonah, Paige was discovering more and more, had a way about him that elicited respect regardless of circumstances. Yet somehow he was different from...he wasn't like— The comparison slid away as she listened to the paramedic, who shrugged, then ticked off a blunt assessment. "Not too bad, considering. Looks like mostly superficial cuts and the blow to her head. She must have hit it when she came out the window. That's where we found her. I don't know how long she'd been unconscious, though the pupil reaction's okay. I don't think she's concussed. Some slight first-degree burns. Smoke inhalation's probably the most potentially dangerous problem."

"I see." Jonah's hand drifted down to touch her forehead—a soft touch Paige barely felt. "You heard what she said?" he asked the paramedic.

"I heard. People will have to investigate—"

"Good. Investigate," Jonah snapped softly. "Because there was nothing accidental about that fire."

Paige gazed into his face, wondering how she could have ever thought of him as docile and easygoing. She was naive, a farm girl from Kansas with the street smarts of a day-old kitten, at least when it came to men. A bright lady but lacking common sense.

"She can give her statement at the hospital," the paramedic was repeating, sounding uncomfortable.

Jonah studied Paige, the hard, dangerous edge softening, and she wondered what he was reading in her face. He leaned over. "If you want to stay here, you can," he murmured. "I agree with you about the arson. I also agree that you need to tell the police what you know. But at this point I'm afraid the timing isn't as critical." He rested his hand on her shoulder, gently squeezing. "The house is gone, Paige. There's nothing you or anyone else can do. But the decision's yours. If you want to stay here, we will."

For some reason, his willingness to back *her* up instead of the frowning paramedic released Paige from the last dregs of panicked confusion. Guilt still crouched, lurking in the shadows—she should have saved the papers—but a crushing weight had momentarily lifted. Jonah was right. At this particular moment, there was nothing more she could do. She felt her body relax, trembling with relief. Jonah had finally believed her about the professor's death; he believed her about the cause of the fire. *I won't let you down, Professor.*

But tomorrow she'd be better equipped to fight back.

Somehow, she managed a feeble smile. "You're right. I'm just in the way here." She turned her head to the paramedic. "The police will come to the hospital for my statement?"

"Yes, ma'am. I'll tell them."

"Thanks." Drained, she allowed him and Jonah to lay her back on the grass. For some reason, she felt herself drifting off into a surreal world of melting color and heat. "Jonah?"

"I'm here. Don't worry."

Two men approached, wheeling a stretcher. They lifted

Paige. She felt Jonah's hand enfold hers. "Jonah? I don't suppose...would you mind—?"

"I won't leave you, Paige."

As they wheeled her past the burning house, Paige turned her head aside and closed her eyes, the utterly calm reassurance of Jonah's words blocking out the destructive sound and fury of the fire. Blocking as well the memory of Professor K.'s gruff voice promising to talk to her in a couple of days....

She had to stay at the hospital overnight, though a sore throat, bruised forehead, singed hair and skin that felt and looked sunburned were the extent of her injuries. Her interviews with a stream of officials early the following morning yielded a lot of unpleasant information. Not only had the fire been deliberate—but traffic and a false alarm had prevented the fire department from responding any sooner. By the time they arrived, the house and all its contents were beyond saving. The police detective matter-of-factly informed Paige that she herself was lucky to be alive, much less relatively unharmed. He just as matter-of-factly told her there was little they could do to solve the case but they would, as always, do the best they could.

Still feeling detached, almost unnaturally calm, Paige had merely nodded and thanked everyone for their time. When Jonah came to pick her up several hours later, he found her sitting in a waiting-room chair, hands folded in her lap.

"Beautiful day," she greeted him, determined to ignore her sore throat. She knew she looked terrible, but she didn't have to act like she felt. "Is it real hot?"

"High eighties." Jonah looked like he always did—a little shaggy but self-possessed, his boyish grin a bit—strained, Paige thought.

She tried to summon an iota of curiosity as to why Jonah looked strained. "You all right?"

He opened his mouth, then lifted his shoulders in a shrug. "Sorry I was late. Ready to go?"

At Paige's nod, he picked up the small overnight bag he'd brought from her apartment the previous night and ushered her out the door. But instead of taking her home, Jonah drove all the way to a mall a good ten miles from her apartment. "We have to talk," was all he said.

Inside the mall he held her hand, not releasing it until they were in line to order a couple of ham and cheese croissants, which neither of them wanted, from one of the busy mall cafés. Even then he crowded her, hovering near her back almost as though he were a bodyguard. Paige was torn between anxiety and irritation. If she hadn't known better, she would have concluded that the man was acting overly paranoid. On the other hand, after the previous night, perhaps his elaborate precautions were prudent instead of paranoid.

"Okay, Jonah." He had maneuvered her to a corner table at the very back, and she carefully set down the plastic tray, then just as carefully slid into the chair. "What's going on? You've obviously brought me here for a reason, but I can tell you're concerned about telling me. Please don't be. I promise not to dissolve in hysteria. Truthfully, I'm all 'hystericked' out and besides, the emotion's a waste of energy. See—" she extended her arms, displaying rock-steady hands "—not even any shakes. I'm fine. Fine." Or as fine as she could be until she discovered who was responsible for Professor K.'s murder, along with the destruction of his house and a lot of his legacy.

Jonah waited until the waitress finished serving his coffee and some hot tea for Paige. His steady blue gaze was both calming...and a warning. "It's not easy...."

"Easy or difficult, just tell me," she muttered, flexing her sore fingers before picking up the cup of tea. "After the past two weeks you could tell me my apartment was torched and I don't think I'd bat a burned eyelash." She glowered at the steaming tea. "Did you have to insist that I have a *hot* drink?"

"Hot tea's the best restorative there is," Jonah returned comfortably.

"Spoken like a true Brit." Paige took a cautious sip, then confessed rather truculently, "I feel like I've stepped into one of your books. Go ahead. Thicken the plot."

"All right." He continued to watch her, one finger idly stroking his cheek. "Your apartment wasn't torched." He paused, then added calmly, "It was searched and trashed just like the professor's."

The mug tilted precariously. Paige set it down. "What?" Her voice was faint.

"And the reason I wasn't in the professor's house with you last night is because someone arranged for your car to have a puncture. When I got out to change it, a man tried to gun me down. It was too dark to see him clearly—but I'm pretty sure it was the same blighter I chased off at Professor K.'s. I think that's what clued me—his body shape, the way he stood. But I still didn't get a clear view of his face." He drank some coffee, his eyes never leaving Paige. "The police have the punctured tire, and are trying to run a check on all the dark blue compacts with Maryland plates—a formidable task. Beyond that, all they could do is advise me to be extra careful— and leave town for a while, they suggested," he added with a wry laugh.

His hand reached across to rest on top of Paige's, which was lying limply by the forgotten tea. "So, darling, you and I are putting my book on hold while we try our hand at solving our *own* mystery."

Chapter Nine

Paige looked stupefied...and stoic. Jonah decided to give her a few moments to assimilate things, and he picked up his croissant. Eating mechanically, not tasting the food, he admitted to himself that his motives were not entirely altruistic: he wanted to just sit, savor the sight of the woman sitting across the table. *He'd almost lost her.* The previous night, for a few eternity-spanning moments he'd thought she was dead.

He loved her.

The realization had been almost as terrifying as the sight of her unconscious body lying in the grass. But once the knowledge had seeped into Jonah's brain, he could no longer ignore it.

What do I do now, Lord? I'm in love with my research assistant. He'd lost his heart to a mysterious, self-contained woman with No Trespassing signs draped around her like Christmas tree lights. The feelings had been growing for weeks, nurtured by his respect for her skills and quick mind, along with a need to protect he'd only lately realized. In spite of her self-sufficiency, Paige Hawthorne was one of the most vulnerable women he'd ever met, and—particularly since the break-in at Kittridge's house—the need to take care of her had consumed almost as much of his thoughts as his writing.

Jonah glanced across at her again, the tenderness welling up, spilling over, so that he almost blurted out his feelings then and there. A fatal mistake, and only the disciplined writer in him prevented the improperly timed scene. One of these days, he thought wryly, he'd have to thank J. Gregory.

"How can you sit there so calmly, knowing that someone is out there trying to kill us and we don't even know why?"

"Same way you can—what other choice do we have?" His gaze wandered over her, his heart aching. She'd combed her hair into its usual sleek style, but nothing could disguise the singed ends or the reddened line of scalp revealed in her side part. Her face looked sunburned, except this close Jonah could see the waxen paleness beneath, and her eyes...

"I know I look awful."

He gave himself a stern mental shake. "You're here, thank God," he said simply. "The effect of the fire on your appearance is only temporary." He smiled, wanting to take her hand again, knowing he shouldn't. "Actually, you look—" careful, lad, or she'll pull that mental disappearing act you love to hate "—a tad sunburned, but ethereal," he finished, grateful for once that words came easily to him.

"Ethereal." Paige considered that a moment, then shrugged. "I guess you're right. I don't really feel much of anything...none of it seems real." She looked down at her plate. "I know denial is one of the normal stages of grief...and I know that there's a lot of...uncomfortable emotion...facing me." Her hand lifted, dropped, the white bandage covering the cuts looking obscene, marring the delicate grace of her fingers.

She wanted to say more, he saw, but either didn't have the energy or was having difficulty picking her way through the enormity of their circumstances. That made her even more vulnerable, and without a qualm Jonah decided to probe. "How did you react when your husband died?"

Sure enough she closed right up, looking as remote and unreachable as the moon. "That's neither here nor there. Don't worry. I won't fall apart on you. Since we have a...mystery of our own, why don't we organize our research, make sure we have all the known facts in the open. My notebook's in my purse. Let me fetch it and I'll jot down a few notes.'' She avoided Jonah's gaze.

"Paige." He kept his voice mild, nonthreatening. "I don't think you understand." He glanced around the restaurant, feeling like a "right proper" Keystone cop but needing, all the same, to make sure they couldn't be overheard. "There are at least two people actively trying to murder us—because that guy acted like a professional, hired to do a job. The police are sympathetic, but unless and until we can ID someone—we're on our own. They have neither the manpower, time nor money to provide us with round-the-clock protection."

Paige looked as if she'd swallowed her spoon along with her tea. Jonah inwardly winced. "But you're famous. J. Gregory— did you tell them who you were?"

Of course *she* was a nonentity, unworthy of even a token mention, he thought, remembering her self-effacing tendencies. A rare flash of anger tingled his nerve endings. He took a deep breath. "It wouldn't matter," he explained. Then, more gently, "Don't blame them, Paige. They do the best job they can, but they can't do it all. In the end, our best protection is to arm ourselves with knowledge, of our surroundings as well as the circumstances. After that, we'll have to rely on the Lord."

"I...see." She pushed a crumbled bit of crust around that had fallen on the tabletop.

"I'm not sure you do." He waited until she lifted her gaze. "So I'll spell it out for you. We've worked together for over half a year now. I know your eating habits, your personal idiosyncracies. Your work habits and the fact that you don't *have* any leisure habits. I know that living your faith is a constant struggle."

"Jonah..." She glanced around frantically.

Jonah ignored her. "But there's still a lot I don't know— like the reason your faith is a constant struggle. Like the reason you go out of your way to avoid talking about your past, your marriage." His hand whipped out to close around her arm, stilling her effort to rise. "I need to understand you," he finished, his gaze snagging and holding hers as firmly as he held her arm, "because I need to know how you're going to react

to the constant threat of danger. Will you scream and cower—
or attack with a butcher knife?"

Paige's gaze shifted to his hand, then back up to his face.
"I don't know," she whispered finally. "I'd like to think I'd
attack with a butcher knife…but you did a pretty thorough job
of convincing me how useless I am at defending myself."

"That can be changed. Now that you bring it up, I definitely
think some fundamental lessons of self-defense would be a
good idea." *For both of us*, he added silently, deliberately ignoring the deeper ramifications of her self-abasing statement.

Beneath his clasp her arm quivered. "Where is this going,
Jonah?" She hesitated, then continued in a voice shorn of emotion. "I'm still a little shaky from last night, so my mental
acuity is fuzzy, but I think you're trying in a convoluted way
to tell me to be careful." A smile ghosted across the pale lips.
"It wasn't necessary. I plan to be—but I also plan to find out
who killed Professor K., and destroyed his home. His papers—" She bit her lip.

Jonah sat without moving, absorbing the implication. This
willowy, fragile-looking woman planned to track down a killer?
What did she think this was—a mystery board game? He stood
abruptly, bringing Paige with him. "You're finished, aren't
you? Good." He took her elbow as they threaded their way
toward the cash register. Her bones were slender, her wrist
delicate. And she planned to track down a killer? As they
threaded their way through the crowd of shoppers, Jonah sent
up pages of prayers. He needed—they both needed, all the di-
vine help the Lord saw fit to provide.

Neither of them spoke until after they were back in the privacy of Paige's car. Jonah locked the doors and put the key in
the ignition, but didn't start the motor. "What would you
think," he asked, watching her, "of putting up in a hotel near
my apartment until this is over? I can't very well move in to
yours—and my place in the mountains is too far away." Regret
stabbed him, the pain sharp and deep. He'd like nothing better
than to whisk Paige off to the tri-level log home he had built
in the heart of the Blue Ridge Mountains when he took out
U.S. citizenship. She belonged there….

"That's probably not a bad idea," Paige responded, sounding remote. Almost indifferent. "The Bergman Arms is only a couple of blocks from your apartment, isn't it? Would that do?"

"As long as they have good security."

"What about you? Is it safe for you to stay in—"

"It's Jay's apartment, remember? I'm just leasing it while he finishes his studies in England. The killer wouldn't be able to look up my address, since the apartment's in Jay's name."

"He could have followed you."

"No one has—yet." That thought had already occurred to him, and to the police, as well.

"Why are you smiling?"

Jonah started the engine, then glanced across. "They didn't believe me, down at the station, when I told the two detectives in charge that I'd know if I was being followed. One of them decided to see for himself."

"Well?"

Interest had stirred to life at last, and she was even leaning closer, impatient to hear the rest of the story. As the muscles in his neck and shoulders relaxed Jonah realized how on edge he'd been, wondering how he would ever break through the massive protective fences Paige had built. He headed out of the parking lot. "I led him a merry chase for four blocks, then lost him. Three blocks after that, I came up behind him," he admitted, albeit sheepishly. Gary Fontana, the detective, had been impressed, but he'd still read Jonah the riot act for his amateur attempts at investigation.

He sneaked a peek at Paige, and almost rear-ended a van. She was staring at him as if he'd sprouted two heads and was belching green smoke.

"How did—never mind, I don't want to know." She leaned back against the seat and closed her eyes. "I'm beginning to realize I know very little about you after all these months together. Strange, isn't it, how you think you know·everything about a person...and then you discover how wrong you are?" Her voice dropped to a whisper.

Jonah headed back toward the city, chewing over her words.

Her shock at his, well, *survival skills* was probably as accurate a description as any, if he had to pin a label to them. He shook his head. Paige, now...he'd never appreciated how sheltered she really was, because she hid her vulnerabilities so skillfully. Articulate, intelligent and resourceful, the woman without doubt was a historian of the first water. As a research assistant her value was above rubies, diamonds, pearls and possibly his royalty checks for the next ten years. She'd unearthed oddments of information that would give his next book enormous added depth, and she could charm obdurate old ladies out of a half-century's worth of family papers.

But she was also, from the little that Kittridge had shared, a home-and-hearth Kansas farm girl, whose greatest adventure had been the move to D.C., away from her family.

Apparently nothing in her life had ever prepared her to cope with physical violence. Unless—

A very unpleasant possibility surfaced, and beneath the mustache Jonah's lips thinned to an ominous straight line. One day soon they were going to have a little talk about a lot of things. Particularly her dear, departed husband.

A century-old hotel stashed in the middle of Georgetown, the Bergman Arms catered to people in all walks of life, from wealthy, aged widows to pinstripe-suited businessmen, to the never-ending flow of tourists. Gleaming brass fixtures and oiled oak trim, polished to a dull sheen over the decades, attested to the low-key elegance of an earlier generation. Faded, but still rich, burgundy carpets and drapes were complemented by strategically placed live greenery.

Fortunately the hotel had maintained its quality; the atmosphere exuded peace and efficient service. Here Paige would be inconspicuous, just another lodger—and Jonah heartily approved the presence of a spry, observant doorman whose sharp eyes missed little. There was also a security guard leased through a local agency. In his nine years at the front desk, the desk manager assured them, not a breath of scandalous activity had smirched the good name of the hotel.

Let it stay that way, Lord, Jonah silently prayed as they

waited for the elevator. His roaming gaze combed the foyer, and he felt the adrenaline pumping through his bloodstream, keeping his body on knife-edged alertness. When another couple entered the elevator right after them, Jonah moved Paige into a corner, placing his body between her and the couple. He relaxed marginally when the couple exited on the second floor, leaving them alone and momentarily safe.

When they reached her room, without a word Paige held out the security key card. "Doubtless you want to search it first," she murmured, her voice very dry.

He couldn't resist tapping the reddened tip of her narrow nose. "You're learning, *chate*. I'm taking no chances with your safety. So you wait right here—hold the door open, where I can see you while I check things out."

It was a small but comfortable room with two double beds. There was even a table beneath the window which could function as a desk. Jonah called her inside, then began a lengthy lecture on safeguards. Paige patiently promised that she still remembered Jay's unlisted phone number, and that she'd call Jonah—regardless of time—if she had so much as a transient nightmare.

"I'll even call you every fifteen minutes, if you'll trust me the other fourteen," she finally said. "Jonah...enough. I'm not Lois Lane, but I'm not totally helpless, either."

Jonah felt like the slime in the bottom of a bucket. "Sorry, love. Guess I am overdoing it a bit. Perhaps." His eyes caressed her face, but at least she was too tired, too distracted to notice. Fortunately. "You've had about all you can take." He deeply regretted the brutal truths he had had to reveal, when she'd just gotten out of the hospital—but the alternative was unacceptable.

"I'm fine," Paige promised, giving him a flickering smile that had all the light of a spent match. "Give me an hour, then I'll be ready for work. I have a couple of ideas—" she sputtered to a halt when Jonah pressed his fingers over her mouth.

You don't give up, do you, darling? he thought. He removed his hand and stuffed it inside his waistband. "The hotel is fine. The weather is fine. You are not. Quit pretending and, just this once—don't argue," he added quietly when she opened her mouth. He moved to the window, drew the drapes closed, then walked back over to Paige. "Lie down...take your nap. I'll go back to the station and talk to the police, find out the latest on the professor's house."

"If you're going, I want to—"

"You want to do as I suggest, right?" He met her gaze. After a moment, Paige shrugged and turned to her suitcase. Jonah smiled in satisfaction, rubbed his hands together. "That's the ticket. All right then, I'll see you later. Lock the door. Don't open it unless you hear this sequence—" He rapped out a rhythm on the wall. "Paige?" He checked, an eyebrow lifting.

"All right."

Jonah frowned. He couldn't quite put his finger on it, but something wasn't right. She had agreed with him, hadn't she? He ran back over the last exchange, trying to figure out if he'd done or said anything that could possibly be interpreted as dictatorial or unreasonable. He'd tried to subtly remind her that he valued her as a person who had feelings instead of a professional automaton, by encouraging her to rest for a while. He'd apologized for treating her as though she were a helpless child.

Yet Paige stood there, looking...what? Jonah shook his head, impatient to be on his way so she could rest. "Well...I'll be going, then..."

"Will you—" She bit her lip, then sent him an empty smile. "All right," she repeated. "I'll see you later."

"Mmm." Jonah closed the door, waited until he heard her shoot home the dead bolt, then took the stairs instead of the elevator. Since the apartment was only two blocks away, he decided to trade Paige's car for his motorcycle. He could think more clearly on the bike. Over the next couple of hours, maybe he could figure out what was going on behind those cloudy-day eyes, in the tortured labyrinth of her brain. A lot had happened to her outside her experience, but in spite of shock and fear and pain, she'd rallied—until a few moments ago, when, in spite of her pose of serenity, she had looked...defeated.

Jonah pushed through the heavy outside doors of the Bergman into the hazy late-August afternoon, grimly determined that the mystery of Professor Kittridge's murder was not the only one he planned to solve.

Chapter Ten

For the next twenty-four hours, Paige remained holed up in her room at the Bergman Arms, plowing through scattered notes Jonah had retrieved from the mess in her apartment. Nothing was left of Professor Kittridge's house. All his research—files, books...the legacy of a quarter century—was gone. Thankful for the anesthetizing haze that left her efficient but numb, Paige worked sixteen hours straight. Pain was irrelevant, as was fatigue. Until Professor K.'s death was vindicated, she didn't want respite from either.

At least the POW book was already in galley form. She had called the publisher, securing a promise to send out an extra set; she also needed to go through the professor's campus office, but sitting behind his scarred cherry desk, in his massive desk chair, would have penetrated the merciful haze that was protecting her from feeling too much.

Tomorrow, she promised herself in Scarlett O'Hara fashion. She would think about it tomorrow. Besides, the police had sealed off his office while they conducted their investigation, though the detective in charge had requested that Paige be allowed access as soon as she felt up to it. Perhaps something there would jog her memory, help the investigation....

The clock radio beside her bed clicked onto the classical

station to which she had tuned it. Paige glanced at her watch. Seven forty-five. Time for her next ten-minute break. Dutifully she rose from the table, wincing as her various aches and pains protested. "All right, Jonah...since you're not here right now I'll admit you were right." He had wanted her to take a break once an hour; she had negotiated for two, but had promised to reset the radio each time so she wouldn't forget.

Amazingly, the ten-minute pauses *had* refreshed, but she still felt as though she was shirking her responsibility. Jonah, she knew, didn't need any breaks. He'd been working with a cadre of officials most of the day, handling an endless hodgepodge of details. Being Jonah, of course, he'd still dug out enough time to interrupt her with three phone calls to make sure she was taking her breaks.

For some reason, his concern made her vaguely uncomfortable, yet—cherished. No, that was too strong a word. Moving stiffly, Paige wandered around the hotel bedroom, her thoughts disjointed. Painful memories, uncomfortable feelings, half-baked theories. Running through them all like yeast spreading through dough, the undercurrent of fear bubbled and rose higher with each passing hour. Would it be a sin, she wondered when her gaze wandered over the Gideon Bible, if she begged God to help her discover why Professor K. had been killed?

She scooped up her purse from one of the double dressers, tugging out the now-crumpled envelope with the tiny key and list of names—and a much folded piece of paper torn from a notebook, with more names. A bitter smile twisted Paige's mouth, tugging at the sore facial muscles.

What if she hadn't left her purse in the car?

It was ironic, when she thought about it. All along, the information had been in her purse, and she had left it lying on the floor, in her car. Professor K. had been murdered, his house burned, Paige's apartment ransacked—and the clues were in her purse, lying forgotten in the car. Even Jonah hadn't noticed its presence until he and the police were searching for the car registration in the glove compartment.

Paige unfolded both lists, sinking back down in her chair. Minton. Rand. Hoffelmeyer. Her fingers clenched, further rumpling the papers. If only she knew how to piece everything together....

Go ahead, she thought. Let's play the If Only game. You're an expert at it, after all. Let's see... If only she'd tried harder to talk to Professor K. when they flew to Georgia. If only she hadn't left him alone the night they flew home. If only shock and panic hadn't wiped completely from her memory the addresses she'd found the night of the fire. *If only he hadn't died.*

"Why did You let him die?" The whispered cry burst free. "It isn't fair, Lord. It isn't right..."

There was no answer, but then she hadn't really expected one. It didn't matter. She wasn't going to rest until she had atoned for her grievous lack of judgment. Perhaps, if she worked diligently enough and long enough and hard enough, God would finally grant her a measure of peace. She rotated a few more kinks out of her neck, carefully flexed her sore hands and spread the two lists out on the table.

One or more of the names on the World War II list had caused such an exaggerated response from the professor that he had dropped everything else and spent his last hours on earth searching for *something* related to that list. Bending over the table, Paige pored over both lists until her vision blurred. One or more of the names on both lists had to be related—except none of them matched. As for the mysterious *B-E-N*...the closest set of letters matching those in the World War II list was someone named Belner.

If only she could remember what she'd dug out of the files before the fire—

Don't go there, Paige.

Three fast, two slow raps on the door provided a convenient way of escape. Jonah's prearranged signal. Paige peered through the peephole, anyway, then slipped back the dead bolt.

He smiled down at her as he stepped inside. His hair was tousled, his oxford cloth shirt clinging in damp patches from the stifling heat outside. No doubt he'd been running around on that wretched motorcycle he loved so much.

"Don't knock my bike until you've tried it."

Paige jumped, only then realizing she'd spoken aloud, so

used to being alone that the words had popped out without a thought. She colored. "No thanks. I prefer air-conditioning and no bugs."

He laughed, then stood examining her with a strange expression on his face until Paige wanted to squirm in embarrassment. She stood straight. "I have an appointment to trim the singed hair off in the morning, but there's nothing I can do but slather cream on my skin. You'll just have to put up with my appearance, I'm afraid."

Something deep stirred in his eyes, and his hand half lifted toward her before he swiped at the perspiration dotting his face and forehead instead. "Your appearance is lovely as it is," he murmured. "Ah...let's go down to the lobby, shall we. We need to make some plans, and I think you need a change of scenery."

She glanced around the cluttered room. "Good idea." Paige gathered her purse and crammed all her notes inside her leather portfolio. But the trickle of uncertainty over Jonah's expression nagged her subconscious all the way down to the almost deserted lobby.

They chose an out-of-the way corner, and Jonah patted a floral damask chair opposite the sofa where he sat down. "Have a seat. I need to fill you in on my day first, I'm afraid." He gave her the lopsided grin that hurt her heart. "After today, I've decided that we don't have much choice but to pursue matters on our own. You were right. Want to crow a few moments?"

Dumbfounded, she shook her head. "Just explain." She couldn't remember the last time someone had told her that she was right about something.

"Well...it's likely to be time-consuming, and a bit dicey, but I thought we'd better have a go at doing a follow-up about the names on those two lists. Did you bring them?"

Paige dug the papers out of her portfolio, held them out. Jonah's fingers brushed against hers, and she stared at them, blinking. Slowly she withdrew her hand, sliding a covert peek at Jonah, who gave no sign that her touch had affected him at all. Paige Elizabeth Hawthorne, that fire must have burned away the last of your brain instead of the ends of your hair. She shook her head. "I'm sorry...my mind was wandering. What did you say?"

One bushy auburn eyebrow lifted, but he repeated his words. "I said that we need to figure out who these people are, track down addresses—maybe pay them a visit. According to the professor's secretary, he kept only administrative files at his Georgetown office, so that probably won't help. With his house files gone, it will take longer, but there's not much else to go on."

"We *might* pay a visit to a murderer."

"Mmm. At least we'd have a face to put with a name. Right now we're nothing but a couple of toy ducks at a carnival shooting gallery."

"What did the police say?"

Jonah put his glasses on, scanned the lists. "That it's my fool neck, and if I interfere with *their* investigation they'll arrange to ship me off to my mother, among other things." Beneath the mustache his mouth kicked upward. "You should know that I had to tell them my alter ego, and it didn't matter a particle that I'm J. Gregory, and that Mother is the British grande dame of the archaeology world." He began stroking the corners of his mustache. "If either of us interfere, we'll be both be treated persona non grata."

Paige sighed. "My parents want me to fly home."

"So," Jonah returned very softly, "do I."

"Well, I'm not going to, so put your bag of British charm away. It won't work this time."

"You know me so well." He reached across and touched her hand. "Even though you really don't. Are you better today, Paige? Did working help you come to terms a bit?"

What, she wondered, had *that* crack meant? "A little. I still have trouble talking about it." Her fingers followed the flower pattern on the chair arm. "I feel like such a failure." The words burst out as though with a mind of their own.

"Don't be ridiculous." He tilted his head. "You've a fair-sized complex for such an intelligent, attractive, eminently *professional* lady. I find that rather puzzling—have for months."

He stopped stroking his mustache and reached for the portfolio, his manner becoming brisk. "And...I give you fair warning that I'll be getting to the bottom of it, too. But not right now. Right now we've work to do, Ms. Hawthorne."

"Who do we start with?" Paige congratulated herself for her "eminently professional" tone, in spite of the tumult rioting through her bloodstream. Over the past few weeks Jonah had begun tossing out comments like that. He'd also developed a disconcerting habit of touching her, fleeting fingertip brushes not even a militant feminist would object to. If she hadn't been so distracted by everything else she would have interrogated him about it, pushed until he...well, *explained*. But then he might not touch her at all.

She marshaled her unruly thoughts. "I've spent most of the day going through the stuff you salvaged from my apartment, trying to find a connection. Nothing. There was—" she wearily arranged the two lists of names on the low table between them "—nothing yet, at any rate. So...pick your poison—the names on Professor K.'s list or the ones on the World War II list."

Jonah spread his hands wide. "Your call." He hesitated. "Paige, I know you'd prefer to go one way while I dig the other so we could accomplish twice as much with half the time. But I can't. I won't." He leaned forward, the deep blue eyes searching her face. "Because the situation is only going to get more dangerous. Like we discussed yesterday, for the time being we're pretty much on our own."

"I know that. Don't worry about me. I'll be okay."

"I plan to try and ensure that," Jonah drawled. "But face it—you *have* led a rather sheltered life, *hana*."

"Would you quit calling me those foreign names?"

"Not a chance." He lounged back on the sofa, stretching his legs beneath the table. "I love to watch you bristle. Um...as I was saying, you might have scraped up the grit to brandish a butcher knife, but we both know you're not really equipped to cope well with violence. Few sane people are."

"The famous J. Gregory, of course, being one of them." She wanted to be offended by his masculine confidence, but he was right. A rueful smile tickled her mouth, widening when she met his twinkling gaze.

"The streets I grew up on were a little more rigorous than yours, yes."

Paige found herself voicing aloud questions she'd been too reserved to ask—until now. "Where *did* you grow up, Jonah? I've always wondered." Almost unconsciously she steeled herself for rejection, or at least another vague reply that revealed nothing.

But Jonah surprised her this time. "I had a rather... unusual...childhood, probably largely due to the unique relationship with my parents." He smiled a smile full of nostalgia. "Mother and Father...two Oxford dons who could have won an award for eccentricity. Don't shake your head—it's quite true. Now, during the school year I was at prep school with a lot of other little boys. Like small boys everywhere, they liked to torment the smallest, the odd man out, which always seemed to be me. Father, bless his soul, used to bring me into his study and tell me stories to try and ease the humiliation."

Paige's heart lurched, struggling with dangerous emotions. "Children can be cruel. I'm sorry, Jonah."

"I survived." His voice was peaceful. "In the summers I traveled with my mother to her archaeological digs, and that made up for the little boys. By the time I was twelve, I'd visited all over the world, places even my father couldn't pronounce."

"Is that why—" She stopped, not knowing how to phrase her question.

"Why I write books? Settled in America? Drive you to distraction calling you names in an assortment of languages?"

"Why you know how to take out a prowler and a man with a gun without batting an eye," Paige snapped in exasperation. "You must have lived in some awfully dangerous places, considering your mother's profession. Is that why you learned all that kung fu stuff?"

Jonah leaned forward, humor fading as he planted his elbows on his knees. Behind the midnight eyes his expression had turned deadly serious. "I got tired of being picked on because I was undersized and wore glasses," he stated flatly. "Because

I wouldn't conform to their image of the son of a professor emeritus of English and a famous mother. You're right. Children are cruel—and sometimes they never outgrow it." His hand shot out to Paige's hair, tucking it behind her ears. "Did you get teased a lot about your ears? Is that why you try to make sure your hair always covers them—even when you're half-dead from a fire?"

Her face burned as hot as fire, and she jerked backward, hands automatically flying up to prove Jonah's point. He'd never commented on her ears before, or even let on that he knew how self-conscious she was about their size. As for the night of the fire— "I don't know what you're talking about," she mumbled. "I was barely conscious. I can't be held responsible for what I said and did."

"See what I mean?"

"I thought we were going to discuss the names, not our personal shortcomings."

"Actually, I believe it's time to tackle both." He smiled gently. "Ease up, love. I wasn't trying to denigrate. But you're right, too. Perhaps we should save the personal stuff for an intimate supper, in between sketching out a sound plan of logistics." He sat back, and Paige released a pent-up sigh of relief. "How about if we stop by for a chat with your old chums at the Smithsonian? Since you used to work at the Museum of American History, they should be willing to spare a few moments."

"I should have thought of that," she admitted. "I'll call first thing in the morning."

"Well done!" He stood, pulled Paige to her feet. "We're both top researchers so it won't be difficult to keep our eyes skinned for necessary info as opposed to oddments that tend to trip one up."

"Thank you," Paige murmured quietly. Jonah paused from gathering up the lists, querying her with a lifted brow. Paige waved her hand, at a loss to explain. "For not treating me like a—like I was—"

"You're welcome." He looked down at her a minute longer, that baffling intensity rekindling in his eyes. Suddenly his head lowered, and he kissed her, a brief touch of his lips to hers that scorched all the way to her toes.

Completely flustered, Paige stood, unable to move, her thoughts scattered. Why had he done that? "Why did you do that?" she asked. But her mouth still felt the imprint of his, still tingled from the surprising softness of his mustache.

Jonah's hand lifted to cup her heated face. "You're an exceptional woman in many ways, Paige Hawthorne, far beyond your research skills." His hand slid beneath her hair, the fingers tracing the shell of her ear. "And that includes your ears. It's time you started believing it. Now...let's grab a bite of supper, and discuss our itinerary." He released her with a final lingering caress down her flaming cheek. "There are a dozen or so needles in acres of haystacks waiting for us to dig them out."

Three days later, Paige's contact at the Army Pentagon Library caught up with her at the professor's Georgetown office. He provided their first lead, but it was a name from the World War II list instead of the list of names Professor K. had hidden.

"Minton, Gerald Payne." Paige hung up the phone and looked across at Jonah. "He served in the Diplomatic Corps— was stationed in England during the war. Permanent home address listed as Dayton, Ohio."

"Too bad it wasn't a name on the professor's list. On the other hand, it might turn out to be the name that launched a thousand questions."

"That was bad, Jonah. You'll ruin your professional reputation."

He grinned at her, unperturbed, unflappable. In the past three days they'd worked side by side, but never once had Jonah become impatient or irritable. On the other hand, he hadn't kissed her again, either. Frankly Paige didn't blame him. According to the bathroom mirror, her eyes were permanently bloodshot, her complexion was peeling, and her nose was permanently wrinkled from hours and hours of searching through files, microfiche, the Smithsonian's database...even old court records.

"Are you game for a lot of undoubtedly wasted travel time?"

She looked up with a start, realizing that her mind had wandered again—a disconcerting habit that over the past years she'd successfully eliminated. Until Jonah. "If a trip to Ohio will help uncover who murdered the professor, as well as who tried to murder us, it's not wasted time."

She knew she sounded like a grouch, but even as Paige opened her mouth to apologize, Jonah had crossed over to stand right in front of her. She forced herself not to retreat, though she felt like a cat trying to tiptoe through a yard full of pit bulls. If he started to chew her out, she didn't know what her reaction would be. With David, she had learned to play the part of chastened wife until she believed what he was saying and didn't have to pretend.

Somehow in the past year a mustard-size seed of the old Paige had sprouted so that now—against all common sense— if Jonah wanted a fight, she'd give him a doozy.

Jonah reached for the phone, his eyes never leaving Paige. "I'll phone the airline," he murmured.

"I can do it." She pressed her fingers against her temples. "I need to do something before I take out my rotten mood on you." She tried to laugh. "I keep trying to pretend what we're doing is for your book—for a work of fiction. But I know it's real, that somewhere out there is a madman who might still be tracking *us* like we're tracking him."

The police had found the dark blue compact the gunman had used. Stolen from a computer programmer in Maryland, it had been ditched at Dulles International Airport. No fingerprints other than smeared ones of the owner. No other clues. Since Jonah had never had a clear view of the man's face, there was no way to ID him.

They needed a break. She needed a break.

"Paige."

That was all. Just her name, and yet she felt the bone-grinding tension crumble all of a sudden, leaving her quivering and vulnerable. Her head lifted, and she met his gaze.

"I'll keep you as safe as I can, and God will take care of us both." He picked up her hand and held it in a warm, comforting grip. "He'll also provide the peace, if you let Him."

Paige closed her eyes so he wouldn't see how much his gentle touch moved her. "I know. I'll do better. I promise."

"Let's go to Ohio, then."

He dropped her hand and picked up the phone, and Paige turned to gather up all the papers. As always, her hand tingled from the brief contact with Jonah's. With a yearning that shocked her by its depth, she longed for even more.

She was in trouble up to her ears, and could blame nobody but herself.

Chapter Eleven

Gerald Payne Minton had died in 1989, but they found his son in Columbus. A former city manager, Patrick Payne Minton now served as a state senator in the Ohio General Assembly. After securing a late-afternoon appointment, Jonah and Paige rented a car and drove from the airport to his office.

The honorable Mr. Minton was a large man, well over six feet, with short-cropped ash blond hair and wary brown eyes. Standing to shake hands, he stayed behind his massive oak desk, his long arm reaching across easily. The firm grip contained little personal warmth, Jonah noted. Remaining behind his desk—a power tactic—revealed even more about his personality. Jonah kept his own face as blank as a fresh sheet of computer paper. Minton wasn't the only one who knew how to play nonverbal games.

"I understand you needed information on my father," the senator announced without preamble after waving them to sit down. Glancing at his watch, he shuffled a few papers, then placed his hands flat on the desk. "I'm still a little unclear as to why."

Jonah relaxed back in the leather chair and nodded to Paige. Some months earlier he had discovered that Paige's interviewing skills surpassed his own—particularly with men. She disarmed the people they interviewed with her genuine interest and lack of aggression. He waited to see how she went about charming a savvy politician like Minton.

"As I explained over the phone, I'm trying to complete a book written by Professor Emil Kittridge," Paige began. "It's actually a revised edition of one he wrote some years ago—he compares POWs in the various wars. The book is actually part of a multiauthored series under the auspices of the American History Association. Did I explain this already?" She paused, face arranged in a pleasant waiting expression until Minton gave a curt nod.

That's my darling, Jonah wanted to crow. Force the man to listen and respond. He was proud of her and bursting with the need to tell her so, but he sat in the chair and tried to look vague.

"The professor...recently died, rather suddenly," Paige continued. "I'm having to backtrack a few sources and came upon your father's name on a list."

"My father spent the last twenty years of his life in a nursing home," Minton said, brown eyes as unrevealing as polished stones. "He suffered from Alzheimer's."

"I'm so sorry." Her face flooded with compassion, and Jonah watched Minton respond in spite of himself. "I know that was painful."

"Well, yes. It was. I'm afraid those years pretty much wiped out most of my memories of my dad when I was growing up. I used to have an older sister, but she died in a car accident, back in the seventies." He picked up an onyx letter opener, fiddled with it, then laid it back down. "You did tell me you were particularly interested in my father's war experiences, but I'm not sure why. He was never a prisoner of war."

Jonah cleared his throat. "He was in the Diplomatic Corp, wasn't he?" He crossed his legs and contemplated the worn-out sole of his shoe. "In England?"

"I believe so, but that's as much as I know. My folks never liked to talk about the war." A long moment of silence passed. "Look—I hate to be rude, but I've got another appointment in five minutes. I'm sorry you flew all the way out here for nothing, but I did warn you when you called from Dayton that I probably couldn't tell you anything.''

Paige's expression remained sympathetic, but Jonah could see the whites of her knuckles as she clenched the pen she was using to take notes. "Senator Minton, we're certainly not trying to open old wounds, but is there a chance you might have some boxes of memorabilia—old letters, newspapers? Anything that might give us a clue about your father's experiences? It would be beneficial to determine which of these names should be eliminated from mention in Professor Kittridge's book.''

"There might be some stuff in the attic, but I don't know when I'll have time—'' An intercom buzzed, and the secretary's voice informed him that Mr. Larchant had arrived.

Minton stood. "Tell you what. Give me a month or so. Maybe when we're in recess over the holidays I can do a little checking, see if there's anything useful.''

"And anything after,'' Paige added. "Even if you think it's irrelevant. Your father's name was on a list, and it would be nice, don't you think, to find out why.'' She looked at Jonah, who rose lazily to his feet.

"You're running again next year?'' he asked as Minton walked them to his door. "I noticed the campaign posters.''

"That's the name of the game. I'd like to be able to spend more time with my constituents, of course, but raising funds for the campaign is the name of the game.'' He opened the door, stepped back. "Thanks for stopping by. Sorry I couldn't be more help.''

"What do you think?'' Paige idly stirred her soft drink with a straw in the fast-food restaurant near Minton's office.

Jonah shrugged. "Evasive, but very smooth. You handled him well, considering you wanted to throw your pen at him, there at the last.''

"I didn't—'' She blushed, then conceded. "All right. It would have been a relief. He was so...so *plastic*.''

Jonah laughed. "The perfect politician. I suppose it would have been much too pat to have everything fall together the first time. I don't even allow that in my books.''

"I really can't picture Senator Picture-Perfect Minton coming after you with a gun, much less dirtying his hands by hiring someone," Paige agreed. "But he didn't want to talk about his father, did he?" She shoved the drink aside and leaned across to search Jonah's face. "Did you notice how he tensed up?"

"Mmm...could have been because the memories are still uncomfortable. Be careful not to read more into—what is it?" Paige's eyes had widened suddenly, her mouth dropping open, then shutting. Jonah waited in tense silence, alert, poised for action.

"There's a man standing in line—I think it's the same man I noticed when you were filling out the paperwork for the rental car in Dayton." She spoke quietly, but the gray eyes betrayed her rising anxiety.

Jonah leaned forward until their noses were almost touching. "Describe him," he murmured. "No—don't back away from me. I want to look like we're—um—oblivious to the rest of the world." He smiled deliberately. "Just look at me, my *gladje*, and talk."

Exasperation replaced anxiety. "Someday, Jonah Sterling..." She flashed a brilliant, Senator Minton smile back. "He's wearing tan slacks—casual style, not dress, a striped shirt. Loafers. Sort of lanky, longish dark hair. He looks...uncomfortable." She bit her lip. "I'm not sure. I could be wrong. But if he followed us to Ohio, that means he probably knows where you live and where I'm staying in D.C."

Jonah's hand closed over hers. He lowered his voice. "Let's try a little experiment, then." He squeezed the cold trembling fingers. "Paige, I'm going to kiss you, so don't jump or pull away. Then I'm going to go order some fries or something. It'll be natural if you follow me with your eyes." He watched her, his smile deepening. "But only if you look appropriately smitten instead of like a startled deer."

Without waiting for a response, he touched his mouth to hers, hearing her quick intake of breath. Her lips quivered, then relaxed. "I'll go order some more," Jonah declared in a normal tone.

He sauntered up and joined the queue of people, nodding at

everyone in general as he pulled out his wallet. Two lines over, the dark-haired bloke shifted and turned around. Indifferent brown eyes slid right over Jonah. Jonah felt his skin tighten in response.

When he strolled back to Paige with a pack of fries, the man had moved to a table that maintained a good view of all the exits. "Let's go. We can eat this in the car." He clasped her wrist and urged Paige to her feet, resisting with difficulty the urge to wrap his arm around her waist. "Our flight leaves in less than two hours."

"Why did you say that loud enough for him to hear?" Paige hissed the minute they were inside the car.

"To see his reaction." He glanced across, adding gently, "And because it's better to know your enemies than to walk in ignorance. This way I can see if he follows and, if so, I'll also know what kind of car he's driving."

"Jonah…"

He waited, dividing his eyes between traffic and a low-slung black sports car in the rearview mirror. They were five miles down the freeway before Paige spoke again.

"I'm sorry, Jonah. I…hate to admit it, but I'm scared."

The apologetic confession ripped through Jonah's insides like a grenade, because he knew what it cost her to have made it. He gripped the steering wheel tighter. "I know." He risked a quick survey of her rigidly upright body. "I am, too."

Her head snapped around. "You're scared?"

Her astonishment made him want to shout with laughter. "I never deluded myself into thinking I was some superhero, after about the age of eight. I can defend myself, and I've had to a time or two in some tricky situations, but I was petrified every time." Behind them, the sports car passed two cars and settled four vehicles back. "Want to hear a story?"

A strained laugh escaped. "Trying to divert me?"

"Of course." He turned his head, winked. "Well?"

Her shy smile told Jonah he'd stumbled onto the right code, even if he wasn't too wild about it. "I'd like that, if you're sure you wouldn't mind."

"For you, I don't mind." But only for you, he told her silently, wondering if she had the slightest clue what she did to him. He was about to share a part of his life that he had never shared with anyone else, including his ex-fiancée and a world-wide assortment of friends.

The black sports car moved closer. Jonah began weighing options while he tried to keep Paige distracted. "Remember I told you I used to spend summers with my mother? Well, I suppose it would have been more accurate to say, that, after she gave me the standard greeting upon my arrival, she'd be off to the archaeological dig, and I'd pretty much be on my own."

"That's terrible."

"Not really. While I was still a pint-size boy, she'd hire a couple of locals to more or less watch out for me. One of them—when we were in the Hokkaido region of Japan—was a wiry little old man who'd been a master in the art of *nin-jutsu*."

The sports car pulled in directly behind them. The man driving lifted his hand—and drank from a large plastic cup. Jonah's shoulders relaxed infinitesimally. The next time the bloke might raise a loaded pistol instead of a drink.

"I was about nine or ten, as I recall, and an eager pupil. By the time I flew back to England to resume courses, I was skilled enough that the next time the school bully filched my glasses and wouldn't give them back, I...um...made him. He didn't bother me or my glasses the rest of the year."

He pressed the accelerator, speeding up a little, because the sports car had closed the distance between them. "When I was fifteen, I spent a summer with Mother in Germany. By that time of course, I was too old to have a nanny. I'd also gotten used to shifting for myself. Thought I could take on the world and win, I'm afraid." He glanced across at Paige. "I joined a local gang and learned a particularly nasty form of street fighting. I'm ashamed to admit that I rather enjoyed it." He glanced out the rearview mirror, then risked another quick perusal of Paige, trying to gauge her response. "Of course I wasn't a Christian then."

"No wonder you take all this in stride...."

"Not always. Relax, Paige. I'm pretty sure the bloke isn't following us deliberately. He's much too obvious. Besides— he's eating." There had also been too many opportunities had his intention been to kill or injure, all of which the man had ignored—definitely not the mark of a professional.

Paige turned and looked over her shoulder. "He's eating a burger."

About that time their car drove by an exit...and the black car disappeared down the ramp.

Jonah glanced across at Paige. "There you go. False alarm. Can't say that bothers me." He surreptitiously wiped his palms, one at the time, on his slacks.

Paige's head drooped. She wouldn't look at him. "I was just being paranoid, wasn't I?"

"Would you stop—" Jonah gnawed on the corner of his mustache a full minute before he knew that his voice as well as his temper was under control. "Until we know what's going on, a certain amount of paranoia is to be expected, not to mention desired. Try to keep a lid on that overreactive guilt complex of yours, love."

Paige sat, wooden and unresponsive.

He reached across the seat and gave her hair a light tug. "Smile for me," he commanded, "or I'll call you something frivolous and frightfully obnoxious in, hmm—German, perhaps? Haven't used that language on you lately."

Paige finally shook her head, but he could see her trying not to smile. Relieved, they drove the rest of the way in companionable silence, enjoying the brief respite from shadow dodging.

But Jonah couldn't help wondering what waited for them back in Washington.

"I told you not to call me. You were fired. Your ineptitude was inexcusable."

"Maybe you need to realize you're not dealing with some punk. So I missed a time or two—I got a handle on 'em now. All I needed was a plane ticket, and I had both of 'em."

"You have been replaced." The cold, calm voice sent a shiver snaking up his spine.

"You can't do that!"

"I already have. You're nothing but a trigger-happy pyromaniac. You were told to produce those names, and you failed. It will be interesting to see how long it takes until you fail at the task of guarding your own back."

He slammed down the phone, then viciously kicked the side of the phone booth. "I'll show that armchair general," he snarled. "I'll nail those two if it's the last thing I do. Then we'll see who gets what."

Chapter Twelve

Paige and Jonah took a taxi from the airport to Jonah's apartment. Paige waited in the cab while he dashed up the steps to drop off his hang-up bag and check the answering machine. He returned less than five minutes later and smoothly ducked into the taxi.

"What is it?" Paige asked, pulse skittering at the thunderous expression on his face. "Did you see someone? Were we followed from the airport? What?"

Jonah stared out the window. "Later," he murmured, his gaze not leaving the window.

Biting her lip, Paige stifled further words. Goose bumps raced over her skin, and she hugged her arms, wishing her imagination wasn't so graphic.

At the hotel Jonah once again made her wait in the hall until he made sure her room was empty. Then he quietly told her to pack up—she was checking out. Paige looked around the clean, innocent-looking room, then studied Jonah's impassive face. "All right," she said after a moment. He'd either explain later, or he wouldn't, but this was not the time to push. Without a fuss she began to pack.

Thirty minutes later, after paying for her week's stay, she joined Jonah, who waited for her in their usual secluded corner of the lobby. "Is this a safe enough spot for you to tell me what's going on?" Good. That was good—her voice sounded collected, no trace of pettishness or worse, panic. Years ago Paige had learned how to keep her expression masked, how to keep herself insulated from verbal arrows. As added reinforcement she kept her clammy hands behind her back. There. With any luck Jonah might not guess that she was well on the way to being downright terrified.

Jonah Sterling's opinion of her shouldn't matter a snapped pencil's worth—but it did.

His hooded gaze dissected the lobby and every unsuspecting guest before returning to rest on her face. The faint wash of approval she read there calmed Paige, even after he answered her question. "Jay's apartment got the same treatment as yours."

She had suspected as much, but hearing the words was still a punch in the stomach. "I'm...sorry. What about your manuscript? Did you remember to leave it at the bank?" She had discovered the first week she'd worked with him and he'd had to fly to New York, that J. Gregory was as protective of his manuscripts as a collector over a priceless uncut diamond. If Jonah left town, the manuscript was stored in a bank vault, safe from fire or theft.

He gave her a smug look. "Sure did. Only useful angle to this whole bizarre incident—maybe my editor will have to forgo his endless digs about my author paranoia."

"But...that means they found out where you live." Paige took a deep breath. "It's too much of a coincidence to consider this a random break-in, isn't it?"

"'Fraid so. And they'll soon be able to trace *you*. I can't figure out..." His voice trailed away, and he shrugged. "At any rate I called the police, and we'll meet them at the apartment. But we're leaving here, now. Know another hotel we can both use as a bolt-hole?"

"The Castille," Paige said after a moment's thought. "It's only a couple of blocks off the Mall, so it's fairly central to our research." She was proud of her even tone. Two years earlier, Professor K. had wheedled Paige into accompanying him to a dinner lecture at the Castille. He'd also bullied her into buying an absurdly expensive designer dress to wear, grouchily telling her that it wasn't a crime for an attractive girl to wear a pretty dress.

For a moment the memory threatened to buckle her knees. Paige thrust the pain back into a small dark corner, silently promising Professor K. that she would not give up until his killer was routed out and brought to justice. She looked up at Jonah. "It's expensive, but under the circumstances, probably worth it. You…said 'we.' You'll be staying there as well, then?" She pretended a fascination with the cabbage roses woven into the lobby carpet so Jonah wouldn't read the flood of relief she knew would be nakedly showing on her face. Maintaining her reserve around Jonah was growing more difficult by the hour.

"That's right, little *blume*. We'll both enjoy living in the lap of luxury for a while."

"You do it on purpose, don't you?" Light dawning, Paige watched the slow grin spreading across his face. "That's why—" A painful knot of emotion slowly unraveled, deep inside, loosing a trickle of gratitude, and something more, something gentle and affirming. "Whenever you think I'm too serious—or tense or—or frightened, that's when you trot out one of those names."

Jonah wrapped his hand about her elbow. "I've always known you were a woman of insight. Glad to see you're starting to utilize it with me. If I'm not careful, soon you'll have unearthed all my darkest secrets."

The words were lightly spoken, but the look he gave her zinged through Paige like a force field. "Including the meanings of all those words?" she retorted, just as lightly.

Jonah's response, naturally, was in some incomprehensible dialect.

They left the Bergman through a side entrance. While Jonah watched the street, Paige called another cab from a pay phone, and moments later Jonah was crowding her into the back seat, shielding her with his back. After a couple of tense blocks he leaned over, his breath washing into her ear. "All clear. Even if someone was watching when we went in, I don't think they saw us leave.''

At the Castille, they were booked into rooms with an adjoining door on the second floor. Instead of an elevator, they climbed a wide, *Gone With the Wind*-type staircase covered in a rich, soft green carpet. Piped music, filtered through invisible speakers, followed them until they turned down the long corridor at the head of the stairs. Once inside, Jonah prowled around the two rooms, searching corners with the relentless diligence of a trained German shepherd sniffing out drugs...or killers. Feeling useless and inept, Paige waited until she saw his shoulder muscles relax.

''We better hurry,'' she reminded him then. ''The police are waiting at Jay's apartment.''

''It will be interesting to see what they have to say this time. Also,'' Jonah added soberly, ''enlightening to hear what they *don't* say.''

The next couple of days, surprisingly, nothing happened. No threats, no suspicious characters lurking about the lobby. Nobody following them as they trundled around searching for information.

A passing rain shower left behind bilious skies and drenching humidity, but Washington wiped its collective brow and waited for autumn. Paige loved just about everything in the nation's capital *except* the humidity, which turned her hair to limp-noodle status and her brain likewise. Jonah's thick hair, on the other hand, curled a little more, which annoyed him. Otherwise he paid little attention to the weather. Paige envied his metabolism and his wavy hair. She was grateful for his even temper.

Late in the afternoon of their second day at the Castille, as they trudged past the front desk, the clerk called them over, handing Jonah two messages and Paige a large parcel.

''The galleys,'' Paige exclaimed, all but stuttering in relief. ''Maybe *now* I can find some information on those names the professor went to such lengths to hide.''

''Right-o,'' Jonah murmured absently.

Paige bumped the galleys against his arm. "Hey. Wake up. We should be able to make some headway now."

Without commenting, Jonah handed her one of the messages, which was from a research contact, then tucked the galleys under his arm and steered her away from the front desk.

Paige read the note while they climbed the stairs to their rooms. "Yuck." Her voice was as dry as Jonah's quirky smile. "*Another* politician, this one a U.S. congressman, right in our own backyard." She sighed. "And we didn't even recognize it when we found it on the list."

"How many people know all the names of congressional members?"

"My political science prof at Georgetown my junior year. Other than that, probably nobody. Point taken. We'll have to call, see how many secretaries and general go-fers we have to wade through to make an appointment." She slanted a calculating sideways look. "If we told them J. Gregory wanted to meet with him...."

"He's from Georgia," Jonah said, ignoring her last sentence.

"I see that." Her levity drained away, leaving a residue of uncertainty—and determination. She stopped outside the door to her room. "I'll start the calls and meet you for supper at seven."

The Honorable Armand Blackstone, representative from the state of Georgia, arranged to meet them at the prestigious Domingo Club, a favorite haunt of members of Congress. They'd caught him the day before he was planning to return to his home state.

"He must be out to impress us, since we're not his constituents," Jonah observed in the taxi the next afternoon. "Lunch, plus an interview, when he's on the verge of leaving town."

"I've eaten at the Domingo," Paige observed. "It's impressive if you're impressed by that sort of thing."

"Ah, well, at least we get a free lunch out of it."

Paige smiled, but when the cab dropped them off, she still couldn't help checking to make sure her hair was arranged and her linen suit straight, wrinkle free. When she caught Jonah's surprising look of admiration, she colored, then sedately mounted the marble steps leading to the Domingo.

A tall, well-built man with imposing brows, huge beak nose and impeccably styled silver-black hair, Congressman Gladstone welcomed them with a polished smile and outstretched hand. The garnet from a signet ring glittered in the subdued lighting of the foyer. His greeting was so reminiscent of the meeting with Patrick Minton, Paige's answering smile almost broadened into laughter.

"Glad you could make it," he said. "I hope you don't mind, but I took the liberty of ordering ahead." He waved them toward the dining room. "I'm pretty pushed for time." He whispered sotto voce to an aide, who scurried off in the opposite direction.

"We're familiar with the complaint." Jonah's expression was bland. Paige made a face at him behind the congressman's back.

Over shrimp cocktails Gladstone shared his Vietnam experiences and how being awarded the Purple Heart had meant so much to him. He admitted that it had probably helped him win his congressional seat twelve years earlier, but he hoped—he gave a self-deprecating smile—that his subsequent victories had been due to merit.

Over boneless breast of chicken *bagatelle* that looked better than it tasted, he and Jonah exchanged reminiscences about their respective childhoods. Armand's father had been in the Diplomatic Corp, and Armand was almost as well traveled as Jonah.

"Did your father ever meet a man named Gerald Minton?" Paige inserted into a rare moment of silence.

Gladstone turned politely toward her. "The name isn't familiar," he admitted after a minute. He smiled. "But then in this position I meet so many people...."

"What about your father?" Jonah casually reached and speared the circular spiced apple Paige had shoved to one side of her plate. "Is he still alive? He'd be more likely to know, of course."

"Regretfully, though still alive, my father's health is so poor

I'm afraid he wouldn't have much to offer. There aren't too many of the old World War II vets left, are there? You say this book series is funded by a grant from the American History Association? I wonder why I haven't heard of it.''

"I would have thought," Paige ventured carefully, "that Professor Kittridge might have interviewed you at some point in the past couple of years. Even though you're not a former POW, you are a Vietnam veteran, and that's the book he was concentrating on." She grabbed her water glass and took a hasty swallow. She had almost blurted out *Before he was murdered,* which would have been disastrous.

The puzzled frown on Congressman Gladstone's face cleared. "Oh. *That* book. The name didn't register the first time, I'm afraid. As I recall, it was at some university function, and he and I enjoyed an energetic debate over the influence the military has wielded in the legislature. He's a character, isn't he? You should have brought him along. I would have enjoyed chatting with him again.''

During the awkward ensuing silence a waiter removed their plates. "I'm afraid Professor Kittridge was—I'm afraid he died back in August." Beneath the table Paige balled her hands into fists and barely suppressed a reflexive jerk, when a warm masculine hand covered both of hers.

"It was sudden," Jonah explained easily, "which is why Ms. Hawthorne is having to retrace some of his sources so she can proof the galleys. I'm—um—trying to help.''

"The professor's dead?" The icy gray eyes softened. "I am sorry to hear that. I'm sure it's a loss to the academic community as well as to those who knew him on a personal level.''

They ate their raspberry flan in congenial silence, but the minute the waiter whisked the dishes away, Armand rose. "I have a committee meeting before I catch my plane, I'm afraid.'' He gestured to a discreet young man who had miraculously appeared behind them. "Dennis will try to answer any further questions, and if you'd care for a tour of—''

"That won't be necessary." Jonah held Paige's chair. "Thanks for your time. We'll see that you receive a complimentary copy of the professor's book.''

The congressman paused, staring down at Paige. "Ah, yes. The book. It's nice to have someone…conscientious, who can step in and see that all his work was not in vain."

Jonah didn't change expressions, or even move, but Paige had interpreted the congressman's look, as well, and gently insinuated herself between the two men. After thanking him a final time, she turned and headed for the exit, forcing Jonah to follow. Only when they were back in the taxi and moving did Paige release a long pent-up breath.

"He was just playing his role, Jonah. Please don't read anything else into it. At least he displayed a little more personal warmth than Minton, I thought."

The midnight gaze rested on her a minute, and Paige felt old feelings surfacing, swirling in ugly eddies of insecurity and shame. She lifted her chin. "We now have two possible suspects—both men's fathers were in the Diplomatic Corp." Why was he looking at her like that? "D-don't you find that interesting? Maybe that's the key to those nine names."

"I don't know." His hand lifted, and his finger tucked her hair behind her ear. "What's the matter, Paige?"

The gentleness of the question could not disguise the demand. She responded automatically. "It's you," she whispered. "The way you're looking—I mean, of course I'm not trying to criticize. That is…I'm sorry…." Her tongue felt tangled and her vocal cords constricted. Paige shook her head, despising herself.

"Ah." Head tilted, his fingers began stroking the tips of his mustache. "Well, you see—I didn't like the way Gladstone treated you. I didn't like the way he looked at you," the mild-mannered Jonah Sterling replied as though she'd asked him his opinion of the meal. "The honorable congressman's lucky I'm such a peaceable bloke, because if he'd patronized you with one more silver-tongued remark, I might have been tempted to remove it for him."

Nerves jangling, Paige gazed blindly out the window until the taxi stopped in front of their hotel. Who *was* this man?

Chapter Thirteen

After weeks of nothing but fruitless hours and dead ends, Paige fueled her determinations with longer hours—and a snapshot of Professor K. tucked in her wallet. Whenever she entertained a notion to give up, she had only to look at the photograph.

Late Thursday afternoon in mid-September, at the Modern Military Headquarters Branch of the National Archives, she at last found another name on the "Pettigrew list," as they'd dubbed the nine names. "Brewster Covington, charged with embezzling government payroll. Sentenced to five years. Dishonorable discharge," Paige read aloud, excitement skimming through her exhaustion. "This happened in 1948, after the war, but his first name does start with a *B*."

Jonah dropped the paper airplane he'd been constructing out of scrap paper, an indicator of another episode of what he dubbed "creative snags." Most days he spent an hour or two reading whatever Paige thrust under his nose. Then he would bring out his laptop and work on his manuscript.

"Now you know why I desperately need a research assistant," he'd explained once with an apologetic smile.

"I don't mind," Paige promised. Hesitantly she added, "It helps...just your being here."

A warm, unsettling light flickered in his smiling eyes. But he only touched her fingers and murmured, "I'm glad," before turning his attention to his computer screen.

Now he scooted his chair from his study carrel to Paige's and twitched the publication around. While he read, Paige pressed her hands to the small of her back.

"Sure wish Major Pettigrew or whoever wrote those names had included first names as well as last."

"Be grateful we've the last names, instead of a list of initials," Jonah murmured absently. "Let's go for it," he announced a moment later. "If we hurry, we might have an address in time to catch a flight tomorrow afternoon, if it's impractical to drive."

He paused. "I wish you'd let me at least cover transportation costs. The professor left his estate to you for your future security, after all."

"What about you?" Paige retorted, exasperated. "You won't let me pay your expenses, either, even though none of this has anything to do with your book."

"Well, darling—" he ducked his head, then looked her in the eye and shrugged "—I...um...I can afford it. Thanks be to God," he added, the flesh covering his cheekbones deepening in color.

Uncomfortable, Paige gathered up her materials. Jonah never proclaimed his faith in lengthy verbage or flamboyant public displays. He...*lived* it, and she was never more aware of the depth of his commitment than at a moment like this, when with a single heartfelt sentence he put his money where his mouth was: in God's hands.

Last-known address for Brewster Covington was Hamlet, Missouri. A garrulous operator connected them to a friend of a friend of a second cousin who used to live next door to Covington's grandmother. Paige watched Jonah's low-key, amalgamated blend of Oxford English and tidewater drawl work its charm on the unseen woman. Every now and then he'd look at Paige, bathing her in the warmth of his slow smile beneath the bushy auburn mustache.

No wonder the operator wanted to talk his ear off.

They finally learned that Brewster had settled in California sometime in the fifties. By the following afternoon, they had an address, and Paige made reservations on a red-eye flight leaving Dulles a little after eleven that night. Unfortunately, a messy accident on the access road leading into the airport forced them to park in the satellite parking lot.

"We'll still have time," Paige muttered sleepily. "There's a shuttle bus."

Jonah merely grunted in response.

Paige straightened in the seat and tried to wake up. She'd dozed most of the way from the hotel. "Fine. Be grumpy—" The teasing retort caught in her throat. Jonah, grumpy? "Jonah?" Her voice came out hushed, more uncertain than she wished.

He had been cruising up and down the poorly lit rows of cars, searching for a vacant spot. "Keep quiet a minute," he murmured back, turning another corner. Then his breath sucked in, and his foot hit the brakes with enough force to jerk Paige forward in the seat. "I'm afraid we may have trouble."

The terse words galvanized Paige, jarring her to heart-thumping alertness. For the past several weeks there had been no sign of trouble and she had almost forgotten the danger. "What is it?" she whispered, mouth dry.

"I didn't say anything earlier, because I wasn't sure until now. We've had...company, since two blocks after we left the Castille. And just now when I turned down the aisle, I saw the figure of a man whose silhouette was too familiar for my peace of mind."

"What do you think we should do?" Though her initial response had been a nauseating jolt of fear, angry determination rekindled, as consuming as the fire that had destroyed the professor's home. "If we can make it out of this lot, we could alert one of the policemen at that accident. No—we *have* to make that flight. How about if you start honking the horn to attract—"

"Easy, Paige." He released the brake so the car began slowly moving again, and switched to the bright headbeams.

"Slide down in the seat," he instructed her. "You won't be as much of a target that way."

Her heart lurched. "What about you?"

"Well, I don't plan to make either of us easy targets." She'd never heard that tone from him before. "Do you know how often the shuttle runs this time of night?"

"Fifteen minutes, twenty-four hours a day...but I don't know how long it's been since the last one." Perspiration made her fingers slippery, and she surreptitiously wiped her hands on the seat.

"Say a prayer then, love." He pulled into a vacant parking space and killed the engine.

Paige tried to swallow, failed. "Where is he now?"

"He parked his car two aisles over—I saw him when he got out, but he's disappeared." He rapped the steering wheel, frowning.

The makeshift parking lot with its sparsely placed lights turned the area into a potential death trap. In the tomb of their car Paige could barely see Jonah's rugged profile. She peered out into the darkness. Pray, Jonah had said, as though he expected God to miraculously alert the authorities or something. On the other hand...she didn't want to die yet. For the first time in years, she yearned to live, and not just so she could vindicate Professor K. The knowledge illuminated her soul, right there in the dark parking lot in the midst of life-threatening danger. She yearned to live, to explore the strange feelings unfurling, deep inside. Reaching out toward—

Headlights suddenly bathed them in a yellow wash—a car, coming down their aisle. It pulled into an empty spot several spaces down. The lights disappeared; the engine switched off, and silence descended. Raw electricity filled the air inside Paige's car, stirring the hairs on her arms, the back of her neck. Breath suspended, slowly she turned her head, staring at Jonah. His stillness frightened her almost as much as the unknown man lurking in the shadows.

In a soundless whisper of movement he eased the window down a crack.

The two men from the car approached, their voices easily

carrying in the night. Jonah's hand snaked out and pressed Paige's shoulder, keeping her still.

"And then he said if we couldn't deliver the new proposal first thing in the morning we'd lose the sale."

"Harry's always been a pain in—" The voices faded as the men hurried by, heading for the shuttle bus stop.

Businessmen. They were nothing but harmless, harassed...*helpful* businessmen. The idea sprang to life and Paige leaned over. "We can use them as cover."

"Come on." Jonah opened the door the same time as Paige, and they caught up with the two men just as the shuttle bus entered the lot, a good quarter of a mile away.

Paige forced a smile for the men. They barely nodded before resuming their gripe session about flying to L.A. at short notice. Beside her, Jonah's body hummed with tension; his head swiveled constantly, his gaze dissecting the parking lot.

The noise of the bus grinding its gears drew closer.

Paige clutched the briefcase as if it were an armor-proof vest. Surely the gunman wouldn't shoot in front of witnesses. And yet...what if he didn't care, and decided to kill the two businessmen as well?

The bus turned down the aisle next to them. Overhead, a departing plane filled the night with roaring noise, muffling out the sound of the bus—and anything else. Jonah casually took Paige's arm and moved them out from under the light and in between two parked cars. Paige felt the strength of his grip, and knew with a flash of numb certainty that he was steeling himself to hurl her to the pavement. That's what you think, superhero. She pulled free, then grabbed his hand and held on. If he shoved her down, she planned to take him with her.

The shuttle approached, blinding them in the glare of its headlights. The two businessman shifted impatiently, but Paige and Jonah stayed between the cars. With a grinding of gears and a soft hissing as the doors opened, the bus lumbered to a stop. In the aisle directly across, a shadow darted into view, then disappeared.

Jonah reached the steps in four long strides, practically yanking Paige's shoulder out of the socket. He shoved her up the steps right on the heels of one of the businessmen. The whole time Jonah was at her back, once again shielding her with his body. He sat down next to her, and the bus lurched into motion, chugging at a nerve-rattling snail's pace.

As they left the parking lot and turned onto the road to the airport, Paige saw a dark shape weaving quickly down the aisles. She nudged Jonah.

"I see it," he said. His hand, resting on his knee, closed into a fist. Not until a policeman waved the bus around the tangled remains of the three-car pileup did Paige see that hand uncurl, relax. His head turned slightly to Paige. In the dim interior lights, she caught the barely visible movement as a corner of his mustache lifted.

It struck her belatedly that he was tired. Tired, baffled and perhaps even a little bit scared. Yet not once had he spoken sharply to Paige, or blasted her with withering scorn for not being faster or smarter or unafraid. Or a model Christian woman, weathering her tribulation with a smile and confident scripture ready on her lips. In fact, he'd gone out of his way to shield and protect her, reassure her and—unbelievably to Paige—he'd even tried to mask his own feelings, for her sake.

Her hand twined through his arm. Then she laid her head against his shoulder, just for a moment, and hugged the arm she held. Neither of them spoke again, but she felt a puff of breath stir her hair, and the coiled muscles beneath her gradually relaxed like his hand.

Their flight had just been called. Jonah turned away from the public phone, and tried to produce an encouraging smile. To Paige, it looked more like a savage bearing of teeth. Though she'd only heard one side of his call to the police, she'd heard enough to know it had been a waste of time. "I couldn't even give them a license number to his car, much less a physical description. Too blasted dark." His voice was biting, laced with bitter frustration. "We're no better off now than we were two weeks ago."

But he didn't take it out on her. Paige swallowed around a sudden lump. "We'll be okay. You've done everything possible, Jonah. Let it go—we're safe enough right now." And right now all that mattered was easing Jonah's pain with the same generosity of spirit with which he had eased hers.

Even as she voiced the words, Paige was filled with a strange sense of peace. She smiled up at him, a surprised, then serene, heartfelt smile. *And I can't even remember a single verse of scripture. No...there was one.* "I do feel safe with you, even in the valley of the shadow of death," she said.

Beneath his mustache, the grim line of Jonah's mouth softened. "Thanks." He looked down at her a moment, and the gentle warmth bubbling through Paige expanded, bursting upward, light as soap bubbles. "You're a trouper, Paige Hawthorne. The best."

Brewster Covington lived alone in a small house in Southern California, on the edge of the Mojave Desert. A thin layer of dust coated everything including, it seemed, the gaunt, grayhaired Brewster Covington. In the unforgiving light of a blinding morning sun it was plain the years had not been kind. Cold eyes, narrowed with suspicion, appraised Paige and Jonah from behind the screen door.

"We tried to call—" Paige wet her lips, smiled coaxingly, "—but your answering machine—"

"I heard it." He abruptly flung open the door. "Come in. Ya got five minutes."

Brewster volunteered a bucketful of information about his son's successful law practice, but no amount of coaxing persuaded him to share his wartime experiences, much less the crime that put him in prison and ended his military career.

"That war's a dead issue—nobody cares anymore, including me. You want to hear about my son, I talk. Keep pestering me about a book I care nothin' 'bout—and you can just show yourselves right outa here."

Six minutes later they were on the way to San Bernardino, where Brewster Covington's son had established his practice. "He might see ya. Might not. Pretty busy man, my son. He's gonna be a judge, if he plays his cards right."

* * *

"Have you noticed," Paige commented while they ate lunch and fed pigeons in a park near James Covington's firm, "that everyone connected with that list is involved in some kind of politics in one way or another? And that nobody wants to talk about World War II?"

"I noticed." Jonah tossed a piece of bread to a hopeful squirrel inching past the greedy pigeons. "Makes me all the more curious about the story behind those names. I have a feeling it might be bigger than we realized, and an even deeper gut certainty that it isn't very pretty."

Paige sent him a wry look. "I didn't think—considering where we found it—that it was merely a list of people to invite to a tea party."

"Unless," Jonah returned just as wryly, "the tea was laced with arsenic."

"Analogies aside, I'll confess that I'm still hoping to discover the link between the Pettigrew list and Professor K.'s." She watched the squirrel Jonah had fed scamper up a nearby tree. "Would have been nice, wouldn't it, if the 'B. Covington' had been Benjamin or Benedict."

"A name to match the *B-E-N?*" Jonah scattered the last handful of breadcrumbs into the cooing pigeons. "Even if we do stumble across a match, we'll still have to prove it's the one Professor K. was implicating."

"I know." And the labyrinthine dilemma kept her nights full of restive dreams.

They finished lunch in silence, and an hour later a perfectly groomed and coiffed secretary admitted them to James Covington's office. He immediately walked around his desk to meet them, and Paige avoided looking at Jonah or she would have burst out laughing. The secretary brought in a silver tea service with coffee and an assortment of sandwiches, then whisked out, shutting the door behind her.

"It was thoughtful of you to stop by—I don't get out to Dad nearly as much as I should." Covington sat down across from them and helped himself to a sandwich. "Life's pretty hectic around here, and Dad...well, you might have gathered he's not the most sociable creature."

"Only when it comes to telling us about you," Jonah said.

"We really needed to hear about his World War II experience," Paige explained. "I realize it was a long time ago, but—"

"With the world political situation what it is nowadays, somehow World War II seems a little more relevant than it did, even a year ago."

They chatted with the lawyer for almost half an hour—and found out nothing. He was married with three children and had a successful practice. He was planning to run for a judgeship in the elections next year. But the most significant tidbit, Paige thought, was the revelation that throughout his life his father and mother had refused to discuss the war.

"What do you think?" she asked on the way to the L.A. airport.

"I think we have a bucket of worms that's turning into a bucket of snakes, all of them poisonous. The trouble is, we still don't know which of them is about to strike. Much less when."

Chapter Fourteen

October settled over the city with warm Indian summer days and refreshing cool nights. But three days of nonstop rain left Jonah and Paige with claustrophobia along with beleaguered spirits, so on the first clear day they escaped for a ride through the Virginia countryside—on the back of Jonah's powerful motorcycle. Paige hadn't objected with her usual intransigency, in spite of the fact that Jonah had only been able to persuade her to ride behind him on two other occasions. She was too relieved to "get out of Dodge," to quote one of Jonah's favorite Western clichés.

They headed west out Highway 50, then turned onto Route 15, eschewing the interstate for the scenic route. Choking traffic, buildings and shopping centers gradually dwindled, replaced by hardwood forests, rolling hills, sprawling farms and white fences. Scarlet maples and burned orange oaks splashed the countryside with bright dollops of color. Gradually Paige realized that she really *wasn't* going to fall off—Jonah was a superb motorcyclist, and she relaxed her stranglehold on his trim waist enough to soak up some of the blurred scenery. She'd grown up riding horses—mostly bareback—on her father's farm. This wasn't really so very different.

Except that she'd never ridden double with an attractive,

mysterious man whose presence imbued the very air with sparks. Who had only to crinkle his eyes a certain way, smiling that lopsided smile, to turn her knees as well as her brain to the consistency of soggy cereal.

But Paige had come to accept, on a subconscious level she refused to examine, that she could trust Jonah with her spirit as well as her life. Since it had been years since she felt that way—and the last time it had almost destroyed her—the realization was alternately exalting and terrifying.

Invigorating wind pulsed around her helmet, filling her head and blending with the cycle's muted roar. After a while Paige gave in to temptation and closed her eyes, allowing the noise and sensation of speed to lull her battered senses into a semi-hypnotic trance.

When the peaceful October day shattered, she was completely unprepared.

"Hold on!" Jonah yelled.

The motorcycle downshifted, then whipped onto a small dirt road bisecting a state forest. Jonah flung out one booted foot to keep the bike from keeling over and flinging them to the ground. The muscles in his back and shoulders bunched, flowing with astonishing strength as he wrestled with the handlebars.

Paige slipped sideways, grappling desperately for a handhold that wouldn't distract Jonah. Her legs gripped the bike as if she were trying to stay on the back of a rearing bronc. Then Jonah recovered control, and the bike shot down the winding road.

Something whined past Paige's cheek, sharp and stinging. She cringed, ducking her head. Next she felt more than heard a muffled thunk in the vicinity of her left foot. Jonah abruptly turned the bike again, directly into the woods.

We're being shot at. The realization hit Paige with the same impact as a bullet. Someone was trying to kill them—which meant that the killer had finally tracked them down.

She risked turning her head. Fifty yards behind them a blue car skidded to a halt on the dirt road. Then the motorcycle bounced, swerving drunkenly around a dense thicket of low-lying bushes, and she had to concentrate on keeping her balance. They wove an erratic path between pine, oak and hickory trees, and Paige tried to keep her body limber, even though fear hardened her limbs to slabs of concrete.

Without warning Jonah whipped the bike in a tight half circle, skidding to a stop on the pine-needled forest floor; she would have toppled if his arm hadn't hauled her back upright. With a quick flick of his wrist he killed the engine, then he removed his helmet, tucking it beneath his arm. Silence descended.

With her gaze trained back toward the dirt road, Paige fumbled her helmet free as well, trying not to make a sound. Still straddling the bike, Jonah surveyed the woods, watching and listening like a wild stag scenting the hunter.

"There." Paige grabbed his shoulder, urgently pointed, just as a bullet shattered the bark in a white pine two feet away.

"Helmets," Jonah barked and they swiftly crammed them back on their heads.

The motor snarled into life and they plunged down a shallow slope, fighting through a tangle of dying catbrier. Jonah gunned up the other side of the slope, steering the bike into even thicker woods. Navigating more slowly, he maneuvered around rotting logs, dense low-branched trees and clinging shrubs. Blackened trunks attested to the ravages of a forest fire decades earlier.

Paige tried to keep a firm, yet light grip on Jonah's waist. But her fingers were numb, slippery, and she kept losing her grip. She was nothing but a burden, no help to him at all...if they died it would be her fault. *I'm sorry,* she wanted to say—except her mouth was chalk dry. She tried to help him watch, but strands of hair caught between the strap and her cheek had half-blinded her, and she didn't want to move her arm for fear of jarring Jonah. So she clung, mute and unmoving, waiting for a bullet to slam into her back.

Better her than Jonah.

Lord? Forgive me for not being a better person....

Jonah's hands closed over hers, and very gently eased them away from their desperate clasp about his waist. Paige blinked, only then realizing they had stopped. Jonah swung off the Harley and lifted Paige to the ground, steadying her. Just as gently he eased the helmet free of her head.

"Paige? You okay, love?"

She looked up into his face, then turned her head, eyes searching the woods. "Where are they?" The words emerged in a hoarse croak, and she ran her tongue over her dry lips. "You shook them off?"

"I'm pretty sure they didn't follow on foot too long, so I imagine they're either trying to figure out where we'll surface—or they've gone back to the hotel to wait for us." He lifted her chin, smiling down at her, though his gaze remained somber. "Buck up—we'll make it out okay."

Paige pulled free, took two wobbly steps and collapsed beneath a blazing yellow tulip tree. She stared fixedly at her knees until a wave of dizziness subsided. "What a lovely way to spend an afternoon," she mumbled, relieved when this time her voice sounded almost normal.

Jonah placed a hand briefly on her shoulder, then lifted it. "Wait here. I'm going to scout around a bit." He disappeared into the woods, so swiftly and silently she blinked.

Who *was* Jonah Sterling? Even though he'd shared tales of his childhood and in spite of seeing him in action against intruders and killers, Paige still felt as though a complete stranger had stolen the congenial, twinkling-eyed Jonah away. All the past months working with him, and she didn't really know him at all. The shocking metamorphosis from preoccupied writer to intrepid adventurer was too unbelievable. Like…like absent-minded professor to Indiana Jones. Like Jasper the cat to Jasper the jaguar….

A half-gasping giggle erupted. Paige scrambled to her feet and concentrated fiercely on the vivid red berries in a tangle of bushes to keep from bursting into hysterical laughter. Get a grip, Hawthorne. You might be a failure as a worthy companion, but at least you can show a little dignity.

When Jonah returned and saw Paige sitting quietly, twirling a tulip tree leaf, something tight inside him relaxed. Close up he was able to spot a telltale puffiness about her eyelids, and one damp streak had cleaned a pearly trail along her cheek. But she lifted her head and smiled gamely as he approached. His love, and the dregs of fear, wrapped around his heart, squeezing it. He loved this woman with a depth he'd never imagined possible. *Please, God. Help me keep her safe from harm.*

"No sign of anything but deer—I saw some tracks." He dropped down beside her, picking up another leaf and tracing his finger over the intricate play of veins. He wanted to do the same with Paige's wrist. "All quiet on the home front?"

"Like a tomb." She made a jerky motion with her hand. "Guess I should use a different simile. Jonah? There's a hole in the rear fender of your bike." Her voice was stripped of emotion—arid as the Kalahari desert.

"What!" He leaped up and strode over to examine the damaged fender. "Insufferable twit!" he expostulated, turning back to Paige with a ferocious scowl that wasn't all that exaggerated. "Now that's going too far, don't you think? It's one thing to take potshots at us, but when you hit my bike instead..."

Paige was shaking her head, a glimmer of light spilling at last into the terror-darkened gray eyes. She crammed her fist against her mouth, but the amusement escaped, anyway.

Relieved, Jonah walked back over. "You never have exhibited proper respect for my machine," he complained. At least his diversionary attempt had succeeded. He *was* angry about the damage to his bike, of course. But next to Paige, the Harley was just scrap metal.

Then he saw more tears seeping out the corners of her eyes and felt as if he'd taken a bullet in his heart. "Paige...love, don't...." He put a hand on her arm, holding her still when she would have backed away.

"I'm fine, fine." Leaning back, she shoved against his chest. "You're just so funny about the Harley. Let me go, Jonah. I'm fine." Her voice broke. "F-fine..."

"Blast it, woman! Be still and let me hold you!" Jonah all but roared, yanking her right up against his chest. He clamped his arms around her and hugged her, hard. "You don't have to be perfect, Paige. Do you hear me? You don't have to be perfect.''

She went rigid, hands clenched in tight-fisted balls at her sides, only suffering his embrace. Reluctantly Jonah freed her, backing a step. He should have known better, but it was too late now, and abruptly he decided he'd had enough. They were going to have this out, here and now. "Paige," he began cautiously, but she interrupted.

"I know I'm not perfect. I've known for years—you don't have to rub it in.'' She wiped the back of her hand over her eyes, disheveled and haggard.

Jonah dropped down under the tree and patted the ground beside him. "Come on, sit down by me.'' He switched back to the gentle, nonthreatening tone to which she best responded. Slowly she obeyed.

"Do you think,'' he mused, picking up a twig and idly marking random trails in the loamy ground, "that if you don't manifest the courage and dignity of Joan of Arc, waiting for the torch, that I'll somehow think less of you?'' He slanted a quick sideways look into Paige's shame-reddened face. "It's not a sign of weakness, needing comfort after a scare, whether it's from a bad dream or a brush with death. It's a sign of your humanity—I'd go so far as to designate comfort as basic human need. So why won't you let me give you that?'' He tried a smile. "I was scared, too, you know. *I* need a hug as much as you....''

Paige shrugged, her shoulders hunched, posture defensive. Jonah waited, saying nothing. "At least you didn't act like a spineless wimp,'' she finally burst out. "And I can't even find out who's trying to kill us—I can't find out who killed Professor K. The next time, I'll probably get us both killed, because I won't know how to help.'' She clasped her knees. "It's humiliating. I never used to be like that. Never used to feel like that.'' She stopped.

"I see,'' Jonah said. He eased himself to a comfortable reclining position, arms draped behind his head, eyes closed. "What did you used to be like?'' he asked comfortably, as if he'd asked her views on the preacher's sermon at the last church service. "Tell me how you used to feel." Good thing she didn't have a clue about *his* feelings.

Unfortunately Jonah could feel Paige's wariness, practically hear the bars clanging shut in the corridors of her mind. Every time he had tried to explore her past, she retreated, eluding his subtle probing with the grace and skill of a fencing master. He dropped the twig in astonishment when, with a tiny sigh, she began to talk.

"When I was a child, I was always the one my sisters could talk into trying something really dangerous, like jumping out of the hayloft, or cutting across the neighbor's field without letting his Angus bull see us. Standing on the back of one of my grandfather's horses at a full gallop. Nothing nearly as exciting as your life, of course—but at least I wasn't a coward."

"You're not a coward now."

"If you hadn't held on to me back there, I would have fallen off, I was so terrified."

Jonah sat up. Remember, keep it down, keep it light. "I believe," he stated calmly, "that we've already covered this ground." He turned toward her slightly. "Where did you come up with the idea that it's a sin for you to admit any weakness? Did you know that when I first met you, you intimidated the socks off my feet?"

Her head whipped up in surprise, and he grinned crookedly. "That's right, Ms. Hawthorne, your formidable reputation had me shaking in my shoes. In fact, I could only think in clichés— every writer's worst nightmare. Brain like a steel trap, mind like a computer. Feminine but professional..." He watched her astonishment in frank enjoyment. "If Professor K. hadn't confided your weakness for animal crackers, I would never have had the nerve to ask you to be my research assistant."

"You thought I was—is that why—" She gaped at him, charmingly incoherent. "That's why you keep buying them, then complaining that they're too small for a grown man and I might as well eat them...."

"You never guessed, then?" Pleased, Jonah chuckled. "Looks like we've both been hiding things from each other, hmm? Just think, all these months you've gone to torturous lengths to prove your invincibility—until one fateful morning when you walked into a situation over your head, and threw yourself in my arms.''

"Don't remind me," Paige muttered, streaks of red climbing up her cheeks.

"But I like the memory." He reached over then and tugged one hand free, tracing the fluttering pulse in her wrist. "You let me hold you, for the first time. Let me glimpse the lovely woman without all her armor in place." Beneath his thumb her pulse had leaped into a gallop. "And I enjoyed holding you very much. I enjoyed even more the...privilege of protecting you. The way I see it, using his strength and his skill to protect a woman—*any* woman, is a man's God-directed responsibility. One of the more noble and rewarding ones, I might add."

"Jonah..."

He ignored the unspoken plea. "The world has done a fair number of muddying the waters, hasn't it? But just because a woman is *physically* weaker than a man, that doesn't make her weak. Do you agree with that, or do you think I sound hopelessly archaic?"

"Hadn't we better be leaving?"

Jonah laughed. "Not yet, little *Schildkröte*. I want to continue this very enlightening conversation."

Finally smiling, Paige grabbed a handful of leaves and soil and tossed it at him. "How many languages *do* you know?"

He grinned. "A working knowledge of four or five. I always picked up the dialect of whatever country Mother and I spent the summer in." He tugged a lock of hair tickling his forehead, feeling awkward. "For some reason God gave me this...ear for languages, as they say. It used to infuriate my world-traveled mother, who couldn't even manage a simple thank-you without a two-language dictionary." He absently brushed the dirt and leaves off his sweater and jeans, lost in a haze of nostalgia and the rare luxury of relaxing with Paige.

"Why don't you ever go on promo tours as J. Gregory?" she asked out of the blue, startling him so much he was momentarily at a loss.

"I—um—I detest the circus atmosphere. You know, being

so mercilessly exposed to the public eye.'' He shook his head. ''What on earth makes you ask?'' Other than the obvious attempt to redirect the conversation.

The color in her cheeks deepened. ''You have to know you're a fascinating, intriguing man. I've been around highly educated people ever since I was a freshman at Georgetown, but I never met anyone who could speak three languages fluently, much less four or five. Or who'd been all the places, experienced what you have. You'd probably sell twice as many books.''

''I want people to read my books for the story and the Christian message—not as a sop to my ego,'' Jonah murmured, feeling his face heat. He absolutely, positively detested talking about his writing with nonwriters. Paige, however, was different, so he made an effort to explain. After all, he was forcing her to peel back the layers of her own ego, allowing him to know her better. ''Public speaking isn't something I ever felt...called to do. Frankly, the thought terrifies me.''

Paige made a disbelieving sound.

''It's true.'' He felt heat creeping under his skin. ''But I agreed, especially after the second book was made into a movie. It was right after that, that my fiancée and I parted. We both realized our priorities were...irreconcilable.''

''Do you ever hear from her?''

''Every Christmas—with a family snapshot. She's married to a solicitor—lawyer to you. They have three kids. Pots of money. Once a year they attend midnight services on Christmas Eve.'' He shook his head. ''I suppose, in a sense, Rhonda helped me understand a Biblical fundamental—you know, the one about the place of money, fame and God's sovereignty?''

''I know it well,'' Paige murmured in a peculiar tone.

Jonah glanced at her, then shrugged. ''Well, Rhonda insisted that I reverse the order. I wouldn't. Anyway, that's one of the reasons behind my adamant refusal to...sell myself, as they say. I don't show well, in the public arena. The few times I agreed to speaking engagements, nobody saw, well—*me*. They saw their own idea of J. Gregory, Christian, world traveler, author, adventurer...a figure somehow larger than life.''

He looked away from Paige. "Um...like I said, I was uncomfortable with the whole circus maximus atmosphere. I feel that God gave me whatever talent and success I've enjoyed to further *His* kingdom—not the popularity of a man called J. Gregory."

Jonah could hear the ragged sound of Paige's breathing—but she didn't speak. Finally he looked at her, and almost panicked at that peculiar, arrested expression on her face. "Paige? Say something. Did I sound pompous? Jaded?" Why was she staring at him like that?

"You sounded—" she shook her head "—not like my husband."

In spite of his own self-consciousness Jonah didn't miss the revealing comment, nor Paige's surprise for having said it. *Finally*. He deliberately relaxed back against the tree, stretching his arms upward until his spine cracked. "Is that bad or good, Paige? Tell me what you're thinking."

"Trust me, that's good. I thank God every day that you're not like David." She waited then, and Jonah sensed her anxiety as though she'd blasted the words through a loudspeaker.

"I'm glad to hear that, actually. It's occurred to me more than once, since getting to know you, that I don't think I would have liked your husband very much."

She seemed to fold in on herself all at once. "He was an intelligent, ambitious man with tremendous gifts. It wasn't his fault that I failed to live up to his expectations." Her hand waved jerkily. "Working with you has been...a revelation. I've enjoyed it, more than I thought possible. But all along I've wondered—"

"Wondered what?" Oops. He needed to watch that tone or she'd be scampering off into the brush. He forced a smile.

She seemed to struggle with the words before finishing in a rush, "I've always wondered how you stay so—*sane* is the word that comes to my mind. You're always under pressure, having to produce a bestseller that's better than the one before. Never knowing if a reviewer will shred your reputation, or propel your book to bestseller status again. Always having to satisfy the demands of the public, regardless of who or what you—oh, never mind. This is ridiculous."

She started to rise, but Jonah reached up an arm, tugging her back down. "I write the books," he said. "It's not up to me how well they sell, if they sell at all. It's up to God." He could feel his back teeth grinding—a bad sign. "Was that how your husband used to make you feel? That you were always on center stage, expected to perform in a superlative manner—according to *his* standards of course—or you were a failure?"

She flushed to her hairline. "I know it's presumptuous to compare my life to yours. I didn't mean—"

"Don't ever let me hear you say something like that again." He rose to his knees, and his hands closed around her elbows. He dragged her close, their faces inches apart. "It's garbage, and a pack of lies. You've been fed a pack of lies, Paige Hawthorne. You're responsible to *God,* same as I am. You don't have to live up to my standards—you didn't have to live up to your husband's. Or your friends'. Even your church doesn't have the right to come between you and your relationship with the Lord. Paige, you know better than that."

"I used to think so." She squirmed, tried to free herself. "We need to leave. Let me go...it's going to be dark in a little while."

"Right. You don't want to talk about it. I get the message, loud and clear." He dropped her arms and stood over her. "In case you were wondering, *Schildkrote* is *turtle* in German. That's exactly what you remind me of right now—a turtle, shrinking back inside your shell because you're uncomfortable with a conversation. It's fine to pick at my scars and insecurities—but never your own."

If he didn't zip his mouth he was going to wreck his chances, possibly forever. He stalked back over to the Harley, and without a word secured the helmets to the bar. He'd been insensitive and undisciplined, lighting into an insecure woman who'd just had the fright of her life. *God, forgive me.*

It would be a miracle if *Paige* forgave him.

He sucked in his breath, staring bleakly across the scant distance separating them. It might as well have been the Arctic Ocean. "Let's go, then."

Chapter Fifteen

Paige stood beneath the tulip tree, her hands brushing her clothes, smoothing her hair...anything to delay the moment when she had to force her feet to move instead. She should never have opened her mouth. A light breeze wove among the tree branches, setting the leaves to whispering like the hushed mutterings of a group of church ladies talking behind their hands. *I can't believe what Paige Hawthorne said to that nice Mr. Sterling... Always said that young woman had a selfish streak... It's a shame, isn't it, and I just know the Lord is offended by her behavior. I know I am....*

She brought herself up short, banishing the long-ago voices even as the breeze drifted away, leaving behind a golden autumn silence. What was it Jonah had just shouted at her—something about her not having to live up to other people's standards? Instead of freezing into the catatonic submissiveness David had demanded, she should march across to Jonah and shout back in his face. Tell him his behavior was insensitive and rude...especially when for weeks now she'd basked in the warmth of his understanding support.

Shout? Christians weren't supposed to shout, David had always said. Besides, shouting equated to anger, which was a sin, an offense to God.

David had been a hypocrite.

Paige took a step forward, stopped. The truth might be freeing, but the chains fell away grudgingly. What if Jonah shouted back?

She took another step, stopped again, her gaze on her scuffed half boots. He hadn't *really* shouted—not like she was used to anyway—but she knew she never wanted to be around a truly angry Jonah Sterling. Better all around just to accept blame, even if she hadn't done anything wrong. Easier. No shouting—less risk all the way around. The cowardly turtle syndrome.

She forced her feet forward, squared her shoulders. Took a deep breath. "Jonah, I—"

"I'd like to apologize."

Nonplussed, Paige stopped in her tracks and gawked as though he'd said he'd like to shave his head and pierce his nose. "What?"

He began dragging his leather gloves through his hand, slapping them in the palm. He avoided her gaze. "I'm sorry. I know confrontations upset you—I should have controlled my temper. We're both...off balance, scared. Regardless, I've no right to bully you."

Paige reached his side and searched the wooden mask of his face. "You didn't bully me. And you didn't shout—actually, you only raised your voice," she admitted candidly. "You were also right, about some things at least." Sighing, she lifted her shoulders in a shrug. "I know I have a knee-jerk reaction to certain situations. I'm sorry, too." She braced herself.

"Mmph." Beneath the mustache his mouth twitched. "Good enough. Let's kiss and make up." The gloves dropped with a soft plop on top of his helmet. "Come here."

Paige blinked at him. "That's a joke, right?" She backed up a step. "Jonah? I don't think this is a good idea."

Jonah stepped around the motorcycle. "On the contrary, this is the best idea I've had in weeks. Months." A light flickered in the night-sky eyes. "Come here—don't retreat into your shell, little *Schildkröte*."

Paige backed up another step. Of all the responses she'd steeled herself for, lighthearted teasing had never crossed her mind. And she wasn't sure she could be lighthearted about kissing Jonah. Just the prospect set a whole battalion of butterflies fluttering in her stomach. "Why are you acting like this? We could be shot dead any minute. This is very unprofessional of you. Jonah——" She bumped into a tree.

He trapped her there by planting his hands on the trunk on either side of her head. "You're absolutely irresistible when you're flustered," he teased with exaggerated British pomposity. Then he leaned forward and dropped a brief kiss on her protesting lips. "There—an apology." Another kiss, even softer. "And a kiss to make it better." His hands dropped away and he stepped back.

Paige touched trembling fingers to her lips. They tingled. She still felt the warm, firm pressure of Jonah's mouth, the raspy brush of his mustache. All coherent thought scattered, along with common sense. "But...you were irritated...you had to walk away. I made you angry."

"I got over it. I'm not a monster, Paige, nor an adolescent who lashes out without regard to the consequences." He lifted her hand, and his thumb began tracing the bones and veins in a mesmerizing caress that turned her legs to soggy strands of kelp. "What I am is a man who——" His eyes abruptly narrowed to black diamond slits, scanning her face. "I begin to see..." His voice trailed away.

"See what?" Oh, no. Was that really her voice, sounding as breathless as a starstruck schoolgirl? Paige closed her eyes, but they flew open when Jonah's hand closed around hers.

Heart somersaulting, she watched in bewilderment as he kissed the back of her hand, then placed it in the crook of his arm. He led her back over to the motorcycle without saying another word, then let her go.

Torn between embarrassment and curiosity, she couldn't let the question hang. "What do you see?" she persisted, lifting her chin.

Jonah pulled on his gloves and was now scanning the surrounding woods. "I see," he said without looking at her, "a lot more every day." Then he glanced over his shoulder and winked at her. "Now, there'll be a certain amount of risk, maneuvering the Harley through these woods. But I think the risk outweighs the greater danger of being trounced on by a gunman if we go back the way we came. Would you agree?''

The door to personal revelation had been gently but firmly closed. He really could be a *very* exasperating man. On the other hand, Paige herself had employed the same tactic many times over the years, and because she understood the instinct, she let the issue drop. Besides, Jonah was right. She scanned the woods herself, then nodded. ''I agree. I'd rather not spend the night here, but what if they hear the motor and follow the sound?''

''I'm pushing the bike. We'll be walking, not riding for a while. Think you can make it, Little Red Riding Hood?''

''I can make it.''

The warm approval in his eyes produced a funny choking sensation in her chest, even more disconcerting than the butterfly battalion in her stomach from his kisses. Panic and pain were waiting for her if she lost her heart to this man, but she was no longer sure she could control it. She wasn't even sure she wanted to. She'd been so lonely for so long.

Paige covered the rush of emotion by flashing a bright smile. ''Maybe Grandma's at the other end with cookies and milk, since hopefully the wolves are engaged elsewhere.''

''That's my—''

''Don't say it! I do *not* want to hear any more foreign words, be they animal, mineral or vegetable!''

In the deepening twilight they grinned at each other and Paige felt, at last, that their relationship rested on solid ground again. Then Jonah's hand lifted and his knuckles skimmed across her cheek. ''You're doing fine, Paige,'' he said in a tone as soft as the featherlight caress. ''Nobody could have behaved better.''

''I'm still scared.''

''That's okay. So am I.''

Over the next hour Paige struggled both with incipient fear and her growing awareness of Jonah as a man. Not J. Gregory, world-famous author. Not even Jonah, professional writer who had employed her to do a job. Just...*Jonah*. Every now and then she found her gaze wandering his way, admiring the supple strength of his deceptively lean body. Admiring even more his attitude.

The motorcycle was heavy, a dead weight, but Jonah didn't complain. He was covered with perspiration, even though the October afternoon had cooled into the fifties, and he gratefully accepted Paige's help when they climbed yet another slope. But he didn't complain. He didn't blame Paige and tell her it was all her fault; he didn't bemoan the uncertainty of their situation or hurl curses and accusations to God like a pious hypocrite. Instead he smiled at Paige, and when he did talk, it was of thankfulness to the Lord for the great weather, or to point out some delicate violet wood sorrel almost hidden beside the gnarled root of a fallen oak tree. Once a bright-eyed chipmunk scampered across their path, and Jonah all but crowed in delight.

But not once did he complain.

The sunset faded to mauve and whitewashed blue. Jonah eyed the sky, then the endless forest, his concern obvious. His breathing labored, he called a halt. Paige collapsed by a sun-warmed boulder and leaned forward to loosen her boot laces.

"It doesn't look too good, does it?" she asked quietly.

"Mmm. How about if you rest a bit, keep an eye on the Harley, while I do some more scouting around."

"Why don't you let me do the scouting instead? I haven't been pushing that ugly monster the last hour or so." She kept her gaze steady on his face and prepared to cope with flat rejection, maybe even another display of coolly controlled irritation. No, she knew better than that. More probably it would be a negative response couched in humor.

"All right. I could use a rest."

For the second time that afternoon Paige could only gawk, too flabbergasted to even close her mouth.

Jonah pulled out a handkerchief and swiped his face and brow, his eyes holding hers in a steady gaze. "Just don't get lost. I haven't the energy to track you down."

Her jaw finally snapped shut. Paige cleared her throat. "I

won't. Actually, my sisters and I tramped the woods all the time, growing up. I made a 'top-drawer' Pocahontas.''

"Great. Think I'll have myself a catnap then, Pocahontas.'' Without another word he flopped backward onto the ground, laced his hands behind his head and closed his eyes.

A smile tickled her mouth as Paige swiftly took stock of their surroundings, establishing bearings and landmarks. There seemed to be a lightness toward the southeast, possibly even a break in the woods, so she headed off in that direction. The smile spread, and suddenly she wanted to laugh. He hadn't put her down, hadn't patronized or ridiculed her, and she was as lighthearted as though he'd filled her arms with a basketful of puppies.

Lifting her head toward the sky, she hugged herself with secret delight. Then she started scouting the terrain.

Chapter Sixteen

A scant ten minutes later she found an abandoned hunting shack on a barely discernible track, leading north. After returning to share the discovery with Jonah and discuss options, they agreed to risk riding the motorcycle. Dusk had fallen, draping the woods in cobwebby shadows that made vision difficult. If they didn't find their way out within the next half hour, they'd have to spend the night in the hunting shack.

The track in front of the cabin led to a dirt road, which cut back southeast and brought them—unscathed—back to the highway twenty-seven minutes later. With a heartfelt "Thank You, Lord," Jonah revved the bike, and they made it to McLean without incident, where they stopped long enough to eat supper.

The prosaic normalcy of the restaurant seeped into Paige, gradually enabling her to relax against the padded booth. The unhurried clatter and clink of silverware on dishes replaced the memories of the high-pitched whine of bullets; all around them clusters of preoccupied diners enjoyed their meal, not a single one of them a killer in disguise. After the waitress finished pouring more water and left, Paige looked across at Jonah, intending to tease him about having the manager announce that the famous J. Gregory had graced his establishment for a meal.

"I'm sorry," he said before she opened her mouth. "I should have been more careful when we left the hotel this afternoon."

"Don't be silly." She studied the taciturn face from which all warmth had vanished. "You took more precautions than a Secret Service agent scouting out the presidential route."

"It was still irresponsible of me to—"

"You sound like me. Stop it." Paige pointed her fork at him. "Just this once, Mr. Sterling, accept the fact that you can't do it all, either. Practice what you've been preaching at me all these weeks. Remember? You don't have to be perfect."

"Thanks. I think."

"You know what I've finally accepted about this whole mess? We're going to have to get out more often…especially after today. I know it's risky, but by getting out in the open, where *we're* vulnerable, the killer is also having to risk showing his hand."

"Now who's donned a red cape, pretending to be invincible?" He scowled across the table. "I think we go back to the police."

"Fine. But we still don't have any evidence except a bullet hole in the Harley. Don't even have the bullet. We just keep searching for clues, and praying for a break, 'cause you know what else I've realized?"

"I'm not sure I care to hear."

Paige ignored both the dry rebuttal as well as the ironic lift of his eyebrow. "Even if we quit nosing around, resume our 'normal' business, I don't think stopping now would alter our situation. Whoever it is doesn't know that we don't know, so they'll keep after us." She took a bite and chewed vigorously. "I have an idea."

Jonah groaned.

"Why don't we try talking to the person who donated Major Pettigrew's uniform? I doubt if the lady—it was his daughter, wasn't it?—is trying to kill us, and maybe she'll have some more memorabilia we can sift through. Snippets of conversation she heard as a child. Something…"

"Maybe she *is* behind it all. Who knows?" Jonah pinched the bridge of his nose between his thumb and index finger.

"Everyone else we've talked to seems to have skeletons rattling, or shaky motives to keep our suspicions lurching around in the dark. Why not her? Maybe she's a secret member of a society that detests college professors."

Paige stood her ground. "Have you got a better idea? Other than setting ourselves up as targets like we did this afternoon?" The moment the words left her mouth she regretted them, especially when Jonah flushed, a veil seeming to blur the brightness of his gaze. "Jonah, I'm sorry."

In a gesture of remorse she reached her hand across the table—and knocked Jonah's drink into his lap. "Oh, no!" All her nascent self-confidence evaporated as mortification caused her to freeze. Guilt consumed her in a relentless spate of remembered insults. Clumsy. Careless. Worthless.

It was as if the clock had spun into the past. Without conscious thought Paige bowed her head, hiding her clenched fists under the table while she waited for the inevitable verbal lashing. She deserved it. She *was* clumsy. She was also cruel—she never should have said those words to Jonah.

"Hey. Paige. Paige!"

A hand appeared in front of her face, waggling back and forth. She focused on the strength of the fingers, visible through the chipped nails and reddened calluses. "Sorry," she whispered.

"Paige, it was just a drink. The glass was almost empty. It's all right, love. Look at me, please. I'm not upset with you."

She managed to lift her gaze as far as the second button of his wool shirt.

"I know you didn't mean what you said," Jonah promised. "We're both exhausted, afraid and probably punch drunk."

He began mopping up the spreading puddle with napkins, and Paige tried to force her atrophied muscles to move her hands so she could help. This was Jonah...she knew better now. The past was irrelevant—David was dead. God had forgiven her.

Jonah leaned over, close enough for his breath to stir tendrils of her hair. His finger slid under her chin, gently forcing it up, and he sucked in his breath. "Don't look like that!" He hurled the sodden napkin to the table.

Paige flinched.

"*He* did this to you, didn't he?"

Startled at last out of her trancelike pose by the ominous tone, Paige met Jonah's gaze, her eyes widening. His shoulders were rigid, and a muscle in his jaw twitched as if he were grinding his teeth. His eyes... Paige's breath caught at the flare of controlled anger leaping from those indigo eyes.

"You're sitting there like a pup, waiting for the master's boot to kick it into submission. Just like this afternoon in the woods. You convinced yourself that you were a worthless coward, deserving only of my scorn. My...debasement of you." He sat back and folded his arms. "Tell me, is that what your husband made you do? Whenever you displeased him, he took it upon himself—the so-called head of the household—to chastise you? And he forced you to sit there and take it, twisting the concept of wifely Christian submission to suit his egotistical needs? Is that it, Paige?"

Paige shook her head, denying the brutal words. Jonah waited, utterly still, his expression commanding the truth. "No!" The word tore past her paralyzed vocal cords. "David wasn't like that. It wasn't—" She stopped, suddenly trembling with the cataclysmic revelation. It had been exactly like that.

"Paige..."

That was all. Her name, spoken in a voice rich with compassion, softening the earlier violence. A violence, she now realized, that had never been directed at *her*. Jonah was outraged on her behalf, because of what she had endured—not because of what she had done. Something warm tugged her spirit, drifted goose down lightly into her heart, infusing her with the courage to face what she had denied for over six years. "I should have handled things better than I did," she admitted painfully. "I...was young, but I still should have realized that our marriage wasn't what God intended the relationship to be."

Jonah's hands reached back across to cover hers, stilling their betraying restless movements. "Was David a Christian when you married him?"

A bitter smile twisted her lips. "Oh, yes. He liked to proclaim his faith at every opportunity."

"A Christian man," Jonah said softly, "is instructed to love his wife as Christ loved the church. If he didn't love you like that, Paige, the fault was in your husband—not you."

The waitress returned to leave the bill and clear the table. Jonah rose, then helped Paige to her feet. But when she started toward the exit the hand holding her arm tightened, holding her still. "About your idea. First thing in the morning why don't we look up Justeen Gilroy's address, then pay her a visit?"

Paige looked blankly at him. "Who?"

One blunt finger tapped the end of her nose. "Your suggestion, remember? Justeen's the lady who donated Major Pettigrew's uniform. And yes, he was her father. I think she lives in North Carolina. A very pleasant lady, as I recall. Should make a nice change from our last few interviews." A corner of his mouth tilted, scrunching his mustache. "Well? What do you say?"

"You really think it's a possible lead? A good use of our time?"

"I think it's a good thing your brain functions more reliably than mine does after being used for target practice."

The humor had returned to his voice, and his twinkling eyes invited her to reciprocate. "Only because they shot your Harley instead of my laptop," she retorted.

They bantered—that was the only word she could use to describe the silly repartee—all the way to the motorcycle. And Paige felt, at last, a little of her ice-encrusted heart beginning to melt.

Chapter Seventeen

Justeen Gilroy's sprawling frame house perched on the edge of a small town an hour west of Raleigh. A cheerful, bustling woman, she insisted on plying Jonah and Paige with cider, fresh-baked bread and homemade preserves.

"I'm so glad you came, though goodness knows if I can be much help." She finally whipped off her apron and sat down at the table with them. "That old trunk with Daddy's stuff gathered dust in the attic for years. I reckon Mama plumb forgot about it."

Jonah polished off the last bit of bread. If nothing else, the food had been worth the trip. "It's amazing what people forget, then remember when they start reminiscing."

"That's why we thought visiting in person might be worth a try," Paige finished, leaning forward toward the older woman. "Something...interesting has come up."

Jonah slowly retrieved the list of names from his shirt pocket and handed it to Justeen. "We found this behind the ribbons mount of your father's dress uniform."

The faded brown eyes sharpened. "Hmph. You don't say." She scanned the list, then gave it back. "I'm sorry—none of them ring any bells. Behind the ribbons, you say? Wonder what on earth they were doing there?"

Just then a loud cheerful voice called through the back porch door, "Yoo-hoo! Anybody home? Justee-en?"

Justeen rolled her eyes. "My next-door neighbor. What she don't know ain't been written, if you know what I mean."

Nodding, Paige and Jonah rose. He lifted Justeen's hand. "If my mother cooked liked you do, I'd never have left England. Thanks for the Southern hospitality, Mrs. Gilroy."

"Aw, get along with you now." She swatted his arm, her cheeks flushed. "I'm only sorry I couldn't be more help. If I think of something, is there any way I can reach you? I plan to finish going through Mama's attic before winter. She was such a pack rat. There's no telling what other goodies might surface. I'd love to help...it must be so exciting, being a writer and all." Blatant hero worship shone from her eyes.

Jonah hesitated. Paige glanced at him, then smiled at Justeen. "We're in and out so much that I think it would be better if I just gave you a call in a week or two. Would that be all right?"

"Give me a call anytime. I'll be here."

They escaped out the front as the nosy neighbor banged the back porch door.

"Well, that was a bust—other than her homemade bread," Jonah observed as he headed the rental car back toward the main highway.

"At least Justeen was *normal,* compared to all our other interviews so far." Paige flopped back against the seat and crossed her arms. "But eating delicious homemade bread isn't going to help find out who killed Professor K."

"I know." Jonah glanced across the seat. For a while now he'd sensed that Paige was turning the search into a personal crusade, heedless of the danger. He knew if he tried to dissuade her that she would agree to his face—and doggedly persist behind his back.

And probably get herself killed. He forced himself to sit back, loosen up, flexing his hands on the steering wheel to relax. Right now Paige needed encouragement, affirmation—a nonemoting male who had relinquished all his protective instincts. The latter role challenged him far more than plotting a book. Sending a prayer upward for wisdom, he set about trying to accommodate Paige as best he could. For right now, anyway. "So far everyone we've seen has a compelling reason *not* to commit a crime, but a just as compelling motivation *to* commit a crime—if buying silence was why Professor K. was killed."

Head against the seat, Paige nodded wearily. "Both Armand Gladstone and Patrick Minton are already in vulnerable positions—especially with the attitude toward politicians nowadays. Seems like the media even tries to *create* scandals, so both of them would want to keep their noses as clean as possible."

"Covington's bucking for a judgeship. If you're going after the political angle, you'll have to include him in the equation."

"It's sad, isn't it, the way we seem to automatically suspect politicians of being morally corrupt? What about Gerald Minton, Patrick's father? He's *not* a politician, and he's committed one crime. Who's to say he wouldn't commit another—especially to save his son's career?"

"Gerald's crime was committed fifty years ago. That doesn't make him a criminal now, but at this point I suppose he's the most viable choice." Jonah's hands tightened on the wheel. Another swift sideways glance had revealed a woman simmering with frustration and exhaustion. Sure enough, she hurled the next words at him as though she were slinging darts.

"Do you honestly think a man living in a dinky little house out in the middle of nowhere would have the money to hire a hit man?"

"Mmm..." Jonah replied, his usual response when he was thinking. "Were the funds he...um...'appropriated,' ever recovered?"

"I don't know."

Jonah reached across and caught her wrist, feeling the tension beneath his fingers. He stroked the back of her hand, savoring the softness of her skin. "We'll work it out, Paige. Eventually, things will work out. Quit kicking against the pricks so, love." His hand slid down and toyed with her fingers. "Tell you what. Let's give it a rest and stop for a spot of supper, hmm? Justeen's homemade bread has reawakened my tastebuds to the joys of good Southern cooking. Shall we have a go at it, then? According to the billboard we just passed, there's a family-style eatery at the next exit."

"We have a plane to catch, and I'm not really hungry."

He released her fingers so he could apply pressure to her knee. It was jigging up and down forcefully enough to wear a hole all the way through to the chassis. "I beg to differ. Whenever your voice goes all frost coated, it usually means your tummy's inches away from revolt. We have time, and you'll feel better. I'll even stop at a petrol station and buy a supply of animal crackers for the flight home...."

Paige yanked her hand free and shoved his away from her knee. "Don't patronize me!" Then, eyes stricken, she retreated against the car door. "Sorry." The word was stiff, barely audible.

Jonah ran his hand around the back of his neck, massaging the kinks, before turning the car into the restaurant parking lot. After stuffing his glasses inside his shirt pocket, he switched off the engine and turned to Paige. "So...you expecting me to retaliate now? Have a row? That's how your husband would have responded, isn't it? Only it would have been more of a one-sided row—David yelling while you...endured it."

Paige's shoulders lifted in a tight little shrug.

Hmm. The nonverbals were deafening, Jonah thought. Let's try diversionary tactics here. "How did you handle displays of temper when you were growing up, whether your own or someone else's?" To keep from obviously watching her he pulled out his glasses and started twirling them in his hand.

She shrugged again. "Before I was married, you mean?" She seemed to turn the question over in her mind, then a corner of her mouth twitched. "I usually laughed. Daddy used to say that when I laughed I sounded like hens cackling, and how could anyone stay mad listening to a bunch of chattering chickens?"

Jonah stopped twirling his glasses and looked directly into the wary gray eyes. "Then remember what your father used to say—not David." He paused, adding roughly, "I'd give anything to hear you laugh like that."

A seething silence filled the air. Abruptly Jonah thrust the car door open. "Let's go eat. Like you said, we do have a plane to catch."

Paige spent the next few days with her nose buried in the galleys of Professor K.'s book. Technically she was proofing the pages for publication, but she refused to stifle the compulsion to search for clues, in spite of hers and Jonah's agreement. She had agreed that she needed the perspective of distance and time. But with possible solutions lurking on every page, she found herself incapable of shelving the sleuthing, even for a few days.

Jonah, she knew, was working on the second draft of his book, which she also knew was one of the underlying motivations behind his request to lay aside the issue of Professor K.'s death. "Well, he may be a bestselling author with a book in every store...but *I* won't put *you* on the shelf, Professor," she promised him. The passionate vow rang out in the quiet hotel room, startling her into dropping the red pen she'd been using.

For days now—no, weeks—she and Jonah had worked so closely together she had almost quit talking aloud to herself. Now she could feel heat stealing into her cheeks, because she couldn't help but wonder what Jonah's response to those particular words would have been.

You're in a high cornfield of trouble, Paige Hawthorne.

At any other time, seeing a book taking shape, knowing she had contributed to its creation, would have filled her with deep satisfaction. Professional pride and, light-years ago, humble gratitude to the Lord. Instead, she was mooning over a man whose behavior toward her zigzagged from indulgence to indifference...protectiveness to preoccupation. And every now and then, when he didn't think she noticed, she glimpsed a disturbing light burning in the dark blue eyes.

Paige shoved aside the galley and rolled off the bed where she'd been working. Her hands swept back strands of irritating hair, and without conscious volition her restless fingers ended up tracing the contours of her ears—just like Jonah had that time. She yanked her hands down, balling them into fists. He was attracted to her...so what? Obviously he wasn't going to profess undying love for her. A godly man like Jonah Sterling wouldn't entangle himself in any kind of permanent relationship with a woman who had lost all of her confidence, much of her faith, and whose level of trust could be measured in micrometers.

Unfortunately, she was well on her way to losing what was left of her common sense, as well—because she was very much afraid that she was falling in love with Jonah.

With an irritated sigh she headed for the bathroom, hoping a long shower would relax her mind as well as her muscles. If nothing else, she could talk in the shower without feeling silly, and maybe at least talk herself out of falling in love, and *into* solving the mystery of the Professor's murder.

Thirty minutes later she returned to the galleys, moving from the bed to the table by the window. Fifteen minutes later she let out a triumphant whoop and leaped for the phone, hoping that Jonah was in his room.

"I think I've found them!" she all but screeched when thankfully he answered. "It was *Metter,* Georgia. *M-E-T-T-E-R.* Not Medder. That's why we never found anything on that one name I remembered finding the night of the fire. But that *is* the name of the man the Professor went to see when he flew down to Georgia with us. I think this might be it, Jonah."

"Slow down, love," Jonah responded with such infuriating absentmindedness Paige blew a raspberry into the phone.

"Jonah, remove yourself from the 1940s and your make-believe plot and *listen.* I'm trying to tell you I've found another clue, probably the most important one. We'll have something to take to the police, and they'll go after the killer finally."

"Mmm—sorry." He heaved a sigh, and she could almost see him stretching his arms over his head, his expression still distracted. "What did you find?"

Infuriating man. "Never mind," Paige said sweetly. "I can tell you're all involved in your book. I'll get hold of this address, then fly down to Georgia. When I return you can—"

"I'll be there in a sec." There was a pause, then he added on a growl, "You little tease. You'll pay for that."

Chapter Eighteen

Thirty seconds later Jonah tapped on Paige's door, and she hurriedly opened it and stepped back, hands trembling in her excitement. Jonah strolled inside with the nonchalance of a tiger pretending to ignore a grazing gazelle. He was twirling his glasses, his coppery hair impossibly shaggy, as though he'd been worrying it with his fingers.

Paige wanted to snatch the glasses and fling them across the room, if only to shake him free of his writer's dreamworld. Instead she slammed the door. "Sorry to disturb the creative flow," she said, though not meaning it. "I know it's hard to surface now that you're at the revision stage."

"So you should be." He tossed his glasses on top of the television and crammed his hands in the backs of his jeans. "It was finally starting to come together, and now my concentration is shot to Sussex and back."

Guilt assaulted her, pummeling the excitement and exultation. She'd been so obsessed with herself she hadn't even considered Jonah's needs. Beyond that, she'd broken her promise not to pursue the professor's death. Despite what she had discovered, Jonah had every right to be upset. "I didn't mean—I am sorry."

He studied her a minute in silence, then abruptly emitted an explosive sigh and flopped into one of the chairs by the table where she'd been working. "It's okay. I knew when I inveigled that promise from you that it was a lost cause. And I suppose what you're trying to do is just as important as my book—probably more so."

Stung, already defensive, she stood straighter and lifted her chin. She had been insensitive, but she wasn't wrong. "Only if you're interested in solving a real mystery."

"You don't have to clothe yourself in your chilly professional armor, Paige. Tell me what you've learned. I'm listening."

Slowly she crossed the room and sat down across from him. "In the process of proofing the galleys, I found the names of some of the POWs Professor K. interviewed without me. One of them includes a James Denmark—from Metter, Georgia. Like I told you, I think that's the name I couldn't read in the professor's notes I found, then lost in the fire. The memory didn't click until I read it again in the galleys."

She began tidying the pages piled on the table, gathering the colored pens and pencils she used to mark changes and make notations. "I thought if we interviewed him, maybe we'd find out what was bothering the professor—and why he was murdered." She took a deep breath. "But I should never have interrupted your work—especially when you've been so patient, putting everything on hold while you traipse all over the country with me. I'm sorry, Jonah. Truly." This time, she meant it.

His hand reached casually and covered hers. The clasp was gentle, but Paige couldn't move. She slanted him a sideways look, then dropped her gaze in confusion at his expression. David would have gone to great lengths to make sure her feelings of guilt turned into a crushing millstone about her neck, convincing her that everything from her insensitivity all the way to Professor K.'s death was her fault. Her personal responsibility.

"I'm the one who should be sorry," was what Jonah said instead. He reached across and squeezed her hand. "What you're doing is infinitely more important. Forgive me, *koneko*—no, wait.'' He gave her a gentle smile. "I've used that one. How about...*min vacker radjur?* Yes, I like that one. *Min vacker radjur.*'' The strange syllables rolled from his tongue. "Will you forgive me?''

Paige swallowed hard, tried without success to free her hand. "Not if you don't stop calling me those names—or at least have the decency to start translating them.'' She darted another quick look across the table and watched an irresistible grin inch across his face.

"You wouldn't like it.''

"Probably not.'' Her voice was resigned. "Tell me, anyway. I'd rather not like it in *English.*''

"Mmph. I'll tell you, if you'll tell me something in return.'' Idly he began stroking her fingers, almost as though he didn't realize what he was doing.

A tingling warmth flowed through Paige in a river of sensation, drowning out the automatic wariness. "What...do you want me to tell you?''

Jonah released her hand, sliding his fingers along her throbbing pulse so that release was more of a caress. Leaning over, he whispered softly, "It's Swedish—and it means 'my pretty deer.' Now—tell me what your worm of a husband did to you that makes you shrivel up whenever you feel like you've done something wrong.''

His translation had brought a warm flush to her cheeks, but his demand froze the blood in her veins. "It's reaction,'' she admitted jerkily. "I'm trying to outgrow it. Bad habits die hard.'' She couldn't tear her gaze away from the strong-fingered masculine hand resting on the table. "And...I *was* insensitive. About your book, I mean.''

"It's okay, Paige. I've worked with you long enough now to know the difference between habitual insensitivity and a momentary abberation caused by conflicting priorities.''

The pompous statement succeeded in bringing her gaze to his, to find a tender smile hovering beneath the mustache, and those disconcerting golden flames turning the navy irises almost to royal blue. "You confuse me,'' she confessed, shaking her head, trying to smile back. "Every time I think I understand you, you manage to yank the rug from beneath my feet."

"You're doing fine. Talk to me about your husband—" his gaze flicked briefly to the galleys "—*then* we'll discuss your discovery. But before we go on any more sleuthing trips, you're going to tell me about your marriage."

"I—all right." It was time, she realized. In spite of the fact that Jonah was gently coercing her, she found she wanted to share the debacle of her life as a Christian wife. Jonah *lived* his faith, far more than David ever had, and she saw the difference more clearly every day. Perhaps he could help her understand where she had gone wrong.

Her grip on the chair tightened. "I met David when I was twenty-one. We were members of the same church. He was considered quite a catch—successful lawyer, church deacon, Sunday school teacher—the perfect Christian."

"Older than you, of course."

"Oh, yes—but at twenty-one I considered myself an adult. What were ten years, after all?"

She looked at Jonah, but she wasn't seeing him anymore. "I'd been working at the Museum of American History for a year, though only full-time after I graduated. I loved it, and I know I was good at my job. But...I loved David more. Or—" she swallowed hard "—I thought I did. He wanted me to quit working, because he said God had blessed him with enough wealth to support us both. And according to him Christian wives are supposed to stay at home, be...submissive. And I wanted to be a good Christian wife. I wanted the home and marriage my parents had built, wanted to be just like my mother...."

"Paige—"

She focused on him briefly. "You wanted to know. Let me finish while I can." She lifted her hands, flexing them as she stared at the ring finger of her left hand. "Within six months I learned that I could never be the perfect Christian wife David demanded. I can't sing—but I joined the choir because he said it set a good example. Taught a primary Sunday School class. Participated in a weekly Bible study. I joined every organization at church, volunteered for every project. If the church doors were open, I was there. David even finagled a spare key, so sometimes I'd be over there when nobody else was, working on some project, even helping the janitor clean."

She was breathing faster, the words tumbling out in a chilling monotone. "It wasn't enough. I was supposed to be a perfect homemaker, too. Immaculate house—but no maid. I didn't have a job, after all. There was no reason why I couldn't keep the house picture-perfect, ready to entertain guests he brought home without prior notice. It was huge—four thousand square feet—his family home. We were going to have lots of children. But we didn't...David couldn't. He blamed me for that, too—" Her voice cracked. "He said I couldn't do anything right. Eventually, I believed him."

"Why?"

Paige laughed, then ground her teeth together to stop the bitter sound. Jonah sounded almost angry. It was so unlike him. Or rather, it was so unlike the Jonah she thought she knew. Now if it had been David...

Restless, she stood and paced the room like a wild animal behind the steel bars of a zoo cage. "Why did I believe him? Because we were both Christians. Our marriage was supposed to be Christ centered. My husband was the head of the family. I never had a problem with that concept—my parents have a wonderful marriage. Did I mention that? My father still makes my mother breakfast on Sundays, before church. She still packs a lunch for him to take out to the field."

"I'd like to meet your parents one day." Jonah stood, approached her.

Paige waved her hand, too embroiled in her catharsis to respond. "I wanted my marriage to be the same. Their love for each other, for God—it shines. And I thought if only I tried hard enough, I'd learn to please David. He'd be proud of me. He'd...he'd—"

"Did he beat you, Paige?"

She turned back to him, shocked. "No! Never. He never lifted a hand against me. He wasn't abusive like that."

"There's all kinds of abuse," Jonah muttered.

The seething energy was dissipating at last, leaving her feeling as though sandbags had been piled on her shoulders. "That's what Daddy tried to tell me after David died."

"How did he die?"

She wandered back over to the table and collapsed back in the chair. "One night I came home late from a church meeting. David met me at the door—he'd been watching for over an hour, growing angrier by the second. He'd lost a case...had a fender bender on the way home—and then I wasn't there."

She lifted tortured eyes to Jonah. "I wasn't there. I tried to explain, ask why he didn't come by the church, so I could have left immediately...but by then he was...raging. So angry. Worse than usual. He kept yelling that it was all my fault. I tried to make up for coming home late—promised to make his supper, take care of the car the next day, the insurance..."

Jonah leaned over, took her hands between his in a warm clasp. "What happened then, love?"

"He—well, he threw a vase across the room, then shouted because it broke and spilled water all over." She tried to take a deep breath, failed. "He had a terrible temper, but he'd never thrown things. I...was scared by that time. His face was all red, except the tips of his ears, and his nose—they always turned white."

She closed her eyes, clinging to Jonah's hands. "He s-stopped so abruptly, and looked at me. I'll never forget that look. Then he collapsed on the carpet. They told me later he died almost instantly. It was a stroke, caused by an aneurysm of the main vessel going to his brain—I forget the term. His father died the same way, I think...."

"And you've been blaming yourself ever since." Jonah shook her hands. "Look at me, Paige." He rose, pulling her along with him and moving out from behind the table.

"If I'd been a better Christian, I—mph."

He kissed her, a hard, brief kiss that effectively stemmed the self-recriminating flow of words. "If you'd been a better Christian, as you say, you would have understood that God's concept of marriage does *not* mean that the wife is a doormat, an unpaid servant begging for the crumbs of her husband's approval. Nor does it mean the husband is lord and master, a despot who takes and never gives.''

Stunned, Paige lifted the back of her hand to her mouth, rubbing the still-tingling lips. He had kissed her…*kissed* her. "How would you know? How many times have *you* been married?"

"None." He tugged her fist away and dropped another kiss on the knuckles. "But I'm widely read—and widely traveled. I also have a very close Friend. I've read everything He ever said—including His words on the subject of marriage." He hesitated, then added with a roughness that prickled Paige's skin, "And I know that the woman I marry won't ever cower from me, or wear herself to the bone trying to live up to some set of rules I demand."

He looked at Paige. "The woman I marry will know she is loved—every day, every way."

"That's easy enough to claim now. But it's different after you're married." She didn't even try to disguise the bitterness. "Trust me on that one."

"Hmm. I think that's a lot of your problem, isn't it? You don't trust anyone anymore, including God. These past years, instead of a God of love you've come to perceive Him as the God of the big stick, waiting to punish every infraction, rap your knuckles when you don't live up to His expectations."

"I don't look at it in quite such extreme terms." Fatigue was dragging her down. Fatigue and bewilderment. Jonah was delivering some theological point, right on the heels of initiating an intimacy he'd never even hinted at before. *Why had he kissed her?* "I know God loves me. I know—"

"Do you *know* that His arms are wrapped around you, sheltering you in His embrace?" Jonah interrupted. "Sort of like this—" Before she grasped his actions he had wrapped his arms around her, holding her close. "Relax—you know I'm not going to hurt you, don't you?"

Her hands had lifted to the firmly muscled chest, intending to push him away. Instead she found herself clinging, as burning moisture gathered beneath her eyelids. "Yes," she choked out, "I know you won't hurt me. Physically, at least." Emotionally he was close to shattering the remaining walls guarding her mind, her heart, and when he left, she wasn't sure she would ever recover.

"Nor any other way," he rumbled above her, his lips brushing against the crown of her head. "God will never harm you, either, Paige. Regardless of what circumstances He chooses to allow in your life, He's always there, waiting to help—not hinder. Shielding. Not shaming. You might not feel the comfort and security of His loving embrace right now—but it's there."

"All I can feel right now are *your* arms," Paige mumbled into the folds of his Georgetown University sweatshirt.

Beneath her hands his chest shook with a silent laugh. "Guess you'll just have to take my word for it, hmm? It's only fair—if I have to trust your word on the aftershocks of married life—you have to trust mine on this. Deal?"

"Deal." Her voice was downright surly, and this time he laughed aloud, then released her.

"Now...let's talk about your discovery." He reached one long arm out and his hand scooped up the notes Paige had made earlier.

"About time," she grumbled, still feeling awkward and off balance. Part of her even wanted to feel guilty, because Jonah was telling her—albeit it ever so subtly—that her spiritual walk had wandered off the path and into a brier patch. He had also held her and kissed her—and turned her life inside out, upside down and topsy-turvy in between.

It was amazing that she even remembered what discovery he was talking about.

But...her heart didn't feel quite as shriveled any longer, as though the purging of her sordid past had given her spirit room to breathe again. After they solved Professor K.'s murder, she'd have to spend some time thinking over Jonah's concept of God's love, which did seem more in line with her upbringing.

On the other hand, David had been a deacon in the church, with a highly regarded reputation as a Bible scholar...

"Paige."

"Sorry." The word came out automatically. "I was thinking about what you said."

"Brooding, more like it." One large hand lifted to clasp her chin. "But it's time to get to work."

She glared up at him. "You were the one who insisted on sidetracking."

"So I was. And I was right, wasn't I?" He pinched her chin lightly, and let it go. "You feel better, even if you still display this tendency toward introspection."

"At least it's not smugness."

Up went a corner of his mustache. "Well...here's something else for you to fume about on the flight to Georgia to interview—" he glanced down at the paper he'd scooped up "—James Denmark." Leaning so close Paige could feel the soft brush of his mustache, he murmured into her ear, "One of the assertions we made earlier—about trust in relationships—is wrong. And Ms. Hawthorne...it wasn't mine."

"The matter of your former employee has been seen to."

"Excellent. How soon can I expect to hear of similar success with the woman and her writer friend?"

"These matters must be planned with meticulous care. Your former employee was a bungler, very clumsy. He made them wary, suspicious. I now must be extra careful."

"I told you they're at the Castille. The information should—"

"I am aware of your requirements, and your timetable. You are aware that your demands introduce a higher level of risk than a simple matter of elimination. We must both cultivate patience."

"I will not risk any loose ends. Not now."

"The matter will be seen to when the timing is...just so. Remember, the hawk who attacks too soon not only remains hungry, it suffers humiliation—because it is no longer master of the skies. You do not risk loose ends. I do not risk humiliation. Ever."

Chapter Nineteen

A sullen, washed-out sky followed Paige and Jonah all the way from Virginia to Georgia, and the small town of Metter. James Denmark—Jimmy, he insisted with a chipped-toothed boyish grin—lived with his second wife and three children in a neat brick ranch house with four white columns supporting the front porch. Aging pecan trees shaded the yard, their dying leaves rustling in the chilly breeze of the wet November day.

Jonah once again deferred to Paige's knack for putting people at ease; they talked to Jimmy in a cluttered family room, for which his sweet-voiced wife apologized effusively as she raced around picking up toys and folding laundry. If it hadn't been for the love shining out of her warm brown eyes she would have reminded Jonah of Paige. Even now the memory of Paige's haunted expression as she told him about her marriage sliced into him like a stiletto.

Mrs. Denmark finally scuttled out the door to return to work. Jimmy watched her through the window, his long bony face both affectionate and bitter. "She wears herself down somethin' fierce, 'cuz I can't work much." He shook his head, then maneuvered his wheelchair back to Paige and Jonah. "Not too many jobs 'round here for a man with only one leg."

"Mr. Denmark—Jimmy." Paige sat down across from him

and smiled. "Like I explained to your wife last night, you apparently were one of the Vietnam veterans Professor Kittridge interviewed this past August."

"Yeah...I remember him. Professor Kittridge, huh? Don't recollect the name, but I remember him—nice old geezer, but pretty strange. He mumbled most of the time I was telling him 'bout my wartime experiences."

Watery blue eyes shifted from Paige to Jonah, then back to Paige. "He asked me about some guy—can't place my tongue around his name right off, either—I'd never heard of him. I told him to try Slicks—that's my buddy. He lives in Eastman now. Don't know whether he ever did or not, but I can give Slicks a call if you like."

"If we showed you a list of names, do you think you'd recognize the one the professor asked about?" Jonah asked casually. He laced his hands around his knees, trying not to betray his intense interest. Beside him, he saw Paige's leg go into its jittering routine, though her expression remained pleasant, serene.

"I don't remember names and stuff too well anymore," Jimmy admitted with a shrug. "Even some of my favorite ball players. The docs told me it's probably from my experiences." He screnched his forehead, then shook his head.

"Perhaps seeing the names on paper..." Paige handed him a list of typed names. "Do any of those look at all familiar?"

Jimmy studied each name, his lips shaping them as he read, but in the end he shook his head. "Nope. Nothin'. Sorry." He handed the list back to Paige. "That old professor, now, he did say he'd get on over to Slicks's. I reckon you'll have to do the same. You say my name's gonna be in that book? What a hoot!"

Before they left, Jonah persuaded Jimmy to call Slicks to make sure he was going to be home. Eastman, he found from studying the map with Paige while Jimmy was on the phone, was about a two-hour drive southwest of Metter. He groaned, and Paige lifted her head, smiling ruefully.

"Slicks can't wait to talk to you." Jimmy wheeled back into the room, face alight with excitement. "He wants to know if y'all have enough evidence this time to convict the guy who set him and the boys in Company C up. And he even remembers the name.''

"I know he's a politician, but he was so *nice*."

Jonah grinned in the gathering darkness of the car. Those were the first words Paige had spoken in the last fifteen miles. "People say Hitler loved little children." He pretended to cower when Paige reached across and swatted his arm. "Let's not condemn the man without hearing what this Slicks fellow has to say."

"Professor K. was convinced. I bet that's why he was so subdued on the flight back to D.C. He knew he was going to be opening a can of worms. Maybe Slicks will also be able to explain the reference to Ben something or other. Whoever it is just might be the piece of the puzzle we've been needing that will help it all make sense."

Jonah glanced across at Paige. "Are you sure you won't consider flying home to Kansas? I have this creepy set of fingers tickling my spine that tells me things are about to heat up again."

"I'm having too much fun in the land of Oz," Paige retorted flippantly.

"Hmm. 'Fun'?"

"Oh, all right—I'm ready to cower under the bed. But I am *not* backing out, so don't waste your breath trying to convince me otherwise. I knew the professor from the time I was old enough to swing on the fingers of his hands—he was my godfather. If it hadn't been for Professor K., after David died I would have crawled back home and never left again." Her voice thickened.

"Paige, I didn't mean—"

She interrupted, her tone passionate. "I will not rest until the man who killed him is behind bars. If you can't deal with that, I understand. In fact, I've been thinking about it ever since we left the Denmarks'. One of the librarians who helps me a lot at Georgetown told me once she'd love to work for you. When we get back to D.C. I'll call her."

Over my dead body. "Easy there, love. I was only concerned about your safety." He waited until the balled hands in her lap relaxed. "I'm concerned about you—about both of us." For a moment or two he chewed on his mustache, then threw caution to the winds. "You're the best research assistant I've ever had, Paige—I've told you that before. But I...care about you as a person, as well. I don't want anything to happen to you."

"I don't want anything to happen to you, either." She moved her hand, a motion quickly subdued. "But your relationship with Professor K. was strictly professional. Besides—" she hesitated "—you are J. Gregory. I'd have to go into the Witness Protection Program, or move to a rock in the middle of the Pacific, if anything happened to you because I dragged you into my problems."

"If I weren't driving—" He bit off the phrase, clenched the steering wheel with enough pressure to crack the plastic. Did *nothing* get through to this woman?

"Before you go ballistic," Paige ventured in a small voice, "that last observation was only reminding you of the facts. You're a household name, regardless of whether you like it or not. I wasn't debasing myself by elevating your importance." A pause, followed by a dry, "That time, anyway."

"Oh." The vise squeezing his insides loosened, but he slowed the car to maneuver around a chugging tractor before speaking again. "In that case—" he turned his head, and flashed her a crooked grin "—we're *definitely* taking any evidence we unearth back to the police immediately. Turn the matter over to the people trained to handle it. Then we are stepping out of the way. I'd hate for you to be hounded by my publisher, much less my editor."

"And millions of fans."

"Right now I'm only concerned about the well-being of the fan sitting in this car."

"And who might that be?" Paige inquired pertly, though she was blushing.

"Me, of course," Jonah shot back without missing a beat. "Who else would it be?" He reached a hand across to tug a lock of her hair, then returned to their previous discussion, before Paige decided to wallop him with her purse. "I'm hoping this bloke named Slicks can produce some hard evidence. If what we suspect turns out to be true, we're in *serious* trouble."

"Because of who it is?"

"That—and because whatever goons he's hired to sniff us out are going to intensify their efforts."

"I know," Paige agreed, the becoming blush fading. "Frankly, I'm still amazed that we made it down here without being followed."

"Mmm. Tell me something. Can you trust me—or at least trust my street smarts—sufficiently to relax on the issue of being tailed, at least?"

He waited in strained silence for almost a mile, the chest-crushing vise tightening its hold again. Since the revelation of her abusive marriage two days earlier, Paige had avoided any personal conversations. And her obsession over Professor Kittridge's murder had intensified.

They reached the turn-off road leading to Eastman. Jonah slowed to make the turn before gently prompting her. "Paige?"

"Yes, I trust you." She'd spoken in a soft voice, face averted—but at least she was willing to admit it. Then her hand fluttered across, rested against his forearm for the space of a single blink. "And...I'm trying to trust even more than your street smarts."

He wanted to shout a victory yell loud enough to shatter the windows. "I'm glad."

In the hard metallic glare of the overcast afternoon her wan profile seemed to soften. "Me, too."

Jonah reached out his arm again, resting his hand on one fragile shoulder for a lot longer than Paige's fleeting brush, and counted himself blessed.

The aging Virgil "Slicks" Malone met them at the door to the filthiest apartment Paige had ever had the misfortune to visit. She plastered a smile on her face, and tried not to brush against the smudged, mildew-covered walls. Feeling like a pharisee, she also avoided shaking Slicks's hand. Jonah, she noted in rising admiration, thrust his hand out immediately, and wasn't in any hurry to let go.

Tall, skinny to the point of emaciation, Slicks acted oblivious to the mess. Talking nonstop, he waved them eagerly over toward a sagging card table laden with yellowing newspapers. Every sentence pouring from his mouth included an offensive obscenity, all of them an opinion of the man they'd come to see him about.

"Can I have a word with you in private?" Jonah interrupted after exchanging glances with Paige.

"Uh—sure."

She hovered over the card table as Slicks led Jonah down a narrow hall, but decided not to examine anything. Her ears still rang from the vitriolic spewing, and the silence was a relief. The two men returned a few moments later, Slick's expression chastened.

"All right now," Jonah said, rubbing his palms together as he divided his attention between Slicks and the table covered with newspapers, "why don't you tell us what you told Professor Kittridge."

The older man began to talk, expletives deleted. Jonah caught Paige's astonished, hastily concealed amusement, and winked at her.

"It was back in '68, and I was a grunt in the First Cavalry— we were s'posed to clean out a nest of Viet Cong." He coughed. "Bah! The, uh, the *lieutenant,* he gave us the coordinates, then sent us poor dumb slobs ahead." Slicks fumbled in the papers, tugged one out and handed it to Jonah. "That's *his* story there."

Jonah held the paper out so Paige could read, as well, and she tried to focus on the task instead of Jonah's warmth and the faint woodsy scent of his aftershave, so refreshing in this fetid room. As she scanned the thirty-year-old article, her heart began to pound in a thick, hard rhythm—because the journalist was praising one Lieutenant Armand Gladstone for his fearless courage in trying to recover his men from an ambush. Tragically, he was unable to succeed, and over half his unit was killed or captured. Gladstone himself was wounded and received a Purple Heart. Details were on page sixteen of the paper.

Paige looked back at Slicks. "I gather your version is not the one here in the paper?"

Slicks opened his mouth, glanced at Jonah, then hastily closed it. "Uh, no, ma'am. Truth is, the one in the paper's baloney—the whole thing's baloney. He didn't rescue us...he sold us down the river."

"What?" Paige gasped, not even pulling away when she felt Jonah's arm close hard around her shoulders.

He squeezed once, then let her go and carefully lifted a wrinkled shirt and a pile of magazines from a straightback chair. His look dared her to refuse, so Paige gingerly sat down, only then realizing that her legs were trembling.

"Why didn't you bring the matter to the authorities when you finally made it home?" Jonah asked.

Slicks's answering laugh reflected all the bitterness, disillusionment and pain of the past thirty years. "It was '73 by the time I finally made it home, and ol' Gladstone was sittin' purty. Whole blamed state bragged on the war hero. Made me sick."

For a long moment he gazed down at the pile of papers, his eyes burning. "He'd been home close to five years by then— honorably discharged, of course. Probably bribed who knows all to git that Purple Heart. There he was, already elected to the state legislature—and you think some dumb old private who looked like a dead man and didn't have two dimes of his own's going to influence public opinion?"

"Why didn't you try?" Paige burst out passionately. "You weren't the only man—you could have contacted the others, written letters." Jonah's hand came back, resting on her shoulder, the fingers stroking her neck, calming. Paige clamped her lips together, but she heeded the nonverbal warning.

The corner of his mouth quirked. "Why didn't you?" he repeated mildly, turning to Slicks. "A lot of heinous actions occurred during that war. Even though at the time it *was* controversial, I'm sure someone would have listened to you."

Slicks coughed again. "I ain't no fool. People like Gladstone don't turn the other cheek. It was still my word agin' his—you look like a halfway smart fella, so I reckon you can figure where *I* would have ended up. And it ain't Congress."

Paige finally asked the question that had burned her tongue for the past fifteen minutes. "So why did you bring it up when Professor Kittridge came to talk to you? Didn't it occur to you that you were placing *him* in danger?"

Slicks hunched his shoulders, eyeing her suspiciously. Above her, Jonah cleared his throat, but he didn't say a word, only stroked his fingers in that soothing motion along the taut line of her neck and shoulder.

Paige grimaced, hearing in the silence the echo of condemnation in her question. She of all people knew the pain of mental bruises inflicted by words without thought. "I'm sorry, Slicks." Without conscious volition she reached across the table in a gesture of remorse. "I shouldn't have said what I did. It's just that the professor was...Professor Kittridge died this past August. He was an old family friend—my godfather, actually, as well as my boss." She tried a smile. "I guess I haven't handled things too well."

Slicks shrugged. "Sorry the old geezer's dead. As I recall, he didn't look so hot the day he came here." The dark, bitter gaze skimmed Paige, softening a little before returning to the yellowing article on top of the table. "Only reason I talked to him was because he promised he'd found another ex-POW whose story more or less matched mine. And he said it was time for the whole truth to be told, that he was writing a book and promised to tell my story, if it could be proved by at least one other witness."

"'The testimony of two men,'" Jonah quoted beneath his breath, but Paige heard, and she couldn't help, just for a moment, leaning her head against his side.

"I reckon," Slicks added resignedly, "that he ain't writing no more, huh?" He wiped a trembling hand across his mouth and eyes. "I need a drink. Y'all want a drink?"

Paige stood. "No, thank you." A strange, gentle tugging inside her heart urged her to reassure the broken man in front of her. To...touch him. She took two steps and laid her hand on the bony arm. "The book is already written," she promised, hoping he could read the truth in her eyes. "We're inputting the final changes—changes that will reflect the *truth*. You can still help, Slicks. Um...did Professor Kittridge by any chance mention the name of that other POW?"

Chapter Twenty

"So what do you suggest we do?" Paige asked the next day as she gathered up all their notes, cramming them back in her portfolio. She stifled the urge to grind her teeth at Jonah, sprawled with outstretched legs opposite her at a still-damp picnic table.

Overnight a downpour had drenched the earth, but the day had dawned bright and clear. Chewing on a piece of grass, Jonah was dreamily contemplating the deep blue of the November sky. "Shh...let's enjoy the peace and quiet, hmm? We have plenty of time to make our flight."

Thanks to the pounding rainstorm, they had spent the night—for Paige at least, a largely sleepless night—in a roadside motel. She had been up since dawn, poring over notes and pacing the floor, frantic with the need to get *on* with it. Jonah, looking rested, relaxed and fit, of course, had refused to drive any faster than a sedate sixty-five because he had been "savoring the Deep South scenery."

When he had pulled into this rest stop on a deserted stretch of I-16, Paige seriously had considered leaving him behind to savor the scenery while she smoked the car's tires the rest of the way to Atlanta. Now she tapped impatient fingers on the flap of her portfolio and tried one more time to persuade him to fly directly to Detroit.

"I still say we wait until *after* we visit Andrew McPhearson to go to the police. It will establish more credibility—two witnesses, remember?"

Jonah sat up. "Paige..." He tossed the piece of grass away and studied her silently, so long that Paige's throat tightened up. "I think I'd better make something a little clearer to you than I'd prefer," he finally murmured in a tone as implacable as it was gentle.

Paige shifted uneasily. "What do you mean?"

He ran a hand through his hair, around the back of his neck, then sighed deeply. "We weren't followed down here because we managed to give our watchdog the slip by sneaking out the hotel's service entrance. That isn't likely to happen again. If Armand Gladstone is behind the professor's murder—and it looks likely—then he knows where you were staying."

"We'll just have to be more careful—we agreed all along that checking out these names was a risk."

Jonah slanted her a hooded, oblique look. "The odds were against it. I frankly never expected to discover anything. The most I'd been hoping was for you to finally accept that the professor's death was not your fault."

If he'd slapped her face it wouldn't have hurt more. "Thank you for sharing your skepticism." Her lips felt numb, framing the stiff words with difficulty. "Now that I know how you feel, the first thing you can do when we return to Washington is to find yourself a new assistant."

Jonah's palm slapped down on the table with a resounding whack. Paige's head reared back, and she would have risen except her legs were frozen to the ground. "Paige," he rumbled in a soft but ominous tone. "*Please* do *not* threaten me with a new assistant again."

"Then don't patronize me!" Paige burst out, erupting in the first outpouring of temper she'd risked in over eight years. Too hurt, and too angry to question why she felt free to loose the emotion, she glared across the picnic table.

"I'm not trying to patronize you. I'm trying to protect you!"

He leaned across until their noses were almost touching. "Think about it, Paige. Think. All right, I apologize if I sounded patronizing, and you can rub my face in it later because I was wrong." His gaze burned into hers. "I don't want to be *dead* wrong. I know how to fight if I have to, and I know how to lose a tail. But I'm a professional writer, Paige—and we've stumbled onto a professional killer, and a man without a shred of conscience or morality left within him."

"Then it's even more imperative to *do* something." She swiped an angry hand across her moistening eyes. "We have to finish what Professor K. started before it's too late for us, too."

Jonah uncoiled, standing and crossing around to Paige's side of the table before she managed to untangle her frozen limbs. Even as she clambered to her feet he was there, and hauling her into his arms. "I don't want anything to happen to you!" he whispered hoarsely into her ear. "Paige...I don't want anything to happen to you." He muttered something else she didn't understand, and buried his face in her hair.

Paige began to tremble. He wasn't angry with her—he was afraid, and the revelation crashed through all her barriers. She wanted to pull back, yet she longed to surrender, cling to the sanctuary promised in his words as well as his arms. Her heart hammered a frantic tattoo against her ribs when Jonah's hands slid beneath her hair. Long fingers cupped her head, holding it so that she had no choice but to meet the stormy depths of his turbulent gaze. With a broken sigh, she closed her eyes, her hands circling his waist to cling to the bunched muscles of his back.

"Paige." He breathed her name in a husky voice. Then his mouth nuzzled behind her ear, slid down her neck and back up her jaw, trailing whispery kisses that burned her heart. In between he murmured incoherent words and phrases in a mixture of languages that carried her off on a raging river.

She had never felt like this before, not even in the first euphoric weeks of her courtship with David. She wanted to submerse herself in Jonah's warmth, in the shelter of his arms. And yet...unlike her relationship with David, she didn't feel swamped, overwhelmed, at the mercy of a man's towering passion she was helpless to control, much less match.

She was in the middle of a whirlwind. But the swirling tornado itself protected her, cherished her.

The impenetrable facade carefully buttressed over the past years crumbled, falling away in a sweeping tide. When Jonah's mouth finally covered hers, Paige melted against him, her arms holding him every bit as fiercely as he held her.

Eventually Jonah lifted his head, resting his forehead against hers. "This isn't—" Paige felt him struggle to draw a breath "—exactly the strategy I had in mind." He pressed a kiss to her temple, a breath of laughter stirring damp tendrils of her hair. "But I'm not complaining."

Paige hugged him, basking in his strength and humor. How could she ever have been afraid of Jonah? "Well, we still face a life-threatening situation," she teased, lifting her face. "That *is* the only condition under which you can kiss me, isn't it?"

"What would happen if I admitted I don't mind kissing you under any conditions?"

Paige knew her face burned scarlet, because the heat in her cheeks was scorching her skin. *What would happen if I admitted the same thing?* But she swallowed the words, still unable to wholly trust in spite of the closeness they had just shared. Jonah had only talked about attraction—not undying love. "I'd say," she finally suggested, "that we need to decide what to do with this information in order to allow for...for any other conditions."

"Hmm," Jonah grunted, his favorite response when he didn't want to commit himself to words.

"Well," Paige persisted, her voice turning brisk, "how about this—the minute we land at National Airport, we go straight to the police? Since Gladstone doesn't know where we are right now, we should be safe."

He propped one hip on the picnic table and crossed his ankles. "I'd considered that, and on the surface it seems the safest course. Trouble is, I understand how Professor K. felt. I have this distinct reluctance to start smearing the name of an eminently respected congressman without some pretty substantial evidence.''

Paige's teeth snapped together. They'd done nothing but argue in circles ever since Slicks told them the name of the other POW. "What do you call Slicks, and hopefully Andrew McPhearson?''

"Two unknown men who've kept silent about the matter thirty years," he returned. "It's also an election year, which makes their motives for spilling the beans doubly suspect." He met her frustration with the low-key iron will Paige didn't know how to circumvent. "We need something more, love. We need to be able to prove that the man or men who are trying to kill us, who torched the professor's house and searched our apartments, are doing so under Armand Gladstone's orders. That, I'm afraid, is the only credible evidence the police are going to listen to.''

"I don't see how we can," she mused after a while without looking at Jonah, "unless we can trap them into compromising themselves...*before* they can kill us off.''

"God help us both," Jonah intoned with deep sincerity, "because I know that." He straightened, took two long strides to stand in front of Paige. His mouth opened, shut. One hand lifted to tenderly comb through her hair, tease her ears.

For some reason her heart lurched. "Jonah?''

He closed his eyes, then opened them to look intently into hers. "I need for you to know," he said, "on a deep subconscious level you never have to question—that I could never treat a woman like your husband did you.''

Paige felt a fine trembling through her limbs all over again. Why was he bringing this up *now?*

"You still don't understand, do you?" Jonah said after a minute. He raised his eyes heavenward, almost reached for her, then abruptly stuffed his hands in the pockets of his pants. "Paige...there's more at stake here than the changing status of our relationship. It's important—vitally important—that you trust me. Trust me implicitly—like Isaac and Abraham.''

"I trust my parents like that. I...trusted God like that once,''

Paige replied slowly. "And I guess I still do, as far as trusting His promise. If I die tomorrow...I'll be with God. But—"

She dropped her gaze, staring at her fingernails. They needed a manicure. "What I'm fumbling around with is that I—well, I don't understand why God allowed the professor to die so unfairly. I don't understand why He allowed me to marry a man like David." She lifted her chin and somehow managed to meet the midnight gaze without flinching. "And—I don't know if I can ever again trust a man that blindly."

"If you can't trust the Lord, or me, with the faith of Abraham, you may get us both killed." The blunt word fell between them like stones. "I didn't urge you to tell me about your marriage just to exorcise David and free you from your past, though I don't deny that was part of it." Very gently he took her hand, held it between both of his. "Like I told you before—I have to know you. I have to know how you react under life-threatening circumstances."

He began tracing the veins on the back of her hand, like he had that long-ago day in the woods—when his quick action had saved their lives. "I have to know, if I tell you to jump, and it's pitch-black so you have no idea where you're jumping, whether or not you'll jump anyway—because you trust me—or whether you'll freeze. And end up with a knife or bullet in your back."

Paige couldn't move, couldn't speak around the unforgiving stone lodged in her throat. Vignettes flashed through her brain like snapshots in a child's viewfinder: Jonah, the day she met him, looking diffident and very British in his heather green sweater, reading glasses slipping off his nose while he petitioned for her help; Jonah, gently shutting a book she'd been scouring for some esoteric detail and hauling her off to dinner in the manner of a small boy sheepishly requesting a treat; Jonah, smiling that slow smile, eyes twinkling as he called her one of those ridiculous foreign endearments, just to rattle her....

Jonah roaring up to Professor's K.'s office on his motorcycle, himself looking incongruously like an absentminded professor while he explained to Paige that he loved the bike but hated the noise so he'd had the engine modified; Jonah—dispatching a criminal twice his size with the ease of a trained professional, in spite of his assertion that he was just a writer.

Jonah.

"I'm trying," she promised, her voice cracking. "I'm trying, Jonah." And she wanted to. *God? Why can't I trust him—and You—enough?*

A bleak look entered Jonah's eyes. "It's not enough," he replied in a flat monotone. The echo of her silent cry left welts on her heart. "It's not enough."

Paige blinked back hot tears, ducking her head. When she tugged her hand away from his, he let her go, and she turned blindly toward the table, fumbling for the portfolio.

"Paige?"

She stopped, keeping her back to him. "Yes?" The tears crowded her throat, strangling the word. She gripped the portfolio tighter, hating the weakness. Hating herself.

"I plan to win that trust." She felt something stir her hair, like the merest breath of a breeze. "Just like I plan—with God's help—to keep you safe."

"I don't deserve that," she whispered. "Jonah...it isn't fair."

Unbelievably she heard a dry chuckle. "But didn't you know, my darling, that life isn't? Don't worry 'bout it. My mother always claimed I had the head of a desert donkey and the soul of David facing Goliath. I think she was trying to tell me I'm a royal pain. Now let's go. We have a real-life murder mystery to solve, so we can return to our lives and I can return to the fantasy life mystery I created."

He helped her into the car. "That, by the way, is what isn't fair. Professor K.'s mystery is far more exciting than the one in my next book."

Chapter Twenty-One

After landing in D.C., they took a taxi to yet another hotel, this time one of the chains off I-95, in Virginia. Jonah had phoned the Castille the previous night, arranging for their belongings to be packed and sent over when they had checked in at a new hotel.

"Why don't you let me call and tell them the address?" he suggested after making sure both their rooms were secure and next door to each other. "Lie down, grab yourself a nap. I'll let you know when the luggage arrives."

Exhausted, Paige didn't argue; she took time only to kick off her shoes before flopping down across the bed. Some time later the ringing phone woke her. "Yes?" she answered sleepily, yawning as she sat up.

"Paige? Our luggage is here. I thought I'd trot down and pick it up myself, to avoid letting anyone know what rooms we're in. Risky enough that the concierge and whoever packed our stuff knows we're here. At least this way..." He paused.

"Mmm."

"I woke you, didn't I? Sorry, love." His voice was contrite now, and around another jaw-popping yawn Paige hastened to reassure him.

"I shouldn't have fallen asleep—you haven't. I'll come

down to the lobby with you so you don't have to carry everything by yourself or make a second trip.''

''I can manage fine. I only rang you so you wouldn't be frightened when I knock on your door.''

Awake now, Paige bristled. Solicitousness was fine—to a point. ''I think I'd like to stretch my legs, anyway. I appreciate the gesture, but I'll meet you in the lobby.'' She hung up, rose and slipped on her shoes, trying not to think about the needle of guilt pricking her skin.

When she opened the door, Jonah stood in front of her, waiting with folded arms. ''You're being difficult,'' he pronounced with lazy humor.

''I know.'' Paige moved into the hallway, checked the door to be sure it was locked and shoved the key in the pocket of her slacks. ''And I'm not going to apologize.'' She slanted him a belligerent look. ''Because I'm not being difficult on purpose.''

''Mmph.'' Suddenly he grinned. ''Now that I think about it, if you *were* doing it on purpose, I wouldn't stand a chance. Neither, for that matter, would anyone else. You're a formidable sight when you set your mind on a track, Ms. Hawthorne.''

''Well, right now that track does not allow for coddling. I feel guilty enough as it is, with all the time you're losing from your book.''

''Can't have that,'' he said, and tweaked her nose. ''Your guilt, I mean. The book will write itself, when the time's right. At least leave that worry up to me, all right?''

''Mmph,'' Paige retorted.

When they reached the lobby the young man who had brought their luggage from the Castille was waiting, shifting from one foot to the other while one eye monitored the clock behind the check-in desk. ''Thanks, man,'' he muttered when Jonah passed him a liberal tip. He nodded once to Paige, then headed out the door.

Paige began checking the luggage.

''Does it look like everything's there?'' Jonah queried a moment later.

"Two suitcases, two hang-up bags, my cosmetic case and your shaving bag. Is that—oh, no. No!" She glanced frantically around. "Where's my briefcase? The galleys are in there."

They searched, even went so far as to inquire at the front desk, but the softsided leather briefcase was nowhere to be found. "I knew I should have taken it with me," Paige groaned. "But we were just going to be gone that one night...." A sudden thought leaped across her mind. "Jonah, is there a possibility—"

"That this was deliberate?"

They stared at each other. "I'll find out," Jonah promised. "Let's get this stuff to our rooms, and I'll get over to the Castille. If I'm careful—use the service entrance again, possibly blend in with some other incoming guests or something, maybe I won't be spotted."

"We'll both go." She picked up her cosmetic bag and suitcase, hoping he wouldn't notice her trembling hands. Not since the first years of her marriage had she chosen to disagree openly with another person. Even with Professor K. she had usually accommodated instead of argued.

"I was going to take the motorcycle. I retrieved it earlier from the garage while you were sleeping. You know how much you detest maneuvering through traffic on the back of that thing...."

"I'll take a taxi then." She added on a placating note, "Jonah, *I'm* responsible for those galleys. Not you. You don't—" *You don't have the right to tell me what to do.* She swallowed. Why couldn't she just say the words? "You don't have—" Her throat dried up.

"What?" Jonah growled as he snatched up his suitcase and hang-up bag. He looked down at her, and a strange expression came over his face. Without taking his gaze from hers, he set the luggage down. "I don't have what, Paige?" he repeated, a disconcertingly tender note in the question. "Go ahead—tell me what you're dying to say. I won't bite your head off." He waited a beat, then snapped very softly, "Do it."

"You don't have the right to tell me what to do," she said to her shoes.

"Sorry. I didn't understand. Could you repeat that, please...slowly?"

A glorious sensation of release unlocked her throat. He was pushing her deliberately—goading her, giving her the freedom to stand up for what she thought was the right thing to do. He *understood*. Paige lifted her head. "You *don't* have the right to tell *me* what to do. The galleys are my responsibility, and I'll accept, as well, the responsibility for my decision."

"You'd be safer here." Not a muscle in his face moved.

"I know." She almost faltered then, because Jonah just stood there looking implacable. Perspiration beaded her temples, dampened her palms. She opened her mouth—and he smiled.

"Don't back down now." His index finger stroked her cheek. "I don't like it, Paige, but you really are right. It's your briefcase and your responsibility."

"You're right, too," she managed in an almost normal tone. "I plan to be very discreet, cautious...and quick."

"Then let's carry our stuff upstairs and trot on over to the Castille."

They didn't speak on the elevator, but just before Paige unlocked the door to her room she turned to Jonah. Now that words were practically dripping off her tongue, she found that not a single one was adequate. "Thanks." It came out lame, almost, but not quite, apologetic—but somehow the simple expression was enough.

The bushy mustache twitched upward. "Don't thank me yet. I have a bad feeling about this...."

Paige couldn't see Jonah following her taxi to the Castille. Maybe he would have been there if the cabbie hadn't run a yellow light a few blocks after they exited the Beltway, then ducked down a back road to avoid a road construction crew. Paige tried to ignore the anxiety twining about her in insidious tendrils, but it was as if she were trying to ignore a column of smoke writhing beside her in the back seat. Almost every block she twisted around to search out the back window, but she never caught sight of Jonah's motorcycle.

The desk clerk at the Castille remembered her and immediately called a bellboy to escort her to her old room and unlock the door. It was a little past four o'clock. Paige hesitated, wondering if she should wait for Jonah in the lobby as they'd planned. She opened her mouth to tell the bellboy, then stopped. She was being paranoid—living on the edge these past few weeks had her seeing assassins behind every tree, suspicious intent in every eye.

She would be careful, but she was through being afraid. Through. By the time Jonah arrived, she'd be waiting downstairs with the briefcase. He might even indulge her desire to gloat in her newfound freedom. *Lord...I do want to be free, in my heart. My spirit.* She realized, as she followed the bellboy up the staircase, that she also wanted to be free to love again, both Jonah and God—the way she had grown up...spiritual freedom as well as emotional.

The most powerful force in the universe.

Just look at her now—marching up the stairs because her budding self-confidence outweighed the fear and anxiety of the past weeks. The past years. In fact, forty minutes earlier she had actually done what *she* felt was the right thing to do instead of what Jonah wanted her to do. Didn't even matter that Jonah himself had had to all but pull the words out of her throat. She had done it.

Heady stuff, that. By the time this whole mess was resolved, she might actually be a functioning human being again. Might even be able to rebuild a relationship with the Lord she thought she had lost forever. *Thank You...*

"Here we are, miss."

The bellboy unlocked the door and opened it, standing back so Paige could enter. "I'll only be a minute." She handed him a two-dollar tip.

"Thanks, miss. Take your time. No one's scheduled for this room tonight. Have a nice evening." Whistling, he headed back down the hall.

Paige started to call after him to wait, then caught herself. She prudently flipped the door guard so the door couldn't close all the way, then began searching the room. Relief almost made her laugh aloud when she found the briefcase right where she'd left it, on the shelf above the clothes hangers. Whoever had packed her clothes had obviously—

"I knew that briefcase would bring at least one of you scurrying back. How fortunate for me it turned out to be you."

Paige cried out, jerking around—and froze. Just inside the bathroom stood a small, slim man dressed all in black. He moved toward her with sinuous grace. A wicked-looking knife extended his left hand by a good eight inches. The point danced in front of Paige's face like a cobra poised to strike.

She didn't think. Lunging, she tried to dodge past him in an attempt to reach the door. The man's foot shot out and sent her crashing to the floor, knocking the breath from her lungs. Then he was on her. Some sort of cloth sack was yanked completely over her head, and his hand gathered the edges and twisted. His other hand pressed the tip of the knife to her backbone.

"Do not be foolish," he hissed, dragging her to her feet and hauling her backward. Paige writhed, choking, her hands lifting to claw at her neck. She was unable to see or breathe, unable to hear beyond an angry buzzing in her ears. Desperately she lifted her foot and lashed out in the direction of his voice.

She felt the keen, cold edge of a blade pressed to the back of her hand.

"Do not move. The next time, it will be to your throat." She was pushed down onto a chair. The constriction at her throat eased. "Where's your friend? Or have you come alone— the modern emancipated American woman?"

"He'll be here any minute." Paige felt disembodied. Her hoarse, barely audible voice sounded as though it belonged to somebody else. In spite of his warning she shifted, instinctively trying to escape the stranglehold—and the shiny silver knife that would haunt her in nightmares. "You won't trap him as easily...."

The knife pressed harder. Paige gasped in pain, feeling something warm trickle down the side of her neck. "Do not move or speak unless I tell you to," he warned.

A primitive survival instinct she hadn't known she possessed refused to listen to the dictates of a murderous little thug. She focused all her energy on thinking of a way—even at the cost of life-threatening injuries—to keep him distracted, throw him off balance. "No matter what you do to me, Jonah won't give in."

"I think," the cold, emotionless voice continued from somewhere above and behind, "that he will cooperate without too much...persuasion."

"What is it you want?"

Jonah's quiet voice boomed like a thunderclap into the room. Paige heard a sudden hiss of surprise from the man behind her, and the knife jerked against her skin. She cringed away, then forced herself to stillness. Jonah was smart...street-smart...now all she had to do was to be prepared to help.

"Let her go, and I'll do whatever you want."

"I think you'll do what I want to regardless, Mr. Sterling." The pedantic voice was filled with terrifying confidence.

Fighting for breath now, Paige tried to keep the buzzing blackness at bay. She had to help Jonah. He'd told her she could do anything she set her mind to...he thought she was smart, capable. *Think. Stop focusing on the fear and think.*

"Perhaps I will—perhaps I won't," Jonah was responding with the same utter lack of emotion. "But if you hurt her more, I might forget that vengeance belongs to God."

The man emitted a dry chuckle, like the sound of rattling skeletal bones. "To your Christian deity perhaps—who doesn't exist. You make idle threats." His voice changed abruptly. "The woman and I will walk out of here quietly. Without notice."

"Hmm. I take it I'm not invited to the party."

The calm cadence of Jonah's voice remained. But beneath the suffocating folds of the sack covering Paige's head, black and scarlet silence thickened—because her terror-heightened senses detected a subtle shift in the assailant's attitude. Not uneasiness...more of a thoughtfulness, the calculated weighing of options. *God? What can I do?* She tried closing her eyes to concentrate—her mind's eye threw out nothing beyond the searing image of cold eyes in an expressionless face. *What if this man had a partner?*

"Partner..." She managed the single word before the flat

side of the knife caressed her throat, the blade smooth and cold against her skin. Paige's stomach clenched as she fought the gagging reflex.

"If she panics, you'll kill her unless you pull that knife away," Jonah said.

"A valid observation," her assailant mused. "You display admirable courage, even though you have lost. Now, Mr. Sterling—there is the matter of some missing information."

The briefcase! He would have searched it, of course, and found nothing. If she could persuade him to look again...have Jonah look. Delay. Distract. "I'll tell you...where it is. Let Jonah go." Unlike Jonah's, her voice came out hoarse, a thin dribble of sound.

"Quiet! You will tell me, but Mr. Sterling is not going anywhere."

"I'm sure you think so," Jonah murmured. "Hold on, Paige. He's sweating."

The fist at Paige's throat twisted viciously. "Your words grow annoying, Mr. Sterling."

"You won't get away," Jonah persisted, the low voice relentless. "Regardless of what you do to either of us, you won't succeed."

"I am not the clumsy, stupid predecessor of my employer. The woman and I will walk out of here." His voice tightened with impatience, the first sign of emotion Paige had heard. "You will check the corridor, make sure it is empty. The woman will die now—very painfully—if you're gone longer than five seconds."

Paige reopened her eyes, but the covering was too opaque, the blackness total. Her feeble attempt at diversion had failed. Then think of something else! she railed at herself fiercely.

The door opened. She could hear the quiet breathing of the man behind her, as well as the rasp of her own labored breaths. Her heartbeat pounded a relentless rhythm in her eardrums.

"Corridor's deserted."

"If you are lying, the woman dies." The hand at her neck tugged, forcing Paige up, stumbling and clumsy. "Just stand over there...that's far enough, Mr. Sterling!"

Paige felt movement at her elbow, heard a whisper of sound, as if he were searching for something in his pocket. But the knife against her neck did not waver, so Paige didn't move. "Stay back!"

He urged Paige forward, controlling her by the choke hold grip around her neck so that each breath had to force its way past her heaving lungs. She dragged her steps, fighting panic. If only she could see Jonah's eyes so she would know what he wanted her to do. *Divert. Distract.*

"Where are you taking me?" The words emerged garbled, meaningless sounds. She wet her lips, tried again. "Where are you taking me?"

"Be quiet."

"Why don't you ask what you wanted to know, and leave her here? I'll come with you as a hostage."

"No thank you, Mr. Sterling. My employer may be unaware of your many and varied...talents, outside your questionable writing skills. But I am not."

"I hope Gladstone paid you up front."

"I don't know who you're talking about." Paige was jerked backward, right against the man's chest.

Still blind, gasping, she had no way of knowing for sure where the knife was pointed. No way of knowing when Jonah would try to make a move.

"You do realize that guns with silencers aren't as accurate," Jonah stated calmly, then added, "Lighten up—she's going to faint on you."

A gun! No wonder Jonah hadn't tried anything yet. With just the knife, there might have been a chance. But a gun! Then his second sentence registered, and she realized at last that he was trying to give her instruction, as well as information. *Faint.* Without further thought she relaxed her knees, sagging, praying her weight would drag the killer down as well. All they needed was a fraction of a second.

"Stay back!"

It happened so fast—too fast. The man holding her jerked, and she heard an ugly spitting cough. Then silence.

"Jonah!" she screamed. "Jonah, no! *No!*" Beyond fear, beyond hysteria, she threw herself backward, arms flailing, fingers arched like talons. Something hard slammed into the side of her head, and she hurtled into oblivion.

Chapter Twenty-Two

The solid thunk of the room door closing brought Jonah back to full awareness, though his head hurt like blazes. For a couple of seconds he didn't move, didn't wince or try to take a much-needed breath to signal that he was, in fact, alive.

His right temple burned and throbbed where the bullet had grazed him, but he ignored the pain. *Paige.* He had to follow or he'd lose her. Slitting his eyes open, he searched as much of the dark hotel room as he could without moving his head. Apparently he'd fallen half inside the bathroom entryway. So...nobody in the bathroom. Made it easier, only having to check the bedroom area without alerting a partner who'd been left behind.

Gritting his teeth, he managed to squirm his way around so that he could peer into the room. Nobody jumped him. Room seemed empty. Silent as the proverbial tomb, except for the subdued roar of traffic in the street below. Near as he could figure, the slamming door hadn't been a ruse.

The hazy memory of Paige's anguished cry propelled him to his feet, though he swayed and almost fell before he braced his hand against the wall.... Had to follow them, immediately. Door had slammed. How long had passed? One minute? Ten?

Pain reverberated through his skull in an anvil chorus, but

compared to the terror for Paige's life the pain was insignificant. Sweating, moving slower than he needed, Jonah opened the door and checked the corridor. Then he ran down the hall to the back stairs.

One flight below he heard the echoing slam of a door—one that exited into a narrow alley between the hotel and a cluster of brownstones. He knew that because he and Paige had used it several times when they'd stayed here. *Lord God...help. I don't want to lose her now.*

He vaulted down the stairs, pain lashing his forehead with every pounding step. At the bottom he opened the door slowly, carefully, wiping sweat and blood away with a hand that shook. From the front of the alley an engine roared to life.

Adrenaline flooded his veins, and Jonah sprinted toward the sound, staying hunched and in the shadows. All he needed was three seconds and a glimpse of the killer's vehicle, and he'd be on the back of his bike. A grim smile twisted his mouth as he reached the head of the alley. God had already helped him. He was still alive—and the killer didn't know.

You should have taken the time to make sure I was dead, he thought. He wondered if Paige had helped in some manner—she'd picked up on his hint almost instantly. She was smart, a survivor in spite of her massive insecurity. She would keep that hired slimeball in knots....

She couldn't die....

A van with an electrician's logo on the side was waiting to pull into the stream of rush hour traffic. A primitive tingle of awareness shot through Jonah, and he ducked behind some pedestrians, following them while his gaze remained fixed on the front of the van. Paige and the killer were in that van—he knew it, deep inside. Headlights and the darkening shadows prevented him from making out the license plate, but in the glare of a streetlight he caught just enough of a glimpse of the driver to confirm his suspicions. *Thanks, Lord.*

The Harley waited at the curb, sandwiched illegally between two parked cars. Jonah swung onto its seat, crammed on his helmet—wincing at the fresh pain—and tore off in pursuit. There was no time to call the police. No time.

He followed the van carefully. The killer would know that Jonah rode a motorcycle. Who was he, anyway? The man who had come up to Jonah the night of the fire, the one who had tailed them out to Dulles when they flew to Ohio, had been bigger, clumsier looking. Either Gladstone felt safe in hiring an army of professional killers—in which case he and Paige would need ten thousand angels...or this thug was the first man's replacement. No matter...without police backup, rescuing Paige without getting them both killed promised to be the challenge of his life.

Twice he almost lost them in the welter of blinding lights and the confusion of rush hour traffic. The taste of fear burned all the way to his belly, receding only marginally when, both times, he was able to spot the van again.

With each passing mile, each tick of his watch, the image of a hooded, bleeding Paige intensified. He knew he had to fight the fear or he'd be less than worthless. But Jonah had never known this level of terror, not even in the most reckless of his non-Christian years. She was helplessly blindfolded, a knife to her throat and blood—

Can't think about that now, Lord. Help me.

The van headed south on I-95. Traffic was heavier now, often crawling along at less than twenty miles an hour. He was careful to maneuver behind large trucks and delivery vans during the slow times. They crossed a river, and for no reason the speed leaped to fifty-five...sixty.

The van pulled into the far right lane. Jonah stayed concealed behind a semi traveling at about the same speed as the van, and prayed. Twenty minutes later the van exited. Jonah hung back, watching until they made a right turn, heading west. He followed, maintaining a good two-block buffer, down a section of road flanked with fast-food restaurants, truck stops, filling stations and a new residential block of half-built houses.

Finally the road narrowed to two lanes, winding out of sight into the darkness beyond the glaring signs of encroaching civilization. Jonah turned off the headlight, using the Bot's dots in the center of the road, and the white lines highlighting the edge of the road to guide him. And he prayed.

About ten miles later the van turned again, drove several hundred yards down a rough county road and pulled into the empty parking lot of an abandoned gas station. Jonah killed the engine and dismounted. Whoever this guy was, he knew how to plan his moves. After turning the bike around, making sure it was well off the road but easily accessible, Jonah cat footed in a crouch toward the van.

A cold, white three-quarter moon shed streamers of chilly light on the earth below. He shivered, abruptly feeling the bite of the late-autumn evening. A breeze ruffled his hair as it sifted through the trees. The van's door opened, and Jonah melted behind a convenient tree trunk.

A shard of moonlight silhouetted the slim form of the man who had kidnapped Paige. Jonah felt the anger bite deep, fisting his hands and shaking his soul, because at that moment he knew with dismal certainty that he could deliberately take the life of another human being. Saving Paige would test the limit of his physical and mental capabilities. Sparing her kidnapper would test the limit of his faith.

The man opened the sliding panel doors and reached inside, hefting out Paige's limp body. For one shattered second that spanned eternity Jonah froze, the pain crippling. One hand blindly groped for the rough bark of the tree trunk, and he leaned against it, biting back a howl of rage and grief.

Paige moaned.

Riveted, Jonah lifted his head, his gaze following the movements of the dark amorphous shapes as they blended into one. The man was carrying her as though she were nothing but a sack of garbage. When they disappeared around the side of the building, Jonah ran, blood surging through his body in the same pounding rhythm as his soundless steps.

Two minutes later he was crouched beneath a window, peering through the grimy pane and waiting for an opportunity to strike. The kidnapper had carried Paige inside the store and dumped her on the concrete floor. Next he lit a kerosene lantern, placing it on a dusty countertop. In the flickering light, his impassive face seemed flattened, a mask hiding a soul stripped of its humanity.

Jonah watched. And waited.

Paige returned to consciousness slowly, reluctantly. Her head hurt, and a queasiness in her stomach warned her not to make any sudden moves. An annoying stinging sensation in her neck, coupled with a sticky wetness, eventually prompted her to feebly lift her hand to check things out. Her hand barely lifted, as though it were buried beneath a pile of sandbags. What on earth was wrong with her? She tried to move her head but the movement, though slight, was a mistake. She moaned in pain.

"Ah. You are finally awake."

The voice ripped through her muddled senses like a drop of acid on a hundred-year-old piece of cloth. The hotel room. A killer with a knife. A gun. *Jonah.* Tears flooded her eyes, soaking her face. "You killed him," she choked, barely capable of framing the words. "You killed Jonah."

"Regrettable but necessary. He was a worthy opponent." He came and stood over her, the empty pit eyes darker than the bottom of a well. Some sort of illumination in the background threw out macabre patterns of light and shadow that danced around his black-clad body.

He looked...evil.

Paige blinked through the scalding tears. She could see. At some point he'd removed the hood she'd worn. She could see, but she almost would have preferred the covering.

"My employer is adamant on the subject of—a list of names? Information hidden by the professor for whom you worked—information you now possess?"

He could whistle for the information. "I don't know what you're talking about," she hurled recklessly, her voice breaking. Professor K.'s death had been devastating, but Jonah... Jonah—

Suddenly he swooped, lifting her to a sitting position. Clawlike hands tightened on her arms, administering a slight shake. Pain shrieked through her, and she bit her lip to keep from sobbing aloud. "Tell me what I wish to know. You will tell me at once."

"No! I won't tell you anything now..." She tried to pull

free, grief suddenly boiling up into an irrational anger so violent she no longer felt the pain. She glared straight into the dark, opaque eyes. "You killed Jonah! I'll never tell you what you want! Go ahead—kill me—why not use the same gun you killed him with? A bullet for us both," she raged.

"A romantic concept, but regrettably not possible." His grip tightened. "That particular weapon is now at the bottom of a trash bin. And for you, I think, a knife will prove more persuasive." He paused. "I can make you tell me, before you die." His hand gathered up her hair and twisted. "You are not used to pain, Ms. Hawthorne."

Unfortunately he was right. Light-headed, Paige heard the words, but she heard them from a distance. She tried to gather herself, tried to summon the strength to defy until the end. Pain swamped her, battered. She couldn't do it...couldn't...

A whispering Voice floated somewhere inside her head, enticing, energizing? Not quite intelligible. Not quite audible. But she understood, anyway. Something about strength beyond her human frailty? Fragments of scripture reminded her of the grace to bear whatever portion was meted out to her. *Lord? Don't let me go. I hear...I hear You.* Like a pinpoint of clear light, the memory shone through the pain.

Delay. Distract.

Paige could think of only one way to accomplish that goal. She caught her lower lip between her teeth and willed her body to relax, even though tremors were causing her left leg to perform a Saint Vitus' dance. Tough. Don't think about the stupid leg. Somehow she raised her head, filling her eyes with what she hoped conveyed fear and pleading. She pretended to cower. "You're right. Please...don't hurt me anymore."

A thin, satisfied smile flickered on the expressionless moon face.

"Wh-what do you want to know?"

"That is better." He let her go, and she sagged back against the cold concrete wall.

"I feel sick."

"An irrelevant detail," was the indifferent reply. "One that will not prevent you from telling me what I want to know."

Suddenly he leaned over, his hot breath right in her face. The knife appeared like magic in front of her eyes, mesmerizing, the steel blade winking in the flickering light. "Where have you hidden the information Professor Kittridge discovered concerning my employer?"

"You mean Alonso...Goldwin?"

For a fraction of a second he hesitated, a flash of bewilderment cracking the stonewall facade. Then he backhanded her. "I will ask the questions. Each time I do not like the answers you will feel—"

The knife point pressed against the opposite side of her neck, drawing blood. Paige shrank back, no longer having to exaggerate her fear. "Answer...I'll answer."

"I want that list of names."

Probably wouldn't survive tossing out a second fake name. "My...purse," she gasped. Delay. Divert. *Thank You.* "There's a list of names in...my purse."

She felt his hesitation; even the air vibrated with suspicion. "I have checked the contents of your purse." The knife lifted, rested against her throat.

"There's a hidden compartment. I'll have to show you." If he let her go, she planned to make a run for it. If he saw through the ploy and brought it to her himself, perhaps she could hit him with it at least. Dropping her head, she waited. And listened.

"Do not move."

She shook her head violently.

"If I am disappointed..." The threat trailed away as he rose.

Through the screen of her lashes Paige watched, waiting until he was all the way across the room. Five more steps...four. He reached the counter, where her purse lay next to the kerosene lantern which illuminated the room. He picked up the purse.

Paige took a deep breath and lurched to her feet. *I will go down fighting, Jonah. You'd be proud...*

"You fool!" He started back across the room. In his eyes she saw her death.

There were no weapons within reach. The battle would be short.

The sound of breaking glass exploded in the dank room. Even as the man pivoted toward the sound, Paige scrambled past, dragging herself behind the counter. A rusted piece of pipe, covered with dust, lay on a shelf. A weapon! She grabbed it, then froze in utter stupefaction.

Jonah—real, very alive—hurtled through the window, landing amid the shattered glass in a graceful roll an Olympic gymnast would envy. He surged to his feet in a blur of speed, adopted the same menacing stance Paige had seen him utilize months ago, with the intruder in Professor K.'s house.

A savage grin Paige had never seen before distorted his face. His unexpected appearance was astounding. A gift from God she could never have anticipated. But she never wanted to see that look on his face again.

Chapter Twenty-Three

Jonah stalked the assassin, watching every flicker of the calculating eyes, even the slight rise and fall of his chest as he breathed. He held the same nasty-looking knife, but there was no sign of the gun. Was it hidden, or disposed of? Jonah wondered.

"Paige," he said without looking at her, keeping his voice calm, "get out the door and take the van—the keys are in the ignition."

"No!" Her voice broke. "I won't leave you—"

The man suddenly leaped—toward Paige. Jonah rushed him, catching the back of his knees in a low tackle that sent them both sprawling. Paige jumped back behind the counter as both men leaped to their feet.

They fought in silence. The assassin had dropped the knife when Jonah tackled him—it lay on the floor in front of the counter, momentarily out of reach. Jonah blocked a blow to his solar plexus, countering with a right jab to the attacker's cheekbone. The thug staggered back, then fell sideways as he grabbed for the knife, at the same time savagely kicking out. Jonah sidestepped, sweeping the knife out of reach with his foot.

The man sprang up, reaching for Jonah. Jonah grabbed his

arm and twisted, but the killer retaliated by dropping down, throwing them both off balance. They fell against the counter, and Jonah's head banged against unyielding wood. His vision blurred; he sensed more than saw the hand chopping down toward his neck and barely blocked the blow. Then he caught the assailant's foot and sent him flying halfway across the room.

The man rolled with highly trained grace. When he stood, the knife was in his gloved hand, poised to throw.

Every muscle in Jonah's body tensed. Even as he was dropping, rolling across the floor, an object flew through the air straight toward the assassin, who had to duck just as he threw the knife.

Jonah felt the breeze kiss his hair, and then the knife thudded into the counter six inches from his left ear. He jumped to his feet. The man darted through the door with the swift silence of a vampire bat and disappeared into the night. Seconds later the van engine revved, then roared down the road with squealing tires and throbbing motor.

Silence descended.

Jonah stood very still, breathing in labored gasps. His body throbbed in protest at the unaccustomed abuse. He turned his head, wincing at the pain, and watched Paige creep around the counter toward him. In the smoky lantern light her face was a pale oval blur, colorless as chalk dust except for trickles of blood oozing from several cuts on her neck. Bruised gray eyes stared at him without blinking.

She came and stood in front of him, hands clenched tightly together. More blood oozed between her fingers from a knife cut on the back of her hand. "I thought...you were dead."

Jonah took a shallow catch breath. "If you hadn't thrown that pipe...I would have been. So would you." He lifted a shaking finger to brush away the single tear making a wet track down her dust-covered face. "You saved both our lives."

She was still assimilating his presence. "I don't understand. At the hotel I heard a shot. I thought..." Her eyes closed, and her bottom lip began to tremble. "I thought he'd killed you."

"It only grazed my head. I'm fine, hardly even a headache."

Very slowly he enfolded her in his arms, eased her against his chest and began rocking her very gently. "I'm okay, Paige. I'm okay." And so—*Thank You, Lord*—was she.

They stood for a few minutes, holding each other, savoring the relief. Paige's hands couldn't seem to stay still, moving with poignant tentativeness up and down his back. Up and down, so light he could barely feel the trembling touch. After a while she lifted her head.

"I p-prayed. Jonah, I prayed." She blinked rapidly, then scrubbed her face over his filthy shirtfront. "And...God answered me."

Jonah hugged her. "Me, too. You're alive."

"I *heard* Him," she persisted, her voice wobbling. "Jonah, even though I'm weak and helpless, not worthy...God helped me. He talked to me."

He let her go and tugged out his handkerchief, carefully pressed it against the shallow cuts on the side of her neck, beneath the Henley top she'd worn that day. "You're weak as a steel beam, helpless as a wildflower breaking through six inches of concrete sidewalk." He had to swallow, and gave her a crooked smile. "As for worthiness...God loves you...that makes you worthy." *And so do I.*

Don't say it, man—not yet. Not now.

Making a pad of his handkerchief, he laid it against the cut, then held his palm against her cheek. "I'm glad you finally heard His voice—and just when you needed Him the most. Welcome back to the fold, little lost lamb."

She tried to smile back. "Jonah..." She turned her head and pressed a kiss into the palm of his hand. "You're...alive."

"Mmph. Paige...did he hurt you anywhere else, love?"

"Just my hand, and my neck. Back of my head hurts. I think he hit me, in the hotel. After he—" She stopped, biting her lip. The smile faded. "I...well, when I heard the shot I more or less went wild as a rabid weasel, as my aunt used to say."

Jonah hated to think about those nightmarish moments. "I don't know about you, but I think I've had my fill at playing real-life detective."

"We certainly have what constitutes sufficient evidence now, don't you think?'' Their eyes met, and he watched a tiny firefly light dart through the storm-dark gray depths. "He let slip that he tossed the gun in a trash bin—possibly back at the hotel. Can we—"

"Go to the police?" Jonah finished, their voices blending in perfect accord. "The thought did cross my mind." His thumbs brushed the corners of her quivering mouth. "You'll have to ride the bike."

This time her smile stayed. "That's the best offer I've had all night."

For two days they pored over thousands of mug shots, to no avail. One maid and a couple of bellboys at the Castille vaguely remembered seeing a man that fit the assailant's description, but they couldn't recognize him.

A squad of technicians dusted the hotel room at the Castille and the filling station. The only legible fingerprints were Paige's and Jonah's, or hotel employees'. No trace of the van had materialized. The bullet from the gun had been dug out of the doorjamb, but the trash bin had already been emptied. Until a suspect weapon was found, the bullet was of little use.

"A true professional. Never took off the gloves," one of the detectives murmured at one point. "The m.o. sounds like he might be a West Coast or European import."

Clearly, the police were still stymied.

Jonah tested the waters by voicing his suspicion that a member of Congress could be involved, even instigating the series of crimes as far back as the break-in at Professor Kittridge's house.

"Nowadays anything's possible," he was told by the cynical detective. "Especially in this town. But you're right. Without some documented, reputable, ironclad proof...all we have is a lot of finger-pointing and nasty supposition." He grimaced. "Not to mention threats of lawsuits. When you're dealing with politicians, particularly of congressional status, a criminal investigation could mean a lot of rolling heads for the innocent as well as the guilty. One of them, unfortunately, would be mine."

He looked so disgusted Jonah hid a smile under guise of smoothing his mustache as he turned to leave.

"Uh...Mr. Sterling?"

Jonah paused at the door, noticing the band of color streaking the hard-bitten detective's cheekbones.

"I, uh, bought your last 'J. Gregory' book for my daughter. I was wondering...could you autograph it?"

The following afternoon they were finally free to fly to Detroit and pay a visit to former POW Andrew McPhearson.

A foreman at one of the auto plants, McPhearson was a short dynamo of a man with a glorious head of red hair liberally streaked now with gray. He remembered Professor K., was shocked at his death, and his opinion of Armand Gladstone echoed Slicks's, though McPhearson chose his words more carefully.

"At first I thought I must've been mistaken. Even in that bloody, awful war, where right and wrong blurred with every battle, it didn't occur to any soldier that one of our own would deliberately set us up."

"What made you realize that's what he'd done?" Paige asked, taking notes while a miniature tape recorder documented every word.

McPhearson laid down the piece of wood he'd been whittling and gazed into the distance. "The Cong kept taunting us after we were captured, bragging on the guns and ammo we'd been sold out for. At first, I thought it was just another demoralizing tool." He smiled grimly. "They tried hard—" He stopped, shaking his head. "Anyway, about ten months after I'd been taken they moved me to another compound. There were some guys there who'd witnessed something really screwy at the infamous battle of Hill Number 418. They'd been undercover, watching for snipers, when all of a sudden right underneath them comes this army officer—along with a couple of Viet Cong. And they were talking as cozy as buddies in a beer joint. Some money changed hands."

Paige dropped her pen. "That's *treason!*"

"Yes'm. I thought the same thing." He rubbed his thumb

along the edge of his carving knife. "Swore if I got out alive, someday that army officer would pay."

"What happened?" Jonah asked into the little well of silence that had fallen. He saw that Paige was struggling to control her emotions, which had been roller coasting from one extreme to the next these past few days. Jonah understood. His own emotional state was almost as unstable, more so because he labored hourly against the need to tell her that he loved her. For the rest of his life he would carry in his heart images of the terrifying events in that hotel room.

McPhearson shrugged. "I was the only one I knew from my unit who made it. I didn't know about the guy in Georgia. The war ended for most soldiers when President Nixon and Kissinger negotiated us back home in '73. But there were some poor slobs like me—the village where I'd been a prisoner didn't care about any negotiations. They decided I was too useful as a slave. I didn't make it back to the States until '77. By then, all I wanted was to be left alone."

"Nobody could blame you for that." Jonah lifted the notebook out of Paige's lifeless hands, caressing her fingers so that she started, then gave him a grateful look. "I read your story in the galleys of the professor's book. It isn't very pretty. I'm sorry we had to resurrect it."

"It was a long time ago. With God's help, I've made a new life." He began whittling again, gnarled heads steady. "When Professor Kittridge started asking me all those questions, and told me that he thought the worm of a traitor was a congressman, I couldn't just let the matter drop." He looked at them and said very simply, "You need a witness, I'll do what I can. We don't need any more garbage fouling the system. There's already been enough in my lifetime alone."

Chapter Twenty-Four

Based upon police recommendation, the day after they returned from Detroit, Paige and Jonah moved to yet another anonymous motel. Troubled, exhausted but game, Paige elected to spend a day indoors, collating all the evidence. Jonah, she noticed, didn't even bother to hide his relief.

"Naturally, *you're* going to prowl all over town...on that motorcycle," she grumped when he stopped by her room to tell her he was leaving. "You could at least rent a car, like Detective Mabray suggested."

"I'll be careful. I promise. But if you're that worried about the bike, I suppose I could rent a car." He paused, one eyebrow arched. "Takes three times as long to park...."

"How," Paige returned sweetly, "would we be traveling if *I'd* decided to tag along?"

Jonah raised his hands in surrender. "You win. Hope I can beat rush hour traffic...did you have a chance to write down the names and addresses for me?" He planned to touch base with the various individuals who had been helping them trace names, and Paige had volunteered to make a list since he'd volunteered to do the legwork.

"Jonah." She spoke his name abruptly, the rush of panic for his safety catching her by the throat. "Please..." *come back to me unharmed.* She suppressed the words, but something must have shown in her face, because the smile disappeared from his eyes.

"I've promised to be careful, Paige." He stood looking down at her, and after a moment his hand lifted to brush her cheek. He murmured something beneath his breath in a liquid, musical language.

"Am I looking that upset?" she managed, trying to smile.

"I don't have time to tell you how beautiful you look," he said so tenderly she blinked.

"Wh-what did you say this time? Turtle? Shivering rabbit? Crybaby?" Lately she felt as though her eyes were nothing but leaky faucets.

"Nope." He balled his hand and gently cuffed her chin. "I'll tell you when I get back this afternoon."

And he was gone.

For the next several hours Paige managed to focus on her work, in spite of the pervasive anxiety over Jonah...and her growing feelings for this incredible man. Did she love him—*could* she love him? For years she had accepted that her marriage to David had been designed as some sort of punishment from God, because she had not been the kind of wife He, or David, wanted her to be.

Jonah had smashed that erroneous preconception, replacing it with a beautiful word picture that also reflected her parents' marriage: mutual love, based on Christ, where respect, affection and self-sacrifice had created a bond unbroken after half a century. None of which she had shared with David, but, over the past weeks, an unsettling description of her and Jonah's relationship.

They weren't married. They weren't even dating. Yet Jonah had consistently demonstrated his respect for her, at least on a professional level. He teased her—that was a sign of affection, wasn't it? And he had risked his own life to save her from unspeakable pain and certain death. The more she learned about Jonah the more...*trapped* she felt. Couldn't admit she loved him...too dangerous...couldn't deny that she felt far more than respect. Affection. Admiration.

The pencil in her hand snapped in two, leaving a dark smudge of lead smearing the paper. Paige stared, first at the broken pencil, then the paper. Instead of a concise enumeration of facts relating to the mystery, she had written Jonah's name, over and over. With a despairing moan she buried her head in her hands. What should she do? *Lord? I don't know what to do.*

Paige had herself back under control by the time Jonah returned a little after two, looking wind-burned, cold and disheveled from the raw November day. A discreet patch of gauze covering his right temple disappeared beneath tousled rust-colored hair as a strong gust blew into the hotel room with him. Delicious scents filled the stale air—the bittersweet tang of burning leaves and damp asphalt mingling with the woodsy aroma of Jonah's favorite aftershave, and the leather of his jacket.

Relief flooded through her. "About time," she scolded to cover the rush of joy. "I was considering calling for backup."

"Coming right along with police jargon, are we?" He combed back his hair with his fingers, grinning as he plopped down in a chair. "Whew. I'm bushed."

Paige wasn't fooled. Excitement crackled around him, all but shooting sparks. "Sure you are." She dropped down in the chair opposite, plonked her elbows on the tabletop and rested her chin in her laced fingers. "Okay, tell me what you found out. Something spectacular, from the look on your face."

"I can't hide a thing from you, can I?" He patted his pockets, eventually producing his glasses, which he crammed into place, and a folded piece of paper.

"Is that it? Don't tell me it's *another* list." She tried to grab the paper. "Let me see."

"Didn't anyone ever tell you that patience is a virtue?" He easily held the paper out of her reach.

"No more than a dozen times a day. It was one of David's favorites, along with the entire chapter in Proverbs that extols the perfect woman. Jonah...*what does it say?*" All of a sudden she realized what she'd said and—more astonishing—the sub-

lime indifference with which she said it. Her gaze flew from
the paper in Jonah's upraised hand to his face.

"Congratulations," he murmured softly. "I've been waiting
for this day a very long time."

"Me, too," Paige admitted. She shook her head, mentally
testing her feelings. None of the shame. No guilt, no fear. Not
even any long-buried residue of resentment.

Nothing but wry acceptance of the past—coupled with a fe-
ver of impatience. "Can we talk about it later? Right now, if
you don't share the news with me, my hair's going to burst
into flames or something."

"Certainly can't have that, not when you've got such lovely
moonbeam hair."

"Jonah..." She shook a fist under his nose.

Jonah leaned forward and dropped a kiss on her knuckles,
then unfolded the paper and began to read. "Justeen Gilroy's
father, Major Lamar Pettigrew, was in Army Intelligence during World War II. When he died, he'd been in his third year
of tracking down a number of Americans suspected of collab-
orating with the Nazis."

Paige glanced over at the dresser, where she'd neatly arranged copious amounts of information—all of it dealing with
the Vietnam War. Not World War II. "I don't see," she began,
but Jonah dropped the piece of paper in front of her.

"The nine names," he reminded her. "Behind the ribbons
mount? One of which was Gladstone?"

"I know that. But all the evidence we've unearthed concerns
Armand Gladstone and what he purportedly did in Vietnam.
He's much too young to have fought in World War II."

"Mmm. Armand was—but what about his father?" Jonah
leaned back again, closing his eyes. "Remember what Professor K. wrote on the piece of paper he hid?"

Paige slowly lifted her head. She'd read the words on that
piece of paper so many times they were engraved forever in
her brain. How could she have been so blind? "'Has to be the
same family,'" Her breath caught. "Jonah—it's his *father!*"

He reopened his eyes to share a smug look with Paige.
"Sounds like it. I talked with your friend Major Haylee, per-

suaded him to let me take a dekko at some dusty old files from World War II buried in the Pentagon basement.''

"How did you—never mind." Major Haylee had never let her beyond his office door. "When it comes to understated charm, the Lord truly filled your basket to overflowing."

"Mmph." The look he gave her then caused Paige to duck her head. "We'll have to discuss its effect someday soon. In the meantime—" he waved the paper in front of Paige's nose "—I also have here the last known address of one Everett Gladstone, attaché for the American ambassador in England during the last years of the war. Right smack in London he was—and right where our Major Pettigrew was snuffed. I thought a visit might prove informative."

"According to his son, Everett is very ill."

"I don't know—" Jonah drawled "—that we can take as the whole truth the word of the esteemed representative from Georgia."

"There is that," Paige drawled back in butchered British mimicry, and they both laughed. "Where does his father live?"

"State of residence is—where else?—Georgia." He reached down and lazily lifted Paige to her feet. "And I'd be willing to donate my next royalty check to his retirement home if the old gentleman didn't enjoy a visit from Professor K. last August."

"Is that where he lives? In a retirement home?"

Jonah removed his glasses, stuffed them back in his shirt pocket and tapped the end of Paige's nose. "Nope. That's why I felt safe making that statement." He grinned cheekily, then told her, "According to some info I unearthed after my visit to the Pentagon, the possibly not-so-honorable Everett Gladstone resides in the town of Marshall, Georgia."

"How far is that from Warner Robins?"

"About thirty miles."

The humor abruptly died. Paige began gathering up the papers and arranging them neatly back in her briefcase. Her heart had begun a drumroll of anticipation and fear. "We're getting close, aren't we?"

"I think so. Um...Paige. I've been thinking. If we share this with the police, the red tape is going to wrap us all tighter than an Egyptian mummy. So I thought perhaps, while you keep looking for—''

"Don't even think it. I'm coming with you." She looked up at him. "I'm coming with you." The previous night she'd awakened in a cold sweat, the nightmare vision of a snakelike man slithering around her body, which was blindfolded and tied to a stake. "But we leave the police our flight information and call them the minute we leave Everett Gladstone's house."

"All right, love." His voice was very gentle all of a sudden. "All right."

By the time they left D.C., snow was falling; freezing rain met them in Atlanta. The three-hour drive south was tense, with few words shared between them. Jonah, Paige had learned, liked to chew on plot and character development whenever he was confined inside a car for long periods. She left him to it, spending much of her time chewing over their decision to slip the leash from police protection.

Traffic was heavy on I-75, many times moving at a crawl due to the inclement weather. At the Warner Robins exit they stopped to eat and freshen up before confronting a hopefully off guard Everett Gladstone.

"I'd like to swing by the museum here on our way back to Washington," Jonah announced after the waitress left. "When I checked my answering service last night, they told me the curator had called. Someone's donated some more Luftwaffe stuff to the museum. I'd like to check it out."

"All right." Paige shoved her knife and spoon in aimless patterns.

"Paige?" His hand reached across and covered hers. Tiredly she lifted her gaze. *"Luz de la luna,"* the soft lilting words barely tickled her ear, "we'll be okay."

"I know that was Spanish," she sighed, then shrugged, "but I only took two years in high school, so you'll have to translate, if you're after a reaction." A corner of her mouth tipped upward. "Other than indifference."

Jonah's head tilted to one side, and he withdrew his hand to begin stroking his mustache. "A daunting pronouncement. Very well. It means *moonlight*. That's what you remind me of with your gray eyes and silver blond hair."

That did make her smile. "Yuck. That's *really* corny. Am I behaving that badly?"

"Mmph."

They finished eating and left, after securing directions for Marshall, a small community some twenty-eight miles to the southwest. The freezing rain had slowed to a cold drizzle. As he started the car, Jonah glanced over at Paige. "Corny or not, you *do* remind me of moonbeams."

Gray and brown, the gently rolling countryside painted a dreary, depressing picture that did nothing to lighten moods. Traffic at least was sparse—they passed few cars, and the only one behind them turned in to a chain grocery store on the outskirts of Marshall.

They had no trouble locating Everett Gladstone in this small community. Twenty years earlier he and his wife had purchased a huge old antebellum plantation and had it completely restored. According to the friendly convenience store clerk, the Gladstones were virtual hermits, though everybody in town knew who they were. The gum-chewing clerk doubted if Paige and Jonah would be welcomed. She said the place was easy enough to find, however.

Ten minutes later Jonah and Paige were parked in a weed-infested circular gravel drive. For a moment they sat in silence, staring at the two-story structure with its four towering white columns proclaiming the glory of a long-dead era.

"Ionic," Paige offered, watching Jonah's gaze move over the house.

"What?"

"The columns. There are three basic types—Doric, Ionic and Corinthian. These are Ionic." She opened her purse, pulled out mirror and comb to check her appearance. "Don't tell me the widely traveled J. Gregory, author of eight bestsellers, whose mother is a legend of archaeology and whose father is a highly respected professor of history...never learned the basics of Greek architecture."

"If I kissed you right here in the car, do you think the person watching us through the curtains would be scandalized and refuse to admit us?"

Paige dropped the comb and closed the small cosmetic mirror with a distinct snap, after catching sight of the blush heating her winter-pale cheeks. "Too bad we'll never know the answer," she retorted, throwing open the car door. If she hesitated any longer, she would have yielded to temptation and instigated that kiss herself.

Jonah came round the front of the car, put his hand under her elbow and leaned so that his lips brushed her ear. "Coward," he whispered, giving her elbow a gentle squeeze.

"All the way to the bone," Paige admitted, her blithe smile faltering as the truth of the words struck home. She really *was* scared underneath the bantering and professional posturing.

And yet...she was also calmly determined. Oxymoron...or contradiction?

"Me, too," Jonah said as they started walking, startling her so much she stumbled. Jonah's hand tightened its hold. "But you know what? I can ignore the fear, because we're trying to uncover the truth. And I'm confident that God is walking with us. Regardless of what He allows to happen, He'll be right here. One of the most comforting aspects of my faith in Christ, that."

"I'm learning." Paige squared her shoulders, flashed him an insouciant smile. "After all, the worst they can do is kill our bodies."

"Thanks for the reminder."

They were almost to the front door. "I'm okay with being dead," Paige ventured out of the corner of her mouth as she rang the doorbell, "it's the process of *getting* to that point that really scares me."

They both laughed, the smiles still in place when a pleasant-faced black woman dressed in starched pink opened the huge, double front doors. Mr. Gladstone, she informed them, was resting in the library, and could she ask their business.

"Tell him," Jonah said, "that we're here on behalf of Professor Emil Kittridge." His voice abruptly turned formal, authoritative, and the deep midnight blue gaze transformed from teasing laughter to the hardness of polished onyx.

A minute later they were led down a hall and ushered into the library.

Chapter Twenty-Five

Stooped, his yellowish white hair thin and dull, Everett Gladstone looked like a man life had chewed up and jettisoned. When Jonah and Paige entered the room, he turned away from the floor-to-ceiling window, letting the sheer, French lace panel drop back into place.

"I knew someone would come eventually." The gravelly voice was resigned, its cultured accent slurred by age and infirmity. Moving with a slow, shuffling step, he made his way to an overstuffed chair and collapsed. Deep lines scored his face. Blue veins bulged in the bony, almost transparent hands.

Paige hurried to his side and poured a glass of water from the plastic bottle sitting on a piecrust table beside the chair. To Jonah the incongruity of that plastic bottle—cheap standard hospital issue—sitting on a valuable antique table, struck with the force of a physical blow. He waited until Paige finished pouring the water, then sat down beside her on a love seat, across from Gladstone.

"How did you know someone was coming?" he asked, after the older man had sipped some of the liquid.

A look of cunning sharpened Gladstone's face, but it quickly dissipated, leaving him merely an old, defeated man. "Elsie told me you were here on behalf of that bullheaded professor.

I tried to warn him, but he was obsessed. Wouldn't listen..."
He shook his head, his voice trailing away.

"He was also my godfather," Paige put in, and Jonah laid
a warning hand on her arm. She shot a fierce look that scorched
his hair to the roots. "He's dead." Her voice rose. "Someone
killed him, this past August."

Everett Gladstone's hand gestured irritably. "I know nothing
of that," he repeated. "I warned him that some...issues...are
better left unopened. He left. I've heard nothing since."

"Um...did you perhaps warn anyone else?" Jonah picked
up a porcelain figurine and pretended to examine it. "Perhaps
your son, Armand?" Beside him Paige sucked in her breath,
her body tensing. Jonah wasn't comfortable with the blunt approach, but right now he was even less comfortable about their
safety. The car that pulled into the grocery store lot on the way
into town had followed them all the way from Warner Robins,
and Jonah had learned almost at the expense of both his and
Paige's life, the folly of assumptions. The driver might have
been a longtime resident. But he might have been...following
them.

Everett seemed to shrink back into the chair. Beads of sweat
popped out on his brow. "My son?" he said hoarsely. "What
do you mean, my son? What has he done—" He stopped, gasping.

Paige surveyed him in alarm. "Jonah, maybe we should
call—"

"No!" Everett cut across her, the denial forceful. "Just...
give me that bottle. It has pills...." Paige glanced from him to
Jonah, then without a word fetched the pills and held the glass
of water for the old man.

They'd have to tiptoe pretty daintily around the explosive
information he and Paige had discovered, considering Everett
Gladstone's precarious health, Jonah realized. At least Armand
hadn't lied about that. He leaned forward, dangling his hands
between his knees in a deliberately nonthreatening pose, and
waited until a little of the grayness had dissipated from Gladstone's complexion. "Mr. Gladstone," he began, "Ms. Haw-

thorne was more than Professor Kittridge's goddaughter. She was also his research assistant for a book he was writing.''

''You're trying to implicate my son in his death, aren't you?''

The fellow might be feeble physically, but he was a former ambassador...and no fool. ''Yes,'' Jonah answered very gently. ''I'm afraid we are. The police think Professor Kittridge died of a heart attack, but Ms. Hawthorne and I discovered information that indicates otherwise. Unfortunately we've been unable to prove anything in spite of some clues we found.''

''Clues that almost led to our own deaths,'' Paige added. She was sitting on the edge of the love seat, hands clenching and unclenching in her lap. ''Mr. Gladstone...we need your help.''

''I'm an old man, not well—as you can plainly see. My wife's health is worse than mine. What makes you think I could help you try to prove that man was murdered? He was loud, obnoxious, sticking his nose in other people's business. Private matters that the public has *no* need to know. Not now....''

There was no help for it—he'd have to push, and pray Gladstone's heart could weather the knowledge, so Jonah wouldn't carry the weight of the old man's death on his conscience. ''Would it help persuade you if you knew that Professor Kittridge's house has since been burned to the ground—deliberately? That both Ms. Hawthorne's and my apartments have been vandalized?''

''You have no right to implicate my son—''

''Those attempts made on our lives Ms. Hawthorne mentioned included kidnapping and assault with deadly intent. That one was very nearly successful.'' He gestured to the scab on his forehead, then brushed his fingers over the Band-Aids still covering the cuts on Paige's neck and hand. ''The police are now actively investigating. The truth *will* come out eventually, Mr. Gladstone. If your son is innocent, what have you to lose by sharing what you know?'' He didn't include Everett in the assumption of innocence.

Gladstone sat in stony silence for a long moment, his gaze fixed. The muscles in his throat worked spasmodically, however, and the rigid shoulders began to sag.

"We need answers...proof," Jonah persisted finally. "The police are doing everything they can, but we can't dodge knives and bullets forever." He waited until Gladstone looked at him, then held his gaze, allowing him to see his own fear and vulnerability. "I...it's not just myself. I don't want anything to happen to Ms. Hawthorne—Paige. She doesn't deserve to be hunted like a deer. She has a family who loves her very much."

Beside him, Paige stirred. "Mr. Gladstone," she told him with a frayed sincerity that tore Jonah's heart, "please. Help us. Jonah is being too modest. He's—" She stopped suddenly when Jonah's hand shot out and closed over her arm. He shook his head slightly.

She pressed his fingers, then turned back to Gladstone. "We've been moving from motel to motel for over a month now, running for our lives. I'm so tired—so frightened by it all. Tell us about your son—why the mention of him causes you to break into a sweat." She took a deep breath, then added in a softer tone, "Tell us what happened in World War II, so many years ago, that caused your name to be included on a list of names. Because that list is what has brought us here today."

Gladstone buried his face in his hands. "How did you find out?" When neither Jonah nor Paige responded he lifted his head, staring as though into a painful past, a painful reality...and a probable painful future. Fingers trembling violently, he reached to pick up the glass of water. In a gesture that made Jonah's heart swell with pride, Paige put her hand over his to help him drink. Gladstone looked at her in disbelief—and shame.

"How did you find out?" he whispered again in a paper-thin voice.

"I'm a historian," she reminded him. "And I've been helping Mr. Sterling with some World War II research as well as helping Professor Kittridge." She forbore to reveal Jonah's alter ego, having read his unspoken wish quite easily. "I found a piece of paper, along with a tiny key, while I was cleaning and examining the uniform of an army intelligence officer. There were nine names—first initial and surname—on that list. Yours is the 'E. Gladstone,' isn't it?"

"Yes." As though the stark confession had exhausted the last of his reserves, Everett leaned back, his head collapsing on the back of the chair. He closed his eyes. "So long ago...but it seems like yesterday. I never knew—no one ever came forward. Thought I was safe...but I was always waiting...."

His voice faded. Jonah and Paige sat quietly. Jonah glanced out the window, watching the gray dreariness of the day sliding into a sullen twilight without brightness, without the softness of the setting sun. He suddenly felt bone tired, as drained and whipped as Everett Gladstone.

Everett began to talk, his voice a dull monotone. The chilling words painted a stark, ugly picture. "It was 1944. The ambassador told me at a party one night that a man would be attending—a major from army intelligence. He'd been investigating some leaks, some damaging leaks, and had compiled a list of names as possible sources." He passed a still-trembling hand over his eyes. "I, of course, was one of those sources."

"Why?" Paige asked, the word exploding out. Her eyes were wild with grief and anger.

Jonah wanted to take her in his arms and hold her, just hold her. She sounded both bewildered and disillusioned.

Everett shrugged. "It didn't seem so bad at first. I was young, and it was my first really important position. Geneva was proud—she loved the glitz and glamour, even during the war. I was approached, offered a lot of money, even more prestige. They said no one would ever know. All I had to do was phone a certain number, pass on pieces of information. At the time the information seemed arbitrary, pointless, certainly nothing that would seriously damage the Allied cause."

Jonah turned his gaze to examine the shelves lined with volumes of books, fighting to keep his own anger from showing. Some things never seemed to change. He'd lived and traveled all over the world, known people from all walks of life. And it never changed. Satan might be subtle—but the snares seldom varied. Wealth. Power. Prestige. He jerked his attention back to Gladstone, faintly ashamed when he realized the older man was watching him, a look of utter hopelessness deepening the lines in his guilt-ravaged face.

"I passed along information for almost a year. Then Geneva's brother died in battle." His voice faltered. "I found out that the reason he'd probably been killed was because of a piece of information I'd passed over the phone. At the time it had just seemed an arbitrary, largely insignificant— But it helped kill my wife's only brother."

"And countless other brothers, fathers, husbands," Paige whispered beneath her breath. Jonah heard and squeezed her shoulder.

"I told them I wouldn't do it anymore." Everett swallowed. Large droplets of perspiration dotted his forehead and upper lip. "They...they..."

"Offered an alternative," Jonah finished without emphasis.

Shuddering, Everett nodded. "Exposure for me—slow, lingering death for Geneva. I...didn't have any choice. I never realized—"

"And Major Pettigrew?" Paige asked.

Everett's hand lifted, dropped lifelessly back on the chair arm. "I called my number and relayed the information that he was going to be at the party with the list of names. And I hung up the phone." The hands slowly closed into fists. "Making me directly responsible for at least one more death." He stared down at his clenched hands. "'Will all great Neptune's ocean wash this blood clean from my hand?' Shakespeare had the way of it, didn't he?"

For a while after that the three of them sat in silence. Jonah studied the worn-out wreck of a man and mused over God's justice. Pondered as well the ominous warning about the sins of the fathers. "What about your son?" he asked Everett reluctantly. "What about Armand Gladstone?"

The old man quivered. Wetting his lips, he thanked Paige when she held the glass to his lips. "He...found out what I'd done when I was ambassador to Thailand, in 1964. Armand was nineteen. He never forgave me." He lifted a gnarled, age-speckled hand and covered his eyes. "Never," he whispered.

"What happened, Mr. Gladstone?" Paige queried.

Jonah glanced across. All the bitterness had drained from her face as well as her voice, replaced by an almost luminous expression of compassion.

Everett looked at her, as well. "You're a nice girl. Why couldn't someone like you have come into my son's life before it was too late? My son, my son..." He cleared his throat, swallowed more water. "When he found out, my son just stood there—the way he looked at me—" Everett shook his head. "I'll never forget. He said—he said—" his face had turned a mottled, sickly gray again "—he was going to continue in the family tradition, seeing as how it was so...rewarding. I asked him what he meant. He looked at me—through me. He said, 'You'll find out, Father. You'll find out.'"

Restless, edgy, Jonah rose and wandered about the room. It was a warm, attractive room, with Aubusson rugs and oak flooring, waist-high oak paneling with a heavy floral-print wallpaper above. Silk floral arrangements complemented the rose and powder blue colors.

It should have been a peaceful, welcoming room, but it wasn't. Jonah returned to stand behind Paige, his hands dropping over the back of the love seat to rest on her rigid shoulders. She was strong, yet felt so fragile beneath his hands. It hurt his soul in a way he couldn't fathom that she had been a pawn in the self-serving schemes of two despicable men.

"What did your son do?" he asked.

Everett looked at both of them, then out the window. "He joined the army and secured a commission. Ended up in Vietnam, of course. For the first couple of years, he'd make a point of telling me—in graphic detail—of how he was selling guns, ammo and military secrets to the Viet Cong. He knew I wouldn't do anything—couldn't. He shared every detail. He also liked to tell me how he used the Gladstone name to rise in rank and power. About how easy it was, thanks to *my* power and prestige. The one time I threatened to expose him, he laughed in my face—and said he hoped we wouldn't share the same cell at Leavenworth."

Jonah didn't realize how hard he was gripping Paige's shoulders until her hands lifted to cover his, stroking his fingers, *gentling* him as though she herself hadn't been ready to vent her fury on Gladstone only minutes earlier. He bent swiftly. "I'm sorry, love," he whispered next to her ear.

"That was the last time I saw him," Everett finished. He took a deep, quivering breath. "It's been twenty years now. I know he 'won' a seat in Congress—and I know he won it any way he could. My son...has become an evil man, even though the public looks on him as a hero, a powerful man who is also—" his voice thickened "—a true gentleman. And I sit here and watch it happen...and do nothing."

The grandfather clock behind him struck four times. Everett rose. "My wife will be home soon. I don't want—" The plea faltered on his lips. He stared at them with those old, hopeless eyes. "It never ends," he whispered. "The lies, the evasion. The fear. With me it was the prestige, the money. With my son, it started with revenge...but he's beyond that now. He's drunk on the power, as well as the money and position. And I can say nothing—do nothing. I did try to warn him after that professor. I called him. It was hopeless. It's all hopeless—it's a trap, a deadly snare that I couldn't escape...and now it's ruined my only son."

He gazed down at the floor, hands working convulsively at his sides. "If my wife finds out what you've told me—what I've told you—the shock will kill her." His voice trailed off. "It's been slowly killing me for fifty years, and now, my son. My son..."

Chapter Twenty-Six

For most of the drive to Warner Robins, Paige stared out the window, watching in moody silence as the twilight faded into evening. The sky had cleared, and a full moon, barely visible, was slowly rising above the shell pink horizon—a lovely benediction to an *un*lovely day. But instead of enjoying God's handiwork, Paige thought about a broken, dying man sitting alone in his beautiful mansion, his life little more than cold ashes.

"I wonder if that car is going to follow us all the way to the museum."

Paige jumped at the unexpected sound of Jonah's voice—even more at his words. She twisted around to glance out the back at the pair of unwinking headlights less than two hundred yards back. "You don't suppose...?"

Jonah lifted his foot from the gas pedal. "Get ready to duck," he murmured serenely.

Paige glanced across. He looked about as concerned as the moonrise. His intrepid assistant, on the other hand, wove clammy fingers together and listened to the rapid whoosh of her elevated pulse clamoring in her ears. After her encounter with a professional killer, her appetite for danger was nonexistent.

The car caught up, flashed its lights—and passed, the glare of the lights momentarily blinding in the early evening. Ashamed of her knee-jerk response, Paige tried to at least catch a glimpse of the driver. "Did you see him? I think it was a man, but—"

"No. Lights were too bright." Jonah shrugged. "I'll keep an eye on him, though." He brought the car back up to speed. "I don't think we were followed, but the sooner we're back under the aegis of the authorities, the more comfortable I'll feel."

Paige leaned back and closed her eyes. "I just wish it were all over."

"So do I, love. So do I."

The Robins Museum of Aviation was situated out the back gate of Robins Air Force Base. The museum had closed at five, but the curator stayed late to allow Paige and Jonah more privacy to check over the Luftwaffe memorabilia. Occasionally fame had its privileges. With his characteristic singlemindedness, within five minutes of their arrival Jonah was immersed in the task, his eyes behind his glasses intent, absorbed.

Paige fingered an old uniform, but for the first time she could remember, it was difficult to summon up much enthusiasm for research. For several minutes more she pretended an interest, then gave up and watched Jonah, admiration and irritation churning her stomach. In spite of earthquakes, hurricanes, a world war, murder and kidnapping...J. Gregory, consummate writer, would not be swayed from achieving his goal.

When Jonah asked without looking up if she'd take some notes while he talked, she dutifully scratched them down on her pad, waiting without comment while Jonah plowed through a bulging shoe box full of letters. A little before seven, he finally gathered everything up, piled it neatly back in two heavy cardboard boxes, and restuffed the shoe box.

"I think that will do it." He wiped his hands on his slacks, smiling at the curator. "Thank you so much. This was extremely kind of you, especially letting me have photocopies of some of the letters." The eager curator beamed at Jonah's cultured tones, not at all impatient with the delay at being able to leave. A band of red crept across Jonah's cheekbones.

Paige hid an affectionate smile. Though he could play the role of world-renowned aristocratic British author with panache when it was called for, Jonah truly disliked having to adopt his "J. Gregory" persona. Her smile broadened as she watched him trying not to squirm beneath the onslaught of effusive praise for his books.

Diffident, absentminded writer, fanatical about his privacy. Coolly capable adventurer, traveling all over the world with serene insouciance.... Compassionate friend whose faith shone like a lighthouse beacon, bathing everyone in its warmth.

And over it all he was a devastatingly charming man, who, during the past months, had somehow managed to slip past all of Paige's defenses. He had helped restore her positive self-image and her trust in God. For weeks now she had been stubbornly avoiding the truth, but no longer.

She was in love with him.

The feelings had been growing steadily for months now, but until today Paige had been able to delude herself that it was merely liking, respect and a very natural hero worship. Everybody liked Jonah, admired J. Gregory's books. Any woman showered in the genuine warmth of his attention would feel special.

But Paige no longer wanted to be just another woman. She not only wanted to feel special when she was with him, she needed to *be* special *to* him.

Keeping her head averted, she gathered up her notebook and the photocopied letters. Ever since David died she had kept her feelings in cold storage, hiding behind a professional mask even Professor K. hadn't recognized, much less acknowledged. As for sharing her feelings with Jonah...well...she didn't know. Perhaps—she should pray. *Lord? Is this a dilemma You will enlighten me about?* Their working relationship was excellent, after all. Surely she could—

"Paige? Got everything? Harry's ready to leave if we are."

"I'm ready." She smiled at the curator and headed for the exit, her mind twisting itself in impossible mental contortions.

They left through the back door, and after another round of thank-yous and promises to stay in touch, the curator finally said good-night, hurrying down the sidewalk. He disappeared around the corner of the building. Seconds later a car door slammed, an engine started, and the sound faded as the curator's car wound down the drive. Silence descended.

Paige and Jonah lingered in the cool silence of the night, gazing out over the display of planes. Overhead the moon rose through wispy shreds of black clouds, a gigantic luminous pearl so close they could almost pluck it from the sky. It cast a serene mosaic of light and shadow over the long rows of planes and equipment on display.

"Turned into a pretty night," Paige ventured, then winced, silently berating herself. Even to her own ears the banal words sounded artificial, overly bright.

Hands stuffed in back pockets and eyes gazing dreamily upward, Jonah murmured an inarticulate agreement.

So much for feeling, much less being, special. Paige chewed another crumb of humble pie and didn't speak again. On the other hand, if she loved him, she would understand his need to absorb, reflect...to enjoy rare chunks of solitude when his creativity soared. There was a dramatic difference, she had learned painfully, between the kind of love that grasped and bludgeoned and demanded—and the Christlike love that gave of itself freely.

It was time to consider Jonah's feelings, as well as her own.

In other words, Paige Hawthorne—grow up. Her head lifted, her back straightened and she turned an emotional corner, quietly resolved to risk giving of herself again. Jonah might not ever hear the words from her lips, but the love would be there just the same. She inched closer, inhaling the musky masculine warmth, and—at last—opening herself to the joy of the moment.

After a while Jonah's arm dropped across her shoulders, and they began walking toward the parking lot. Paige shivered when they turned the corner of the building, and a cold breeze blew through her hair, down the back of her neck beneath her blouse and bulky sweater. "Brr. Turning colder again," she observed.

"Mmph." His arm hugged her closer.

A moment later Paige stopped abruptly, forcing Jonah to halt. "Did you hear that?"

"Hear what?" He still sounded preoccupied.

"I'm not sure. Wait a moment...."

A rising wind soughed through the trees, rustling and eerie, but in the dimly lit parking lot nothing moved but a lone piece of paper tumbling soundlessly across the driveway.

Paige finally shrugged. "Must be the wind, and my nerves. Sorry."

That finally penetrated. He patted her shoulder comfortingly. "You're just tired. How about if we grab a spot of supper, and—" The hand on her shoulder tightened; tension radiated from his suddenly rigid body.

"What is it?" Her heart began to thud unevenly.

"A puncture," Jonah said slowly, warily.

Paige glanced across at the rental car, noting the slightly tilted rear end. "What a nuisance," she groaned. "Hope there's a real spare in the trunk, instead of one of those ridiculous doughnut things."

Jonah didn't respond. His head was raised, turning, his gaze searching. The wind had died, plunging them into a void of prickling silence. In the utter stillness, goose bumps raced over Paige's skin. "Jonah, what—?"

She didn't have time to complete the question. Jonah shoved her facedown behind some bushes, his body falling on top to shield her just as a sharp cracking sound splintered the night.

Paige knew that sound.

And Jonah wasn't moving. *He wasn't moving.* Beneath the granite slab of his body, Paige began to squirm, panic devouring her in savage tearing bites. "Jonah!" Her hands scrabbled in the cold wet earth, searching, searching in escalating terror. In an instant she was transported back into a hotel room that had almost been a tomb. *She was blind, and he'd shot Jonah. Jonah was dead. Dead...and there was a knife at her throat...a hissing voice promising all manner of unspeakable horrors before she, too would die....*

Hard hands—warm, strong hands—closed over hers, stilling the frantic movement. But the voice whispering urgently in her ear was not threatening pain and death. Instead it kept telling her she was all right—he was all right. They were okay, but she must be quiet.

The swirling blackness receded. Paige abruptly went limp, her breath shuddering out of her in a quivering sob. "Sorry." Her head dropped onto their clasped hands. "For a minute it was the hotel all over again."

Though the choked explanation was delivered in a reed-thin whisper, Paige knew Jonah had heard when she felt his hands slide back up her arms, then release her. He dropped a light kiss on the back of her neck.

"It's okay." The words whispered into her ear like a sigh, soothing, calming. "But I need you to stay absolutely still. Promise me, Paige."

She tensed again, but before she could question him, another resounding crack shattered the night, bouncing in an echoing ricochet off the museum walls. A scant twelve inches from Paige's nose, twigs from the evergreen bush exploded into fragments, and dirt sprayed out from the ground in front of their hiding place.

Jonah yanked Paige deeper beneath the shield of his body, his hands biting into her arms. They froze into absolute stillness, waiting.

"He's off to our left," Jonah finally whispered. "If we can make it to the back, the building will be between us, and we should have enough of a start to make it to the base for help."

Paige managed a jerky nod.

"When I squeeze your hand, roll over and start crawling. Follow the bushes. When you get to the corner, run. I'll be right behind you."

Right behind—and shielding her with his body. "Jonah—" she swallowed, licked dry lips "—don't do anything stupid."

He didn't reply. Seconds later he squeezed her hand, rolling his weight to the side. Paige scrambled to her hands and knees and began crawling, keeping crouched as low as possible. Bits of bark and stone cut into her hands and knees, and the wet earth clung to her in clammy, sodden lumps. The pungent aroma of evergreen and humus stung her nostrils.

Suddenly Jonah's hand closed over her ankle, jerking her flat. Paige lay motionless, not even breathing. Jonah prodded her and she began crawling again, feeling Jonah at her heels, hearing the sound of his even breathing. At the corner she stopped, heart racing as she waited for Jonah's signal.

"Now!"

They leaped to their feet and ran. A bullet slammed through the metal siding of the museum with a harsh metallic ping.

"The planes!" Paige gasped out as she ran. "Hide in the planes!"

Displayed in long rows with narrow concrete pathways between, the assortment of flying machines sat motionless, looking in the moonlight like a grotesque collection of metal insects.

Paige ducked under the wing of a snub-nosed prop job, eyes darting about, trying to decide where to run, where to hide. Jonah grabbed her arm. "Over here!"

Hand in hand they zigzagged an erratic path until Jonah yanked her under the wing of a cumbersome-looking C-47. Shadows closed over them, and they edged backward until they bumped into the slanting fuselage, a characteristic of the old "tail draggers."

Shivering, breathing in uneven gulps, Paige sagged against the cold, rain-wet metal. Jonah's arm came round her shoulders, hugging her close. Beneath her shoulder blades his heart thundered. For an endless span of time they waited, not moving, and Paige concentrated all her energy on breathing quietly. Unfortunately she couldn't seem to do anything about her quivering leg.

Finally Jonah slowly crept forward, one soundless step at a time, under the wing, toward the nose of the plane. Ribbons of moonlight shimmered in streaming patterns, highlighting some of the planes in its day-bright white light, while casting others in impenetrable shadows.

Paige followed, her own gaze searching the area. Right now

shadows protected, concealed them—but they also protected and concealed a professional killer. A *desperate* killer, to be attacking so openly. This time Paige knew with awful certainty that, regardless of risk, he wasn't going to give up until both she and Jonah were dead.

Chapter Twenty-Seven

Across an open space free of planes, a shadow darted through a patch of moonlight, then disappeared.

"There!" Paige whispered, grabbing Jonah's arm. "Near the back of the lot—I think he's trying to cut us off, keep us from making it to the base."

Paige felt Jonah's arms draw her back close against his chest. He was strong, warm—a haven from harm. The knowledge that he was guarding her with his life both humbled and awed Paige. For almost thirty years the only man she had associated with that blend of strength and protectiveness had been her father, who loved her. "I...only saw him a second—" Her voice caught, steadied. "I think he's hiding under those tall pines."

"Okay," Jonah whispered back. "Let's try to make it a little farther, before he has time to move in closer."

Paige turned in his arms, clutching his shoulders. His hands moved comfortingly down her back. "Why not the way we came? If we reach the car, even with a flat—"

His fingers pressed against her lips, stilling the panicked words. "There's nothing beyond the museum but swamp and the highway. Even if we use the car, he could pick us off without any trouble, not to mention any unsuspecting motorist who stopped to help." He cupped her face. "Paige." His voice was urgent, but the hands held her gently. "You've got to trust me. Promise me."

Unbelievingly his voice faltered. *Jonah was scared, too.* And, she realized in painful honesty, part of that fear came from his uncertainty over her willingness to obey. Paige felt as though she were suspended on a tightrope across a deep gorge and the cable had just snapped. The only other time she had trusted another man enough to submit to his dictates, her heart had been broken first and then her spirit.

Trust Me.... I won't let you fall beyond My outstretched arms.

A gentle warmth invaded her soul, drifted into her body, filling her up with a quiet joy not even a killer could destroy. Just as gently the knowledge seeped into her brain of what she needed to do. She gazed up at Jonah's shadowed face, seeing only the pinpoint glitter of his eyes. "I trust you, Jonah," she promised, very softly. "And I trust God. Regardless of what happens." All the love spilling into her shone from her face, echoed in her voice, but she no longer cared. She only wanted to give what she had received.

For a minute Jonah's head bowed, and she thought he closed his eyes. Then he kissed her swiftly, his hand slid to clasp hers, and they began edging toward the front of the plane. The faint, undulating keen of sirens echoed in the distance, but Paige paid scant attention.

"Let's go." Jonah sprinted for the next plane, Paige on his heels.

They paused for only a second before dashing across to a larger EC-123, the huge dome atop the fuselage distinguishing it from all the other planes. The chill November night wrapped around them. Paige shivered, her breath escaping in icy tendrils of steam as she flattened herself against the plane.

Jonah motioned for her to stay put. Then, with his body doubled in a stealthy crouch, he made his way around to the other side of the plane. Paige trained her eyes on the jumbled shapes across the field, searching for any movement. If she glimpsed even a leaf flutter in the breeze, she planned to alert Jonah.

Even when he returned she didn't turn her head. "Did you see anything?"

"No...nothing." There was a pregnant pause, then he said, his voice rough, "I'm going to try to draw his fire—I want you to run for that B-52 over there, near the road. The back gate of the base is just beyond, and maybe—"

Her heart had given a gigantic lurch, and Paige reached up before Jonah completed the sentence to wrap her hands behind his neck. "No—wait!" She tugged until their faces were inches apart. "There has to be a safer way!" she whispered, choking on fear and love. She clutched him tighter. "We'll *both* try to make it to the B-52. We need to stay together. Together." Dimly she knew she was losing control, but she didn't care. Only Jonah mattered—and telling him how she felt before it was too late. "You big lug!" she choked, tears spilling over, "I don't want you playing some superhero anymore! I love you. I don't want anything to happen to you. *I love*—mmph—"

Jonah's mouth stopped the flood of words. He gripped her shoulders, pressing her back against the plane as he unleashed a storm of passion that rocked her to her toes. Paige responded, meeting the kiss with an intensity that underscored her desperation. The world dissolved in a river of colors, dazzling and rich as a waterfall of gemstones. She had never realized the breadth of his shoulders, the power of his strong arms, the texture of his hair, thick and cool as her fingers sifted through the strands.

"I love you," she repeated against his mouth over and over, holding him close. Her fingers slid down to his face, tracing the strong cheekbones, the bristly texture of his mustache. "I'm sorry...had to tell you..."

"Shh," he murmured back, his mouth dropping brief but burning kisses to her lips, her eyes...temples. Back to her lips. "Hush, now. It's okay. I love you, too...." His mouth trailed back up her tear-wet cheeks. Incredibly, she felt him smile. "You do pick your moments, don't you?" he whispered, dropping a last kiss on the tip of her nose.

"I—you what?" she gasped, her ears ringing from his almost casual declaration. "What did you say?"

"About your sense of timing?" he teased, gathering her even closer, his hand stroking damp strands of hair from her face. Then, his own voice choking, he said, "I love you so much it's been eating me alive...weeks. Months. Trying not to let you see. I didn't want to terrify you. And now..."

Paige rested her head against his shoulder and closed her eyes. "We *both* have a terrible sense of timing."

"Mmm. Then I guess we'd better postpone further joyous revelations until—"

A bullet slammed into the hollow fuselage, inches from Paige's head. Jonah threw her to the ground. "Roll," he commanded harshly, his body following hers.

She rolled, over and over like leaves in the wind, Jonah almost on top of her. When she bumped into the nose wheel of a plane, she wriggled onto her stomach. Another shot rang out and beside her, Jonah jerked. *"Jonah..."* The word barely struggled free of her locked throat. *Don't scream. Don't lose it....*

"The helicopter—over there," Jonah ground out. "It's body's close to the ground—better protection." His instructions ended in a choked groan. "Hurry, Paige. Please. I'm right behind you."

Without a word she squeezed his clenched hand, then rolled to her feet and ran, hurling herself behind the ugly squatting 'copter in a diving roll that jarred the breath from her lungs. Seconds later Jonah landed beside her. He lay unmoving, his body taut. Paige scrambled to her hands and knees. "Where?" she asked him, her hands searching, patting his chest and arms.

"Left side," Jonah managed to say. His hand came up to her cheek. "Paige...it's just a flesh wound. Stop...shaking. But I don't know how fast I can run...." His hand dropped.

Paige yanked her sweater off, folded it into a pillow, then manhandled Jonah's belt from around his waist. "Do you have a handkerchief? No—lie still. I'll get it." Her fingers slid under his back, frantically tugging, even though she knew the movement had to hurt. She could see a dark stain spreading over his sweater, feel the sticky warmth as she carefully eased his shirt free and peeled everything away. It was more than just a flesh wound.

Jumbled, almost-incoherent prayers poured forth in a sound-less whisper. A curious ringing sound flooded her eardrums, but she ignored it as well as the light-headedness from a heart threatening to explode out of her chest. All that mattered was Jonah.

Suddenly her head snapped around. That sound—it wasn't a ringing in her ears! "Jonah! Listen." The undulating wail she had barely registered earlier rose to a banshee scream. "Si-rens—do you hear? Hang on. Help is coming...Jonah. Hang on."

"I hear. Pray, love..."

"I haven't stopped." She pressed the handkerchief directly over the spot in back where she felt blood oozing out. There was nothing she could do right now about the point of entry. She probed, trying to be gentle, but he flinched. "I'm sorry." She choked back the sob. "I need to fasten your belt around this now."

Teeth gritted in pain, Jonah managed to sit up, holding the handkerchief while Paige tightened the belt to keep it in place. Next she picked up her sweater and arranged it around his neck and back for extra warmth. He leaned against the helicopter, his breathing harsh and ragged.

The wailing sirens stopped, leaving in their wake a throbbing silence.

Several hundred feet away a shoe scraped on stone. Gravel crunched—then silence descended once more.

With Paige's help, Jonah struggled to his feet. One arm clamped next to his injured side, the other wrapped around Paige's shoulders, he urged them deeper into the shadows. Paige glanced frantically around. The B-52 lay some fifty yards beyond, crouched like an ominous black and green lizard in its camouflage paint. To reach it, they would have to cross a wide swath of bare ground, bathed in moonlight.

"Paige?" The husky syllable brushed against her ear. "I want you to listen to me...we don't have much time...."

Her throat muscles tightened in a spasm of foreboding.

"Don't ask me, Jonah," she begged in a voice thick with anguish.

"Paige...love..." The word sighed a caress into her ear. "I told you once that I needed you to trust me—trust me totally." With melting tenderness he traced a path across her face to her chin, down her throat, with fingers that trembled from pain, fear and emotion. "Love of my heart—the knife is poised. Do what I ask you—and if you can't trust me that much, then trust God to provide the lamb. Please—or we're both going to die."

"If I leave you here, you'll—you might—" She couldn't say it. *Trust me,* he'd pleaded. *Trust Me,* the Lord had reminded her, and she knew she would carry the sound of that Voice in her soul the rest of her life.

Paige closed her eyes, knowing that she must make the most difficult decision of her life—immediately. The longer she hesitated, the closer the assassin crept toward them—and the less chance Jonah had of successfully creating a diversion. Either she obeyed Jonah's wishes or chose to follow her own. Whom did she choose to trust more—herself or the man to whom she had just pledged both her love...*and* her trust?

God had promised that she was never beyond the reach of His loving embrace, and He had sent Jonah Sterling into her life. When everything was said and done, there was really only one choice to make. Paige opened her eyes, lifted Jonah's hand and held it between hers. "What do you need me to do?"

For a timeless second he didn't speak, and Paige could feel the tension dropping from him like heavy, broken chains. Then he leaned down, inhaling sharply when the movement obviously caused pain. "When I give the signal," he breathed next to her ear, "run for that bomber. Once you make it to the other side...you'll have a little protection. Be in sight of the road. Start screaming...bloody murder." Even in the pitch-black darkness she sensed the undaunted smile. "Literally. There's a guard at the back gate—he'll hear. If we're lucky, they've already heard the shots anyway, and are coming to investigate."

He stopped, his breathing labored. Paige waited, hands clenched over his in a death grip. "Stay in the cover of the

B-52 until either the gate guard or the police can protect you,"
he finished.

"All right, Jonah," Paige answered after a minute. She lifted
his hand and brushed a fleeting kiss into his palm. It was damp
with sweat. "What are you going to do?"

His hand turned in hers, squeezing. "I'll tell you later.
Paige?"

"Yes?" Her voice was strangled.

"I love you."

She lifted her chin, swallowing the tears. "I love you, too,
but if you get yourself killed, Jonah Sterling, I might not ever
forgive you."

"Take it up with the Lord." He shifted, moving with painstaking caution toward the front of the chopper. Paige watched
while he slowly crouched down, then just as slowly straightened. "Now!" he called out in a light breath of sound that
barely made it to her ears.

Heart in her throat, Paige tore off across the field like a
spooked doe. She didn't look back.

Chapter Twenty-Eight

At the same instant Paige darted out into the open, Jonah threw a stone in the opposite direction. He heard it ping against metal and then, far closer than he liked, he heard the muffled thud of running footsteps, somewhere off to his right. Fortunately the diversion had worked, because the killer was headed in the direction Jonah had thrown the stone and away from Paige.

Now all he had to do was prolong the game of hide-and-seek until she made it to safety. Suppressing a groan, he pressed his side harder, picturing all the movies where the heroes took a bullet. *They* usually acted as though the injury was about as debilitating as a bee sting. Next time his agent wanted to talk movie rights, Jonah decided muzzily, he'd make sure there was a clause providing for a more realistic depiction.

Don't be some superhero, Paige had begged him. Jonah grimaced. Needles of pain wove a barbwire fence around his rib cage, making him light-headed and less than steady. Superhero, ha! Right now he doubted he could blow out a birthday candle. As for leaping tall buildings—he thought of the remaining rock clenched in his hand. More like David facing Goliath. *You'll be with me, as well, won't You, Lord?*

A sharp pain streaked up his arm from his hand, and he

risked a quick downward glance. Oh. He'd been squeezing the jagged, rough-edged stone so tightly it was biting into his palm. *You're really on the ball, aren't you, pal?* Jonah relaxed his grip, allowing himself a twisted smile. With his side on fire, he was surprised he'd even noticed discomfort elsewhere.

Breathing shallowly, grateful that at least the wound was on his left side instead of his right, Jonah lifted his arm, then threw the second rock, aiming at a spot about ten yards beyond where he'd thrown the last one. The gunman probably wasn't stupid enough to fire, but maybe he was arrogant—or desperate— enough to accidentally reveal his whereabouts. Ignoring the pain, as well as the sweat dribbling down his face, Jonah watched. Listened.

There. Darting behind the C-47 where he and Paige had hidden moments earlier. The gunman disappeared almost instantly, but not before Jonah had glimpsed the lethal barrel of his custom-made rifle and the infrared scope.

Goliath was stalking him with a pretty sophisticated spear.

Jonah inched down the fuselage of the helicopter, keeping his back pressed against the metal, his mind spinning in a thousand useless directions. Had to stay alert, think. Couldn't give in to the fear for Paige. Needed to summon strength...quick reflexes. He could do this. *I can do all things through Christ...the Lord is my strength...greater is He that is in me....*

Like a fresh wind the verses blew through his mind, bringing in their wake an almost electrifying energy. Jonah stood straighter, a true smile of profound gratitude pulling at his cheeks. The makeshift bandage had slowed the bleeding, and the pain was starting to subside into a dull, steady ache, easily ignored. As for the rest, timing would be everything. Right now, all Jonah needed to do was stand still, and wait for Paige to start yelling. *Another promise there, Lord. Standing still until the time is right? Like King Jehoshaphat and his army, three millennia or so earlier.* Didn't matter which millennium a child of God lived on earth—the battle against evil still belonged to the Lord.

He shifted his body, feeling the balance and alertness flood-

ing his muscles. When the scream rang out seconds later, he
was ready.

"Help!" Paige yelled with astonishing volume, the sound
shattering the night as effectively as the sirens. "Please, help!
Someone's shooting at us!"

Jonah's body shifted into overdrive; he barreled out onto the
concrete walkway, smack into the spotlight brightness of the
moon. "Over here, pond scum! Be a man—show yourself!"
Then he dived behind the plane again, springing up immediately, adrenaline masking the white-hot pain. Dodging and
weaving, he worked his way toward the museum and away
from Paige—and waited for the impact of a lethal bullet.

In the background, never wavering, Paige continued to yell.
Jonah catapulted in a flying leap behind the partially restored
wreck of a plane, then lay winded, his ears straining to listen.

Paige's voice stopped midsentence.

Gasping, half passing out with pain and panic, Jonah struggled to his knees. Roaring filled his head, and he shook it,
blinked to clear his vision. *Paige,* he wanted to shout aloud.
Why wasn't she still screaming?

Then, over the roaring in his ears, he heard the sound of a
stern voice talking through a bullhorn, and the relief brought
him right to the edge of passing out. "This is the police. Throw
down your weapon and come out with your hands up."

Spotlights clicked on, flooding the area from four different
directions, including the area where Jonah lay in an untidy
sprawl. Prudence dictated that it would be to his best interest
to lie still a little longer, so he focused his blurred vision on
the dome lights flashing through a stand of trees, and didn't
move.

A different voice spoke into the bullhorn. "This is Sgt.
Wajeskowski of the United States Air Force Military Police.
We have you covered. Please surrender your weapon and show
yourself."

From among the planes on display came the crack of the
gunman's rifle, and a spotlight exploded, plunging a corner of
the museum lot back into darkness. Seconds later Jonah spotted
a black-clad silhouette running a broken path in and out of the

planes, back toward the woods at the far end of the museum. Off to the left an engine growled to life, and a military jeep roared into sight, cutting a diagonal path designed to intercept the fleeing man.

Thanks, Lord.... Gathering his strength, Jonah clambered to his feet, then had to rest his head against the cool metal until the ground stopped undulating.

"Freeze!" commanded a voice behind him. Running feet approached.

"Take it easy. I'm the one being shot at," Jonah told the fuselage, and almost laughed. He started to turn, then froze when he heard the ominous clank of a round being chambered into an M-16. "Um...your bloke's headed toward the swamp."

"Can't take any chances, sir." A radio crackled, and the MP spoke into it without taking his eyes off Jonah. "State your name, please."

"Jonah Sterling." He swayed. "J. Gregory...to a lot of loyal...readers...." *Stuff a sock in it, man, before you make a royal idiot of yourself.*

The young military policeman lowered his weapon slightly and stepped closer. "Sorry, sir. You need medical attention? The lady said something about you being shot?"

"Flesh wound." He grinned crookedly. "But it hurts like...blue blazes."

"Jonah!" Paige's voice called out brokenly, and both men turned toward the sound as she dashed across the grass toward them. "That's Jonah—leave him alone." She skidded to a halt beside both men, looking wild-eyed and rumpled almost beyond recognition.

In the harsh glare of the spotlights, Jonah could see the caked mud and smeared grass stains, along with several scratches running down her cheek. Sweaterless, blouse half untucked and windblown hair flying about her face, she was still the most beautiful sight he'd ever seen. *Lord—I love this woman so very much. Thank You for Your mercies.* He tried to smile at her, but at the moment Paige wasn't even looking his way. Instead, she glared at the MP with one of those Amazon warrior looks of hers. He almost felt sorry for the MP.

"He needs a stretcher and an ambulance!"

"They're on the way, ma'am," the airman politely responded.

Gunfire erupted, a short-lived burst of sound that died as abruptly as it had begun. The radio crackled again, and this time the military policeman moved away to answer it.

Jonah lifted his good arm, but it was such an effort it was already falling when Paige slipped into his woefully weak embrace. She reached up and kissed the corner of his mouth, then pressed his shoulder, urging him to sit back down. He was too dizzy to resist.

Leaning his head back, he allowed Paige to cushion him against her body. Something wet splashed onto his hand, and he managed to twist his head just enough so that he could look up into her face. "Don't cry. It's over."

"I'm not crying." There was a short pause, then, "All right, so maybe my eyes are—" Her voice broke. "Jonah...I was so scared. I kept thinking that I might let you down...that I couldn't yell loud enough. That you might...you might be—"

"I'll be okay, Paige. It's painful, but not fatal. I'm fine." The ground was moving about again, most unpleasantly. "Not some superhero, though. More...David versus Goliath." He knew he was rambling, but could no longer seem to halt the idiocy spilling from his lips. "Goliath with a fancy gun instead...spear...."

"Just be quiet and rest, do you hear?" He felt her hands smoothing through his hair, stroking his back. With great concentration, he lifted his hand and traced the contours of her ear. He loved those ears. "You...were great. Opera quality...."

She gave a gasp of laughter that finished in a sob. "My throat's killing me."

"I love you." He could hear his words slurring and decided it would be just splendid if the stretcher would arrive about now.

Paige's hand had come up to cover his. She began kissing it, then holding it to her damp cheek. "I love you, *mayn heldish leyb....*"

He could barely comprehend what sounded incredibly like...a badly pronounced Yiddish phrase? "Trying...to steal my—'' He sank into the depths of a bottomless black sea, carrying with him the sound of Paige's soft murmuring into his ear. Something about how she was getting a little of her own back, while she had him at a disadvantage.

The last thing he remembered was the touch of her lips dropping a soothing, featherlight kiss on the top of his head.

Chapter Twenty-Nine

Jonah spent the night at the Houston County Memorial Hospital, but the doctor released him in the morning, much to Paige's relief. A cheerful pot-bellied man with kind eyes and a deep-bass Georgia drawl, he stood at the foot of Jonah's bed, twirling his stethoscope while he talked.

"Bullet passed clean through," he promised Paige, then winked at Jonah, who was sitting on the hospital bed, buttoning his shirt. "Didn't even nick a rib. Missed everything that matters. Young fella's lost a little blood, but nothing to get excited about." He chuckled, glancing at Paige. "I'd say someone's sure looking out for that man."

Paige looked beyond the doctor to Jonah. "Yes," she agreed quietly. "Someone is." Her gaze met Jonah's and she felt an uprush of love so powerful she fancied the room glowed with it. "You're *positive* he's okay?"

The doctor had examined the entry and exit wounds, applied fresh bandages and written out a prescription for antibiotics. Paige, banished behind the curtained cubicle, blatantly peeked around to make sure Jonah couldn't hide any medical details from her.

Now he slid off the bed and took two steps to her side. "I've never been better," he said. A corner of his mouth lifted. "Let's go home."

"I'm glad they didn't kill him," she ventured some hours later, leaning back against the airline seat with a weary sigh. The flight attendant had just removed their snack trays, and Paige turned her head toward Jonah. "I know it doesn't make sense, but as much as I hated being stalked by a professional killer, I'm glad he's not dead."

Jonah lifted her hand and pressed a kiss into the palm. "I love you. And anybody who tries to follow the life-style of Jesus would understand exactly what you mean."

Her throat tightened with a funny prickly feeling. "Did you find out how long he'll be in the hospital?" she hurriedly asked. "They wouldn't tell me anything."

Gleaming navy eyes smiled into hers. "You must be slipping." The glint sparked into blue flames as he cupped her chin and leaned over. They kissed, a slow, loving kiss of ineffable sweetness.

It was delicious, Paige reflected muzzily, to kiss when you weren't running for your life...even when sitting in a plane full of people. She smiled against Jonah's mouth, and he lifted his head, rubbing his nose to hers.

"About our assailant," he murmured, sitting back in the seat. He reached for Paige's hand again. "One of the bullets penetrated his lung. He came through the surgery okay, I was told, but will probably be in hospital a week. Then he'll be remanded to the county jail. Doubtless we'll be flying back down for his arraignment some time next year."

"It'll be a while before the fat lady sings, won't it?" Paige groused, dropping her head against the shoulder on his uninjured side. For a few moments they sat in silence, and she debated the wisdom of voicing aloud a need that had turned from a wayward thought to an unrelieved itch. In the end she had to scratch. "I want to visit Armand Gladstone."

Jonah didn't respond beyond a momentary stiffening of his body. Then he said, "Why, love? It's in the authorities' hands now. They have all the proof they need—or will, when our stalker is able to talk.''

"What if he doesn't?'' Paige insisted, sitting back up. "All the information we gave the police is still circumstantial if that paid killer refuses to talk. Besides, it's not just Armand—it's Armand's father, Everett Gladstone. He's as much to blame for Professor K.'s death as Armand. Not to mention countless others.''

She and Jonah had, through the grace of God, survived and been blessed with mutual love. But it was through Professor K. that God had worked to bring about her own miraculous rebirth...while the professor had died, taking unresolved questions with him. Even now the pain of personal failure continued to drag at her, shadowing the joy of newfound love. "And we still haven't discovered the identity of the Ben-something person. What about him?''

"Shh, love.'' His hand stroked down her arm in a calming caress. "Just be still—and rest. Everything's going to be all right. We have Someone watching over us, remember?''

"I know, but—''

Jonah sat up, winced, then carefully grasped Paige's elbows, forcing her to look at him. His thumbs rotated a soothing circle on the insides of her arms. "It's a matter of trust, remember? Trust the Lord's purpose...and also me. I know you've carried the weight of the professor's death on your conscience these past months, but love, it's not necessary. Even Professor K. would tell you—he might even yell—that he knows you've done your best, but it's time to let it go.''

She knew he was right, but she *couldn't* let go. Not yet. "It isn't fair that he died, and men who are responsible for untold deaths live out their lives with impunity.''

"Ah. Your perception of Everett Gladstone's life was one of joy and untroubled peace, was it?''

"I agree that Everett has paid.'' Paige held his gaze, stubbornly resistant. "But it was his *son* who ordered someone to kill the professor.''

"In the end, God's justice will prevail.'' His voice was peaceful. "Yeah, I know that smacks of a glib Christian cliché.

But we both know it's not. It's the truth, the only one that we must accept. Whether in this life, from man's efforts—or when he dies and faces the Almighty God, Armand Gladstone will bear the responsibility for his actions.''

"Oh, all right, all right." She reached up and kissed him. "But I still don't like it."

"I know. You're a loving and loyal woman—with a warrior's heart, I'm beginning to realize." He laughed when Paige gave an unladylike snort. "Look at it this way. We don't have to hide any longer, we don't have to scrounge the country for clues anymore." He slanted her a faint sardonic look. "Do we?"

"Not for a while, at least."

"Like I said—a warrior's heart. Um, would it assuage your conscience if we resumed the other part of our lives? By—" he hesitated, then finished diffidently "—finishing the work on the professor's book. And...mine?"

"I very much need to resume a normal life and work on the books," Paige agreed. She gathered her courage—warrior's heart, indeed!—and looked him in the eye. "But I still want to visit Armand. I'm going to confront him with everything we found out, just to see what he says."

Tension spiked through her, but she didn't back down. And she needed him to understand, needed to know that he would still love and support her, even when they disagreed. She blocked from her mind the ramifications if her stubborn insistence drove him away. "Jonah...I need to do this or it will never be over with in my mind." She kept her gaze averted now, staring blindly at the back of the chair in front of her, because she couldn't bear to see the disillusionment... impatience...withdrawal—

Gentle hands pried her clenched ones apart, lacing warm fingers between hers. "All right. All right, love. We'll go see Armand." He squeezed her hand and released it, but only to wrap his arm around her shoulders and draw her to his side.

She did not deserve this man, or his love, but she fell asleep to the thrum of the plane's engine, thanking God for them both.

* * *

Armand Gladstone stood with his back to them, looking out a window, when they entered his office in the Capitol late the next afternoon. He curtly dismissed his aide without ever turning around. Hands clasped behind his back, tall and imposing, he continued to stand at the window in seemingly indifferent silence.

Sleet splattered against the glass, sliding down the panes in icy trails. Jonah quietly shut the door behind the aide, then followed Paige over to a couple of maroon leather armchairs. They sat, and waited as silently as Armand. Paige was determined not to be intimidated, much less patronized, by an amoral snake of a man. She exchanged a level look with Jonah, who encouraged her with a faint smile.

"You can't prove any of the charges," Gladstone eventually said, his voice cold, confident. "I only agreed to this meeting to warn you not to try." At last he turned, facing them with glacial calm. "If you do, I'll slap you both with a lawsuit that will bury you both for the rest of your lives—and win. You can rest assured that I will win."

Paige held out the large manila envelope she'd been carrying. "You might want to have a look at this." Her own voice matched the congressman's. "It includes all the information Professor Kittridge compiled. I believe you've been, um, 'looking' for it?" She dropped the envelope on a table between her and Jonah, then sat back, crossing one silk-stockinged leg and folding her arms—a deliberate posture not lost on the older man.

His arrogant self-assurance cracked a little. He took a step, his eyes narrowing. "Papers can be forged."

"And witnesses bribed or eliminated." Jonah spoke up for the first time. "We've become painfully aware of your modus operandi. We've already shared every piece of information we've gleaned with the police, FBI and any other interested government agency. What they choose to do with that information will be up to them. I'm not overly concerned, Congressman, but I'd be careful, if I were you, about threatening anyone with a lawsuit."

"You're only digging the hole deeper," Paige added, stifling the urge to throw the envelope at his feet, like a gauntlet.

Gladstone drew himself up even straighter. "That remains to be seen." He wandered casually across the room and scooped it up. "It's amazing what private individuals with axes to grind stoop to nowadays—especially with an election year approaching." With a contemptuous flick of his wrist he opened the envelope and dumped the contents back onto the table. "But my record will stand, and I plan to win a Senate seat, regardless of the attempted defamation of character by some interfering female and a hack Limey writer."

He scanned the neatly typed pages Paige had formulated the previous evening, but ignored the photocopies of original notes, newspaper articles, and a cassette tape. After several moments of thick silence he tossed the papers down. "A loser and a factory worker, trying to smear my name after all these years? A crackpot professor well-known for his eccentricities?" His mouth twitched into a crocodile's smile. "You're wasting my time. Get out."

"What about the man you hired to kill us?" Jonah was stroking his mustache, looking about as ruffled as a sleeping tomcat.

But Paige knew him by now, and she stirred, torn between anticipation and anxiety. She could imagine the headlines: Famous Author Sends Congressman to Hospital. A sidebar would of course include an article on her aiding and abetting Gladstone's subjugation by Jonah's fancy martial arts—maybe by throwing one of the pair of Ming vases displayed on the table under the window?

"The police captured your...employee last night," she told Gladstone, giving him her own version of a crocodile's smile. "He was trying to shoot us down at a museum in Warner Robins, Georgia, at the time. As you can see—once again he failed."

Gladstone's smile turned into a slashing straight line; a tic appeared at the corner of his left jaw. "I don't know who you're talking about."

"I see." Paige studied the ceiling, pursed her lips. "He's also charged with malicious destruction of government property, along with historical artifacts. He's landed himself in a pret-ty sticky swamp. As will the, ah, individual who hired him, when the shooter starts talking.''

"But since you don't know who we're talking about, I guess you've nothing to worry about, right?'' Jonah drawled in his best, bored Oxford accent. He and Paige pretended to exchange commiserating looks. ''Wonder what the penalty for perjury is nowadays.''

Paige's composure was cracking a little by this time. She'd never been terrific at intimidation, much less standing firm in the face of evil. She wished she could touch Jonah, hold his hand, at least. Was Gladstone really capable of calling their bluff, even in the face of all their evidence? In a defensive motion she was unable to arrest, her hands moved to press down on her knee.

"Something the matter, Congressman?'' Jonah inquired then. ''You look, um, a trifle nervous?''

"I told you to get out of here.'' His voice raised the hair on the back of Paige's neck. He began stuffing everything back in the envelope, his movements jerky, vibrant with suppressed rage. ''I'll deny everything—they'll believe me. The two of you can prove nothing. Nothing!''

"We don't have to anymore,'' Paige said, the relief dizzying. ''The police have your hired thug. They also have the original documents of everything we just gave you, along with the evidence that Professor Kittridge's death was murder.'' That was pushing it—all the ''evidence'' provided was still circumstantial. On the other hand: ''And they've proved that arson was the cause of the fire that destroyed his home.''

Gladstone turned on her with a fierce malevolent glare. ''You'll regret this—'' He half raised his hands—and suddenly Jonah was in front of her, shielding her with his body.

"It's over, Gladstone,'' he pronounced with a gentleness far more ominous than the older man's threats. He took a step forward, forcing Gladstone to retreat. With casual fingers he reached into his own shirt pocket and withdrew the list of nine names, his gaze never leaving that of the sweating man in front of him.

Those names, Paige knew, were their trump card. And after the revelatory conversation with her parents the previous night, she also had a feeling her next shot would be the final one. She sat forward, leaning to see around Jonah's broad shoulders, no longer afraid of Armand Gladstone.

"We neglected to include this list of names in your packet there. I believe it's something else you spent a great deal of trouble trying to find." He held it up between two fingers, and Gladstone glared as if Jonah had offered him a cyanide pill. Jonah just as casually folded the list up and put it back in his pocket. "Perhaps I should mention that before going to Warner Robins, we paid a visit to your father. He told us everything he knew—including both his own treason—and yours."

"I talked to my parents last night," Paige continued. "My father and Professor Kittridge's son were best friends, you see, back in the early sixties. Only, the professor's son—his name was Benjamin—went to Vietnam. Imagine my surprise when my father told me last night that his friend Ben had been killed in an ambush, back in 1968. He was part of the First Cavalry, Company C. You recognize the unit, I see."

And her father had unashamedly wept upon learning that his friend's death had been engineered by a traitor. He had also agreed that, to honor the death of both the professor and his son, she and Jonah needed to present Armand Gladstone with their evidence.

"You can't prove any of it!" Gladstone repeated, suddenly almost shouting. "None of it! Not a single spurious word!"

He pivoted and strode angrily behind his desk, as though to preserve the illusion of his power and position. "In two days I'm holding a press conference to announce my bid for the Senate seat. You'll regret this interference—I'll make you regret it." The cold slashing voice spat words like poison-tipped darts.

"Will you hire another hit man?" Paige asked.

Red suffused his face, with the tic in his jaw even more pronounced. "You'll be looking over your shoulders the rest of your lives," he threatened, and Paige realized finally how

well her mission had succeeded. Somehow the victory seemed
a hollow one.

"I hope when they finally get you, it's slow and painful."

"That's enough." Jonah reached the desk in one stride and
leaned over, planting his palms on the top. "You've nowhere
to run, *Congressman*. Your filthy life is about to be exposed,
and you know it. Especially when the press gets hold of the
story. And make no mistake, they will."

"I have contacts—"

Jonah shook his head. Looking at him, Paige saw with a jolt
that he was studying Gladstone with an expression of...pity.
Pity and regret. "Public opinion makes a fickle mistress. Perhaps you could win it back. But the truth won't change...and
all three of us present in this room know what that truth is."

"Truth is whatever I determine it to be," Gladstone insisted,
but there was no longer any confidence in the words.

"Hmm," Jonah dissented. "Situational ethics and so-called
virtual reality do not constitute God's truth." He smiled mirth-
lessly. "God doesn't need editing, Gladstone, regardless of all
attempts to do so by people who claim to be more enlightened.
Let me repeat myself, with one modification." His voice
dropped to a resounding whisper. "All four of us present in
this room know the truth. You can't hide from God, even if
you deny His very existence. And you can't hide from the truth,
even if you deny it for the rest of your life. It will be waiting
for you when you die."

The words hovered in the air, and Paige could tell the exact
second when bitter reality finally sank in. "No. You can't do
this...I won't let you—"

Jonah straightened. "You've done it to yourself. You sowed
the wind, Armand Gladstone. Now you're about to reap the
whirlwind."

"Nobody will believe you." His hands moved spasmodically, opening and shutting. "I'm a United States Congressman,
a war hero—"

Paige stood and came over to Jonah's side. "You're a liar
and a traitor," she announced, her voice breaking. So many
lives lost, destroyed.

And yet... Warmth slowly encircled her like a rainbow embrace, filling her with peace. Faith, she decided, truly was inexplicable. She didn't know if Jonah could feel it, didn't know if she could even explain it—but she *knew,* with a certainty that defied understanding, that God's loving Presence had finally washed away the last of her guilt and bitterness.

Not only could she let the professor rest in peace, she could let the past go. Incredibly, she could even leave Armand Gladstone to God, because she suddenly realized for the first time that Armand himself had been betrayed—by his own father. Standing beside Jonah, she faced the beaten man across the table and felt the pity and regret mirrored on Jonah's face. "Before long the whole world will know exactly who and what you are. We won't have to say another word, to anybody... you're a public figure."

She tucked her hand through Jonah's arm. "You know, if I were you, I'd cancel your press conference unless you plan to...tell the whole truth, and nothing but the truth."

"'So help you God,'" Jonah quoted under his breath beside her.

They started walking toward the door. Jonah opened it, and Paige turned for one last look. The honorable Armand Gladstone had dropped into the chair behind his desk and was sitting there, stone-faced and silent, the manila envelope crushed between his hands.

Chapter Thirty

"**K**now what we need to do now?" Jonah observed the following evening as he helped Paige clear the table after supper in her apartment.

"What?" Paige turned the water on and began rinsing dishes, feeling a profound contentment. It had been pleasure beyond words to prepare, then cook a homemade meal after weeks of restaurants and fast food. Sheer joy to share with Jonah in companionable silence, free of worry and fear. The spectre of David had disappeared completely: Jonah refused to allow her to make dessert as well as the whole meal, purchasing for them a frozen cherry cheesecake, and Paige hadn't felt guilty at all.

She wallowed in the delight of having Jonah help her clean up, brushing arms as he handed her a dish, feeling his lips drop a kiss on the back of her neck. Basking in the simple reality of his presence in the kitchen with her.

"Well, what we don't need to do is make another trek to the police station," Jonah teased, licking the knife she'd used to slice the cheesecake.

"All right, two can play that game." She began loading the dishwasher, ticking off all the errands they'd been running the past twenty-four hours in concert with the placement of each dirty dish. "We don't have to verify that the FBI sent someone to talk to Armand. We don't have to swing by another motel to pay a bill..."

"We don't have to move any more of our stuff back into our respective apartments." He grinned. "And we don't have to check *into* another motel, which for a couple of committed Christians has a faintly scandalous ring, doesn't it?"

"Mmph," Paige said, having decided Jonah's catch-all expression suited her, as well. She flicked droplets of water at him. "I know what it is! I finished proofing the galleys last night, and you're going to take me to—"

"I want to pay a visit to Justeen Gilroy," Jonah said, and Paige almost dropped the emptied broccoli casserole dish.

"Justeen Gilroy?" she repeated blankly.

"Major Pettigrew's daughter. That's the one." He nodded, the helpful embellishment reeking of Jonah-esque diffidence, alerting Paige's suspicions. "I want us to share with her the, um, 'rest of the story.' Within limits, of course." He began fiddling with Paige's ears. "And...I want us to take the bike. I checked the forecast for tomorrow. Clear, sunny, highs in the fifties. A lovely, mild December day, perfect for taking a jaunt on my bike. Think of it—just you and me and the wind. Nobody taking potshots at us, or following us. No uncertain reception by unknown entities waiting at the other end...."

"I am not riding that machine all the way to North Carolina. Especially in December." She wiped her hands on a towel and turned to the man standing at her back. A lock of mahogany-colored hair had fallen across his forehead, brushing the hopefully elevated eyebrow. He'd rolled up the long sleeves of his shirt, exposing his arms, and in spite of the domestic scene, he looked supremely male. His eyes bathed her in a cajoling warmth.

"It's only a couple of hundred miles. We'll be there in four or five hours."

"Fine. You take the motorcycle—I'll take a plane." She looked him over, loving him so much she wanted to weep with the aching joy of it. "And I bet I beat you there."

"I'm sick of flying, aren't you?" He snagged her waist and

whirled her around, completely off her feet. "Just think of the fresh air. The freedom—"

"The millions of cars traveling eighty miles an hour. Thousands of megaton trucks traveling ninety miles an hour."

"Hugging me close?"

"I can do that on the plane. Even better, you can hug me back!"

"Mula terca." He kissed her, then dumped her gently in the chair.

"Cut that out!" Paige laughed up at him. "A friend at the museum only told me how to say *heldish leyb.* I didn't have time for more."

"Ah, yes. I did wonder about that." He faked a cough. "Your accent was—and is—atrocious, love." He stepped back, adroitly dodging her swinging arm. "Though it's flattering that you think I'm a brave lion, even if God has blessed me with a stubborn mule."

"I'm definitely taking the plane!" She jumped up, alive with mischief—and the idea that had popped into her head. "I'll call Justeen to make sure she's going to be home, then make a reservation. For one." She turned around, tilting her head as she shot him a challenging look. "You leave when I leave for the airport, and we'll just see who gets there first!"

"You're on." He caught her close, hugged her. "Paige? You're sure you'll be all right? By yourself, I mean?" The laughter had faded from his voice and eyes.

Paige sighed, listening to the comforting beat of his heart, savoring the loving concern. "I'll be fine. Armand knows he's lost. We both saw it in his face, remember. Besides, there's a good chance he'll be taken into custody soon, and I don't think he'll bother hiring another hit man. It's too risky, especially when he knows that they know what we know—if you know what I mean."

Jonah's chest expanded in a silent laugh, but the arms holding her abruptly crushed her close. "It's going to be hard for me," he confessed quietly, "letting you go by yourself."

She lifted her head, pressed a kiss to the warm skin exposed in the open collar of his shirt. "I know. But it's like going to see Armand—it's something I need to do. Sort of the last test, the final exam, to see if I've passed back to being a normal, self-respecting person. The consummate, well-balanced, Christian professional woman.''

Suddenly self-conscious, she freed herself and started for the phone, pausing when Jonah spoke her name. Her heart twisted in a peculiar spasm at the strained look deepening the lines in his face. Her smile faded. "Jonah? What is it?''

Deep blue eyes searched hers. He started to speak, closed his mouth, then took out his glasses and began whirling them. "I want...um...will you—dash it!" He tossed the glasses on the table, took two quick strides and grabbed her close again. "I love you. And—I want to marry you. Will you...have me?''

Floored, Paige gaped at him, at a loss for words. Only in her most secret dreams...

Before she could answer, he pressed her against his chest, speaking rapidly over her head with a pleading tone she never wanted to hear again. "I know your first marriage was traumatic, full of mental and emotional anguish. But—God as my witness—I would never treat you like David treated you. I want to love you, protect you...cherish you. Help you become whatever *God* wants you to be. The Lord, not me." He began kissing her hair, her ears, her temple. "I love you more than I ever thought it was possible to love someone. I'd given up searching. I realize I have a lot of faults—''

Paige couldn't bear it. She laced her arms around his neck and stopped the flow of pleading words with her lips. "I want to marry you," she whispered. "Because this time I'm ready to be a *good* Christian wife—not a perfect one. I've learned the lesson you've taught me. The one that God has been trying to remind me of for years, only I was too hurt to listen." Emotion swelled, squeezing her heart, her throat. "You helped me see that even Christians can fall into traps—especially when we're blinded into trying to do things man's way instead of God's.''

Jonah held her a little ways away, studying her. "You're absolutely convinced you don't have to live by my standards?''

"Well—'' she traced teasing patterns on the soft knit of his royal blue shirt "—I don't know that there's much wrong with your standards. But no, I plan to live by the Book this time. Not the gospel according to David Bennett or Jonah Sterling— or J. Gregory, for that matter."

"Does that mean 'yes,' then?"

His arms were crushing her, but it was the most wonderful sensation in the world, being held like that. "Only if you promise I don't have to sing in the church choir, join every committee, darn your socks—"

This time his mouth stopped hers.

Naturally, Paige's flight was delayed. Jonah met her at the airport, looking as bland and smug as a row of newly elected politicians. He escorted her out to his motorcycle without gloating too horribly, and by the time they were halfway to Justeen's, Paige was almost ready to admit he'd been right. Almost, but not quite.

Justeen met them at the door, the fragrance of fresh-baked oatmeal cookies and hot spiced cider filling the air. A television blared in the background.

"Come in, come in. I've been about to bust a gullet waiting to hear the story. You say that list of names you found was a list of traitors, and my father had been trying to expose them when he was killed?"

They shared a judiciously edited story with her, having decided it would serve no purpose to expose the tragedy of Everett Gladstone and his son. It was enough for Justeen to learn the circumstances surrounding her father's death, and that the legacy of the list had, at last, been an instrument of justice.

Suddenly Justeen slapped her hand to her face and rose. "Here we've been yakkety-yakking away, and I almost plumb forgot!" She scurried from the room and returned minutes later with an old wooden fruit crate. Inside was a dilapidated cardboard box, almost crushed in half. "I found this last week when I finally got around to finishing up cleaning Mama's attic. Remember I told you I planned to do that, the last time you were here?"

"We remember," Jonah said, his gaze devouring the box.

Paige suppressed an indulgent smile. Her husband-to-be could never resist *some* forms of temptation.

Justeen, bless her, hadn't missed a beat. "I've been so busy, though, that I never got around to checking the contents. Some woman in England sent it to Mama about five years after the war—see, that's her name there on the box."

She poured Jonah some more hot cider, then sat down, propping her feet on the empty chair and sighing with pleasure. "Anyway, I remember when it came—I was so excited." She chuckled, reminiscing. "'Spect I thought it was a present or something. Then Mama never even opened it—said it was some of Daddy's stuff. Apparently the woman's husband and my father had been friends, and Lord what's-it had kept a few personal belongings of Daddy's. Think he died a year or so after Daddy was killed, and his widow eventually gathered up this stuff and sent it to Mama. She stuck it up in the attic without even looking. I was plumb mad..."

While Justeen talked, Jonah opened the box. Inside, along with a packet of faded, crumbling letters, an antique pearl-handled derringer and a penknife, was a diary. He picked it up, looking across at Paige.

She stared a minute, then with numb fingers groped for her purse. Justeen watched with unabashed curiosity as Paige removed the contents of her purse, then felt inside, her fingers hooking under the lining. With its distinct noise, the velcro parted. Paige tugged out the crumpled envelope.

Hands not quite steady, she opened it and took out the dainty key, handing it to Jonah. He inserted it in the rusting lock and twisted. The clasp grated, resisting, then released.

Jonah put on his glasses and began to carefully leaf through the pages. Paige read along with him, her breath whooshing out in an incredulous gasp when the names leaped off the page. Sometimes in neat print, other places a hurried scrawl—but all legible—Major Pettigrew had written down all the details of the sordid betrayal of their country by nine individuals. Gerald Minton...Brewster Covington...Everett Gladstone...

If Justeen had found that box earlier, and they had had this diary...

"How interesting—a diary." Justeen munched a cookie, her voice cheerfully interested. "I don't know if you can use it in your book..." Her voice trailed away into the stunned silence.

Jonah slowly closed the diary and looked up at Paige, his face reflecting disbelief, then rueful humor. Paige looked back. Doubtless her own expression mirrored his. On the whole, she decided that if she'd been given a choice, she still might have chosen to endure the trial and tribulations of these past months, anyway. A whole lot of good had evolved from a whole lot of bad, after all. One of God's many promises she planned to remember, regardless of what the future held.

Turning to Justeen, Jonah gently laid the diary back in the box along with the other items, then gave it back to the be-mused woman. "It was thoughtful of you," he said, "but I think I have all the information I need."

They all rose and traipsed out of the dining room toward the front door. As they passed through the parlor, Paige heard the television announcer's sober voice. She clutched Jonah's arm, stopping them both.

"Late last night. Cause at this time is unknown. To repeat this breaking news—Armand Gladstone, House representative from Georgia, has been found dead in the study of his home. According to one source, the event occurred late last night, but we have no further information at this time. Local authorities are investigating, but have offered no explanations. Stay tuned to this channel for a complete update on the six o'clock re-port."

"Lands!" Justeen shook her head. "What's this world com-ing to, I want to know. So much violence, and right in the nation's capital—a *congressman*." She glanced from Jonah to Paige. "I notice they were real careful not to say whether it was murder or suicide. Sometimes I wonder..."

She made humming little noises in her throat as she held the door open for Paige and Jonah. "Well, I just hope he had his affairs in order and was ready to meet his Maker."

Paige opened her mouth, closed it. A paradoxical blend of heavy sadness and heart-lifting release coursed through her body. She felt Jonah's hand close around hers, the firm clasp of his fingers comforting and solid. They told Justeen goodbye and strolled down the sidewalk. All the love inside Paige was spilling from her eyes when she looked up at Jonah and smiled. "Let's go home and work on a book."

"A wedding."

"Which one first?"

They exploded in laughter and finished the walk arm in arm.

Justeen watched the couple walking down the sidewalk toward their monstrous chrome-and-black motorcycle. She shook her head again, wondering why such an attractive couple would ride one of *those* things. Ah, well, they were young, and so in love with each other they glowed with it. An indulgent smile blossomed when she saw Jonah catch Paige up in his arms. They embraced, exchanged a kiss. Then Jonah swept Paige off her feet and tossed her onto the back of the motorcycle. He was grinning like all the heroes of the old cowboy movies Justeen loved to watch.

Paige was laughing, and it transformed her too-pale complexion into a lovely translucent peach. She shoved playfully at Jonah before strapping on a helmet that engulfed her head. Then she wrapped her arms around Jonah's waist and hugged him close.

Justeen had to admit that they made a nice couple, even if they were riding a motorcycle. She steeled herself for the deafening roar, and her mouth dropped in astonishment when Jonah kicked the starter...and they vanished down the street at a quiet putt-putt.

Justeen went back inside and shut the door. "Would have been perfect," she muttered to herself, "if he wore a mask and rode a white horse."

She could almost hear the *William Tell Overture* playing in the background.

*　*　*　*　*

Dear Reader,

The title of this book, *Shelter of His Arms,* conjures
up several images for me, all of which lend themselves
to the message I hope is conveyed through Paige
and Jonah's story. All Christians, of course, have the
indescribable comfort of being held within the shelter of
God's loving embrace, regardless of marital status. But
way back in Genesis the Lord Himself wrote what can
arguably be the first romance: Adam needed Eve.

Yes, I realize things turned sticky after that—just as
they do for Paige Hawthorne as she struggles to solve
a mystery as well as rethink her views on marriage.
We don't live in a perfect world. We do, however,
have a Perfect Creator, Who somehow manages to work
miracles through the fumbling attempts of His children,
typified in this book by Jonah Sterling. And believe it or
not, sometimes romances in real life do have the same
happy endings as storybook romances. One of the many
reasons I believe God led me to writing in this genre is to
share a little of the joy He's given to me through almost
twenty-eight years of marriage to my very own hero.

Shelter of His Arms tackles—wisely or no—the
thorny issue of how some Christians define the marital
relationship. It is my hope that this entertaining romance
not only lifts a heart and brings a satisfied smile…but
that its presentation "…correctly handles the word of
truth."

Some writers seek to touch minds—my prayer is that
God's grace enables my books to touch hearts.

Joy,

Sara Mitchell